HIGHLAND
ESCAPE

CATHY & DD MACRAE

HIGHLAND ESCAPE
Copyright © 2015 Short Dog Press

Published by Short Dog Press
ISBN-13: 978-0-9966485-2-3

Published in the United States of America

Acknowledgments

We'd like to thank our critique partners and those who had input in this book: Vonda Sinclair, Dawn Marie Hamilton and Cate Park. You are the best!

Thanks and much appreciation to our wonderful editor, Simone Seguin, and fantastic cover artist, Rae Monet.

Chapter One

14th Century
Cheviot Hills, Scottish-English Border

*A*nna glanced over her shoulder. The two plump harts she and her brother Edrick had killed lay secured on the back of the pack horse. She smiled, waiting for Edrick's excuses to begin anew.

"You know mine had more antler points before he stumbled down the ravine and broke a tip," Edrick declared with a pushed tone of frustration.

"Mayhap, but the fact remains my stag has twelve to your ten." Anna's nonchalant answer didn't match the merriment spilling from her eyes, or the tremors of barely contained laughter.

Edrick gave a sigh of annoyance, tempting Anna further toward laughter. They'd been having this argument ever since the ill-fated fall of his winning kill.

"Mine still outweighs yours." His resentment was comical. Anna rolled her eyes.

"Yes, well, if that were the wager, you would be the winner. However, 'twas not." Her curt reply gave no ground. "You have my stable chores for the next sennight, brother mine." She burst into a sputter of giggles she could no longer restrain.

They broke from the forest at the base of a gentle hill. A column of thick black smoke billowed in the sky. The pungent odor of

1

burning drifted to them, interrupting the delicate aroma of spring. A hasty glance at Edrick told Anna they shared the same fear. As she readied to put a heel to her horse, he hooked his reins on his saddle and drew a dagger, grabbing her reins to stop her.

"You must swear you will do nothing but fire your bow from a distance." The fierce look in her brother's eyes was a familiar one. Before she could answer, he cut loose his kill and turned to do the same to hers in order to leave the pack horse unburdened.

"Your word, Anna." He sounded like a hardened warrior, bred and trained to lead.

"'Tis my home, too." She raised her chin in defiance.

He gazed at her for a moment with a sudden softness she rarely glimpsed. "Yes, but I cannot do what needs to be done whilst I worry for your safety. You may cover my charge from a distance, but nothing more. We may already be too late. If the fight is lost, you must flee into Scotland to Grandfather. Your word." The command in his voice mimicked their father's so strongly, it compelled her submission.

Anna stared hard at him as the second stag slid off the pack horse. Her brother's height of six feet two inches made him tower over many. Only four inches shorter than he, she stood head to head with all but the tallest of her father's men. Edrick's straight coal black hair, strong nose and chin mirrored her own, but the dark blue-eyed ancestry of the Braxton line passed to him, while Anna inherited the deep green of their mother's clan.

"You have my word," she conceded reluctantly.

He nodded once and kicked his horse into a gallop. Anna paused long enough to unsling her bow and hook it across her back. Then, giving her horse his head, she sped toward the smoke. Reaching the top of the hill overlooking her village and home, Anna took in the scene below. The sight stole her breath and her stomach churned with anguish.

The roof of their manor house blazed with a fire so intense, 'twas well past saving. The crackle of hungry flames reached her ears. A small group of armored men attempted to breach the gates. She recognized their armor and tactics immediately.

"Bloody English," she spat.

Though her father's soldiers kept the enemy at bay, the opposing numbers appeared too great.

She followed Edrick as he guided his horse to flank a small formation of archers pinning down Baron Braxton's men, leaving them unable to ward off those trying to break through the massive wood-and-iron gate. She halted between two slender trees, sighting the archers, ready to protect her brother. Edrick kept his approach silent, riding through their back line before they could react. His sword rose and fell, cutting through the lightly armored bowmen like a sickle to ripened wheat.

He wheeled his mount to make another pass. Several archers broke formation to flee. Two archers readied to fire as Edrick charged. Prepared for such a reaction, Anna sucked in a steadying breath, then launched an arrow deep into the chest of the first man. Drawn swiftly to prevent the second archer from harming Edrick, her next arrow missed its target, penetrating the man's hip instead of his torso. Knowing she'd fired too quickly, Anna took more time with her third shot. As the wounded archer turned, her arrow slammed into his breast, knocking him onto his back.

Edrick's second pass through their ranks killed or scattered the rest, allowing the men atop the wall to focus on the large group manning a battering ram. He felled two more archers as they made their way toward the main body of the army. A cheer rang from the wall, her father's men recognizing their unexpected allies.

Arrows, crossbow bolts, large stones and oil rained down with renewed fury on the attackers. Lit by torches, the enemy became screaming human bonfires, stalling their assault on the gate. The stench of burning oil and charred flesh soon joined the bitter smell of Anna's home aflame.

A sickening roar pulled Anna's attention from the fight. The roof of her home collapsed, flames and sparks shooting heavenward. A wall of the main keep shifted and crumbled as stone exploded under the heat of fire.

The conflagration continued to the tower where her chamber was located, a level below her father's prized library. The terrible heartache of loss threatened to overwhelm her as the horror of death and smoke assaulted her. Anna violently shoved them aside and focused on protecting her brother.

She urged her horse forward, picking her next position amid the slain archers, and swung down to retrieve quivers of abandoned arrows. A feeling of hopelessness unlike any she'd known gripped her as she realized the odds they faced.

She turned her fear into anger, using it to shower death upon those closest to her brother. His sweeping attack from flank to flank at the rear caught the enemy unaware, and many foot soldiers fell before they could respond to the unexpected threat. Each time one turned to meet Edrick's charge, Anna's shaft pierced his chest, putting an abrupt end to his challenge. Another pass against the men on the ground, and Edrick pushed the enemy death toll well past a score.

Panic dug in like talons as the enemy surrounded her brother. She fired arrow after arrow, carving an opening in the noose of flesh and steel around him. Edrick's sword cleaved death on two more, making use of the gap Anna created. He cleared the group encircling him and flashed her a smile that ended abruptly in a look of shock. He slumped forward in the saddle, a crossbow bolt protruding from the middle of his back.

"NO!"

Frozen, she watched in horror as a crush of men dragged her brother from his horse. The main gate shattered, the sound of splintering heavy oak drowning out all other noise. Soldiers swarmed the bailey of the barony's fortified keep.

"No." Her voice fell to a strangled whisper.

The enemy made short work of the outnumbered men inside the walls. Fixed by grief, unable to move, Anna watched as everything and everyone she loved was violently ripped away by blood, fire and steel.

The sound of horses approaching jarred her from the paralyzing terror. Twisting in the saddle, she spotted men bearing down on her. Remembering her vow to Edrick, she turned Orion and kicked once, spurring him toward the forest. She was instantly at a gallop, clumps of turf tossed high in their wake. Lying flat against her horse's mane, she encouraged him as he lengthened his stride, ears flat against his head. Daring a backward glance, she noted the gap between them and the attackers widened, the men's heavy armor slowing their mounts.

Anna's knowledge of these lands, coupled with Orion's speed, soon left her pursuers far behind. She guided the stallion north across the River Tweed, then into a copse of trees before traversing open ground toward the forest again.

She sought signs of a chase, slowing Orion to a trot as they entered the woodland. With the enemy out of sight, her only goal was to hide. Putting distance between herself and home, she traveled deeper into Scotland, darkness and the dense timberland concealing them.

"Easy, boy." She patted Orion's neck and he dropped to a walk. "Bloody bastards cannot keep up with us. Serves them right for wearing heavy armor and choosing steeds more fit for the plow than war."

The horse flicked an ear in response, then willingly splashed into a swiftly moving stream swollen by the spring melt.

"No oats tonight, my boy." Anna kept her voice low despite the noise created by the fast-moving stream. "We will search for a nice thicket under the stars. Let us hope the night remains clear and dry." Tears streamed down her face as the reason for a night alone flashed across her mind, and she stroked his mane, drawing comfort from the warmth of his massive body.

The current washed away his hoof prints as fast as he made them. After a furlong, she turned him up a graveled bank and into deep shadows. Sliding from his back, she unsaddled him, setting her unsheathed swords close by on the ground for quick access.

She settled in for what rest to be found before dawn, but slumber did not come easy. Edrick's death played over and over again, tormenting her dreams, leaving her more exhausted than restored. Finally giving up, she rose, dawn scarcely a hint in the sky. She wasted no time breaking camp, looking and listening for any sign of pursuers. Satisfied none were about, she mounted and continued deeper into the forest, unsure of her destination.

Anna picked her way through forests and fields, avoiding civilization, questions tormenting her without cease.

Whom did they serve? Had a neighboring lord attacked? With no visible standard, no heraldic device, how could she be sure? *Who is friend? And who is foe?*

Which led to another important question—where would she go? Returning to England was out of the question. Anywhere she appeared, she could unwittingly put herself in the hands of unknown enemies. Though she had promised Edrick, she couldn't go to her grandfather's clan for fear of bringing her father's enemies to his doorstep.

With both her brother and father dead, she was now her father's heir. She would be declared a ward of King Edward and forced into marriage if she returned—and could not live with such a fate. She squinted her eyes at the sky, weighing her options. Her only path lay north—into the Highlands.

One day bled into the next, and then another. Having never traveled this far into Scotland, Anna had only the slimmest idea of her location. The terrible loss of her home and family continually gnawed her heart, but she had no time to indulge grief. For now, stealth and survival were her priorities.

Feminine screams pierced her thoughts, causing her to put Orion to flight. At the edge of a large glen, six men held two young women. One fought, kicking at the man holding her until he threw her down, tearing her dress. Sounds of nearby battle reached her ears. *A raiding party?*

Anna clenched her jaw. *Cursed barbarians, stealing women.* After days of unfulfilled vengeance eating away at her, here was an injustice she could throw herself into.

Leaving Orion in the trees, Anna drew her bow and crept closer to the party. The woman with the torn dress lay on the ground. The men surrounding her laughed and held the other woman roughly until she ceased to struggle. Anna moved nearer for a better look. The two were barely more than girls. A cold rage swept through her.

She stepped from the trees, bow at the ready. Taking careful aim, her first arrow penetrated the back of the man who'd thrown the girl to the ground. Standing menacingly above her a moment ago, he now lay motionless beside her. The fallen young woman released another scream, transporting Anna back to the battle for her home. The ghostly sound of Edrick's battle cry ringing in her ears, she drew her bow again. The next arrow pierced the neck of the man holding the second girl, the weight of his lifeless body snapping the slender shaft as he hit the ground.

The men's attention turned from their hapless captives, seeking their attacker. Anna's third arrow hit the largest brute squarely in the chest, dropping him to his knees. With a shout, the three remaining men charged. Her fourth arrow also found a home, sending another to his death. The last two men were nearly upon her.

Discarding her bow, Anna drew two curved short swords from the sheath on her back. An emotionless detachment descended on her, numbing her to fear. The first man to reach her swung a broadsword she easily avoided by stepping sideways. Striking his sword arm with the first blade, her second blade slid across his throat with little effort.

Only one savage remained. He slowed, glancing at his five fallen companions. He stared at her, his evil smile promising pain and death.

Anna's eyes narrowed. *Arrogant swine!*

His sword strike arced in a slow and predictable manner. Anna deflected the strike with one sword, then spun, stepping past her opponent.

Her other blade bit deeply into the back of his leg, sending him to his knees. Continuing to twirl with the momentum of her previous attack, she struck with each sword again, and he pitched forward into the bloodstained grass.

Scanning the area for more enemies, she spotted two groups of men on horseback racing toward them across the field. She turned to the two women. "Hide in the woods, now!"

Eyes wide with shock, they obeyed without question. Pleased they trusted her, Anna retreated until the forest stood directly behind her, trees and undergrowth forming a protective wall against an organized attack from the mounted men. Head raised, she faced the oncoming threat.

Spying their kinsmen on the ground, the rogues in the first group wheeled their horses to meet the riders behind them. They were cut down without mercy, the sound of steel on steel ringing in the air. Two warriors in the second group waded among the downed riders, dispatching them with brutal effectiveness. Seeing the fierceness of the men now thundering toward her, Anna wished for her bow to even the odds. Fear prickled along her spine, but she refused to pay heed. Her escape into Scotland appeared to be at an end.

A few yards from her, the lead rider held up his arm, calling the group to a halt.

"Da!" The young woman with the torn dress ran to meet the men, the other girl following her.

The leader dismounted, embracing the first girl fiercely. Men gathered around, now too close for Anna's comfort. Alone and exposed, her swords held at guard, she faced two men pointing crossbows at her, ready to fire at their leader's word.

"Hold," the leader commanded. He pulled his daughter behind him and looked to Anna. "Who are ye, lass?"

One bowman stepped closer, his weapon ready. Anna shifted her stance, putting both the leader and bowman in her vision.

"A traveler, my laird," she replied in Gaelic, her instincts screaming for her to run.

He frowned. "What is yer name?"

"Anna," she replied in a flat, emotionless voice. The grip on her swords belied her calm demeanor.

"English?" His voice lowered to a growl.

"No, my laird, Scots." She took a deep breath in an effort to regain her composure.

Eyeing her, he rocked back on his heels. "What clan?"

"I am sorry if I trespass, my laird. I will leave at once." Anna swept her gaze over the group, searching for any threatening movement.

She slowly backed toward her horse. Without warning, the man still aiming at her fired his crossbow. Anna stepped slightly aside, deflecting the missile with her swords. Dropping one sword, she drew a knife from her leather bracer. Flat with no hilt, its design made for flight, it fit her palm perfectly. She spun, launching the knife at the man. The blade penetrated his shoulder deeply, sending his crossbow crashing to the ground.

"I said hold!" the leader roared, making eye contact with each of the men behind him.

Anna regained her sword, continuing to back toward Orion.

"The next man to defy the laird dies by my sword!" a deep baritone growled as it echoed across the glen, causing all to cease moving, including Anna.

A younger version of the leader drew his steed a few feet closer. "This is Kenneth MacGregor, laird of clan MacGregor."

Bowing slightly, Anna replied in disbelief, "Am I to be your prisoner, Laird MacGregor?"

The younger man, clearly the son of the laird, dismounted. The two men exchanged a brief conversation, quietly enough she couldn't hear a word.

Anna took in MacGregor the Younger. He appeared to be a few inches taller than she, arms and shoulders thick with muscle. His uncovered legs appeared as big around as her waist. Sable hair, tied at the back of his neck, reached his shoulders, curling at the ends. His eyes, the lightest blue she could recall, bored through her when he shifted his stare from his father to her.

She swallowed uneasily.

He and his father wore the blood of their enemies liberally on skin and clothing. Knowing the young woman was his sister explained the ferocity with which he fought to reclaim her. It did not explain, however, why Anna was being detained.

"Aye. Ye will come with us."

The laird mounted his horse, picked up his daughter and placed her on the front of his saddle. He then rode back across the field. Another man did the same with the other girl.

The younger man faced her. "I am Sir Duncan MacGregor, the laird's son. Ye will hand over yer weapons and ride with us. It can be done willingly, or ye can fight. The choice is yers."

With a hard look, Anna unbuckled her sword sheath and removed the two daggers from her belt. She then tugged each dagger from her boots, handing them with a growl to the men who approached.

"Will I be allowed to ride, sir?" she asked with as much venom as she dared.

Duncan motioned for her horse. "Aye, the laird put ye in my charge. Ye will ride."

Taking Orion's reins, he indicated she mount. As they headed toward the battle site, she noticed a man speaking with Laird MacGregor, arms flailing, clearly angry.

"He is my brother, laird. 'Tis my right to demand a challenge!"

The laird glanced at Anna then back at the fuming man in front of him, reluctantly nodding his head. "Set camp. See to the wounded first."

So, the brother to the man I knifed demands the right to avenge his injury. Anna's blood boiled. Never mind that he'd disobeyed his laird's orders. *He cannot believe 'twas done by a woman,* she mocked. His rage suddenly made her weary. It was not the first time a man wished to kill her. She shrugged. *He will join the ranks of others who have tried. The only question is, dead or wounded?*

"'Tis what I get for being of assistance." She didn't realize she'd spoken loud enough to be heard, but MacGregor the Younger gave a twitch of a smile at her complaint.

Men set up tents, built fires and gathered the wounded.

"Sir, I am trained as a healer, if I may offer aid," she said as Duncan tied her horse to a nearby tree.

He eyed her suspiciously. "Why would ye assist my men if ye believe yerself our prisoner?"

A good question. Why indeed? "Am I correct in assuming these men were injured rescuing two young women kidnapped by a raiding party?"

He gave a short nod in response.

"Then helping men who were injured putting a stop to such a barbaric practice is reason enough." The opportunity to tend to the wounded drowned out her anger—for now.

Cocking his head slightly, he crooked one corner of his mouth at her response. "A fair answer. We have a tent and some supplies. Do ye require aught else?"

Dismounting, Anna pulled her bag from Orion's back. "Boiling water and whisky if you can spare it."

"Fetch water from the burn and set it to boiling," Duncan ordered one of the men tending the fire. He stared hard at her as if trying to assess the truthfulness of her answer. Anna stood fixed as his gaze penetrated her. After a few unnerving moments of forceful scrutiny, he strode toward the tent.

Opening the flap, Duncan motioned for her to enter. As soon as she did, the stench of impending death struck her. Supplies sat on the ground between two pallets with injured men already on them; they appeared to be the worst of the injured. One man suffered a deep belly wound, the source of the acrid smell. The other bore a long slash down one leg.

Anna spoke quietly to Duncan. "Sir, this man is not likely to survive. I will make a poultice to staunch his wound and give him poppy tea for the pain."

Duncan nodded as a man brought in a pot of steaming water and whispered to him while Anna went about her work.

Finishing with the stomach injury, she turned to the leg wound. Using waxed silk thread and a rounded needle, she closed the extensive gash. She then applied a medicated salve to ward off infection and bound it. One after another, men were brought to her, each staring at her in surprise when they arrived for treatment.

While she worked, she repeatedly caught sight of Duncan MacGregor from the corner of her eye. He watched her, his countenance brooding, angry. Though not an overly tall man, he possessed an imposing presence. He carried himself as a seasoned warrior, the scars visible on his arms also giving testament to his experience. He was a man used to having orders obeyed. When his men made eye contact, a nod gained their compliance. The MacGregors appeared highly trained and well disciplined. The slight number of their injured, compared to the number of their enemies now lying dead on the field, proved this fact.

"May I ask why I am being detained, sir?" Anna asked without turning away from the injured man she tended.

When Duncan did not respond, she glanced in his direction. He hadn't moved. Still standing, legs apart, arms folded across his chest, he wore a grim, inscrutable mask. The heat of anger rose within and her hands clenched around her tools. Held for no perceivable reason, she now endured being ignored as if of no consequence. *I should let them treat their own damned wounded.* With an effort, she resisted the temptation to pack her bags and cease her hard work.

The healer in her wouldn't allow her to let these men suffer. Since MacGregor permitted her to see to his men, she knew they had no healer among them. The wounded played no part in their laird's decision to hold his daughter's rescuer against her will. As much as she wanted to retaliate for his treatment, her honor wouldn't allow it. Her father always said a true man or woman of honor behaved such, whether it was expected or not, whether observed or not. Honor did not, however, prevent her from goading her captor.

She waited to speak again until finished with the last man brought to her. "Is that all the wounded, sir?" She bit back the snarl she wanted to use to punctuate her question.

Duncan nodded once.

"Thank you for allowing me to treat your men. I applaud your efforts in stopping *barbarians* such as those from taking young women against their will." The sarcasm in her voice apparently fell on deaf ears. Again, she inspired no visible response. The urge to challenge him with physical confrontation swelled, then faded. Even if she could get past him, a large group of men outside the tent would not hesitate to stop her.

Surrounded by seasoned warriors, she saw no chance to escape. She would have to bide her time. After watching her dispatch their enemies, Anna knew they would not see her as a helpless female and would thus be on guard.

Now finished treating the wounded, she wanted to wash the blood and filth away and quench her thirst. After a quiet morning, this day seemed to grow more and more disastrous. Tomorrow promised to be more of the same. If she survived the night.

Chapter Two

*T*he camp noises faded from Duncan's thoughts. He and his men had killed the main body of the MacNairn party that had captured his beloved sister and her handmaiden. He'd only needed to find and kill the rest of the raiding party and retrieve the girls. He stared at their prisoner skeptically.

When he first spotted the raiding party across the glen with the women, rage filled every corner of his being. As he and his men charged toward the band, a stranger stepped from the trees and dropped three of the enemy by bow before the raiders could react. Another fell before the mysterious ally had drawn swords. Instead of a long sword, claymore, or axe, he'd wielded two falchions, his movements fluid as he avoided the first attack. Striking the sword arm of the attacker, he then delivered the killing blow. The last MacNairn fared no better. Parrying the attack, the mysterious stranger quickly cut the bastard down.

Reining in his horse several paces away, Duncan had immediately noticed the stranger wasn't a man, but a woman. Impossible! Had he not seen the whole thing played out before him, he never would have believed it. However, 'twas true. This strange woman stopped six Highland warriors with a deadly effectiveness he'd never witnessed before.

Such skill! Such bravery! Never have I seen a woman best a man in combat—much less six men! Heat slid through his veins. *And the bonniest I have ever seen. No pampered lily, this lass, but vital, compelling—alive.*

Her expressive eyes, the color of green only found in nature, reminded him of faerie stories his mam told him as a wean. They reflected strength and courage—viridescent eyes sparking anger.

Long black hair reached her waist, held in a braid thick as his wrist. Her smooth complexion glowed, tanned by time in the sun. The high cheekbones, strong nose and chin, and kissable lips all added up to striking beauty. She'd finished treating his wounded with skills one would expect to have taken half a lifetime to master. His own clan healer was not nearly as proficient, and the old crone had seen many winters.

She claims to be a Scot, but her dress and mannerisms claim her as English. She is, however, well-spoken in Gaelic. For some reason, the lass had a fine teacher. A mystery. Unfortunately, a mystery he would unlikely solve, as his father gave Shamus permission to avenge his brother's shoulder injury. *Fool. His brother faces punishment for disobeying his laird by firing upon the lass, particularly since she'd saved my sister.* Discipline must be maintained. He'd fought in too many battles not to know the lesson well. As captain, it fell to him to see all obeyed without question. Including himself.

I owe her a life-debt. The conundrum twisted him inside. He knew his father did not wish to sentence the woman to death, but could not ignore clan law. *Should I support my kinsman or the lass I just met?* Smiling inside from a feeling he didn't quite understand, he sincerely hoped this Anna survived the night.

He watched her glance about—no doubt searching for a way past him—but ignored her questions about captivity for he had no answer to offer. His only orders were to disarm and detain her. Her body stiffened, fists clenched, a vision of anger. He swallowed the smile on his face when she spun toward him.

"Sir, do you wish me to attend the women? I can treat any injuries they may have sustained." She wielded her sharp tongue with the same ruthless precision as a blade. The play of emotions on her face, as changing as the clouds above, beguiled him.

He took advantage of the opportunity to gaze at her before answering. "'Tis not necessary. They were not injured."

She responded with a slight squint and nod. Did she disbelieve him? Or think he did not trust her?

"We have no shelter for ye. Ye will set up camp outside this tent. Food is being prepared. Ye will eat with us."

"Thank you for the kind offer but that will not be necessary. I can take care of my own meal." Her face and tone were as rigid as the finest steel blade.

Duncan motioned for her to exit the tent. Her saddlebags and bedroll lay deposited on the ground outside, and she replaced the supplies in her pack. Glancing up, she stiffened. He followed her gaze to her stallion on the other side of camp, saddle removed, tethered to the other horses—one more route of escape denied her.

Duncan watched with curiosity as the woman quickly set up her camp. She gathered her belongings and placed them beside a large rock away from the tent. Producing a small folding knife, she cut two saplings, laying them next to her ground cloth, using a third sapling to create a slender trident.

She paced to the burn, moving quietly along the bank, her shadow falling away from the water, he noted with approval. Halting next to a small eddy created by a submerged log, she took a deep breath. With one swift movement, she impaled an unsuspecting trout.

Duncan jerked with a snort of surprise.

After cleaning the fish with precise, neat moves, she returned to her campsite. She dug a small fire pit, collected fallen limbs nearby, then pulled out a flint. When the stone struck the knife, sparks flew into the tinder cradled in the shallow pit. The wood caught and a fire grew.

Duncan doubted he could have done it as quickly. Within a few minutes, she had a fire burning and the fish on a spit. She ignored him, not giving him even a cursory glance.

How can such a lass, scarcely out of her youth, possess such skills? 'Tis unheard of, absurd. Not for hundreds of years have women been trained in combat and woodcraft, and 'twas then only to repel the Roman bastards.

He resisted the growing temptation to approach her, a multitude of questions on his mind. It was clear she wanted nothing to do with him. He couldn't blame her. They treated her as an enemy rather than an ally. *What is Da about? He saw how she rescued Nessa.*

Even dressed like a man, he found her stunning, though the church would call her choice of clothing a sin. Try as he might, Duncan couldn't tear his eyes from her. Her feminine curves weren't completely hidden beneath the leather armor she wore. A matching black tunic and trews covered the rest. Leather bracers along with the cuirass were well fitted and spoke of wealth, as did her horse. *It makes no sense. Why would anyone of means allow a daughter as beautiful as she to dress and behave as a man and travel alone?* A mystery indeed.

He remembered the challenge and his mood shifted. He struggled with a strong need to do something to intervene. He ran a hand over his face in frustration. He could not. Clan law bound him as tightly as his father. He could not even offer to stand in her place.

Stand in her place? St. Filan's teeth! What am I thinking? Go against a clansman for a strange lass? What was wrong with him?

Why did he feel a powerful urge to protect her when she clearly didn't want his protection? *It must be gratitude for saving Nessa and her maid. A curiosity. A riddle to solve, no more.* One of his men handed him a bowl of stew, causing him to push such thoughts away with another curse.

Finishing the fish, Anna produced one of the few remaining apples in her pack. With a pout, she inhaled its sweet fragrance before biting into the succulent flesh. Better to savor this, as there would likely be no such luxuries where they were headed. From the smell of the stew they passed around, she could assume her rations as a prisoner would be similar or worse. Her gut tightened as MacGregor approached, the same dark, brooding expression on his face.

"Come. Did ye hear the request for challenge when we arrived at camp?"

Of course she had. Did he think her daft? She rose without acknowledging the question.

"The rules are simple. The challenger chooses the type of weapon. Ye will have yer pick from several. The winner can allow quarter if he chooses or not. Any grievances are considered fulfilled by the match."

Anna snapped her head around in response. "Is that not convenient for clan MacGregor? No such right to my kinsmen if someone were to wish to avenge my death," she spat, no longer trying to contain the anger she'd held back all afternoon. Every muscle in her body tensed as she struggled against the urge to knock the man next to her on his arse.

"And what clan should I expect to come calling if ye were to lose this eve?"

His tone sounded calm and even, infuriating her more. Stiff with anger, Anna faced the men gathered without answering and strode toward the ring of expectant faces. She could play the game of ignoring questions as well as he.

"Good luck."

"Go to the devil, *sir*," she shot back with enough force to injure.

Laird MacGregor entered the circle and commanded attention. "Shamus has claimed his right to challenge. It should be said that Alasdair was injured disobeying my order. But he is a kinsman. Under the laws of our clan, 'tis his right and I grant it. I demand quarter be offered because the challenged is a woman, and because she killed the MacNairn filth who stole my Nessa." He turned to Anna, nodded slightly and left the circle.

A square of plaide sat between them on the ground, blades scattered on its surface. The knives were of various lengths, none longer than her forearm plus handle. Shamus walked to the cloth, promptly selected a dagger and snarled at her. Looking at the pile, she noticed wooden batons as long as the longest dirks.

She claimed one in each hand and peered at Duncan. "Am I allowed two?"

He turned to Shamus for the answer. His laughter joined that of the rest of the men as he replied, "Only a *Sassenach* would bring a stick to a knife fight."

Allowing the insult to pass, Anna quickly slipped into the mental space her mentor had taught her. *Give no thought to killing or being killed. Give no thought to your enemy. Clear your mind. Take only what is given.*

Zhang's lesson had been drilled into her for longer than she could remember—flowing through her like the air she breathed.

Shamus spat on the ground at her feet, his face contorting with hatred. "English bitch."

He seemed to need no provocation to work himself up to kill a woman. Any blood spilled would be on his hands.

"Barbarians," Anna growled. She brought the batons up and swung them around in circular patterns. Shifting her feet along with the sticks, she fell into a steady rhythm. The rods moved rapidly in a blur of motion, singing low as they cut through the air. Shamus watched with surprised fascination, seemingly uncertain what to make of the unfamiliar movements. She needed to take care. By the way he moved, this man had survived a number of fights.

He moved warily, probing the perimeter of her swings. Where the batons made contact with his blade a distinct *clack* echoed. Cautious not to hit the dagger on the edge, she struck only the flat of his weapon. This pattern went on for a while, his probing, her defending. He sought a weakness. She strove not to show one.

Shamus stepped in for a slash. Anna deflected most of his blow, but the tip grazed her left arm between the elbow and shoulder, causing a familiar sting and warmth as blood flowed.

He tossed her a wicked grin and a taunt. No time to think, only focus on the *here*, the *now*. Another slash and she swung both sticks in response. Each made contact with the wrist holding his blade, creating the distinctive *smack-smack* sound of wood on meat. Shamus dropped his blade. From the force of contact, she hoped for a broken bone.

Allowing the batons to continue to circle after the strike, she brought them both down to crash into the outside of his knee, spinning as she swung to add more force to the blow. The twin strikes buckled his leg, driving his knee into the soft turf. As she continued her spin, Anna used the momentum of her last attack to power the next, aiming for the back of his skull where the spine joined. The double strikes—one after the other—to this vulnerable area rendered him unconscious with a sickening thud, dropping him like a felled tree.

Snatching up his fallen blade, she grabbed the back of his hair and placed the dagger against his throat. The crowd, which she'd ignored during the fight, fell into silence. She scanned the crowd for MacGregor. He stepped into the circle. She issued her challenge.

"Laird, this man owes me a life debt. Agreed?"

The laird stared at her with surprise for a moment before answering. "Aye, agreed."

She dropped her unconscious opponent, turned and stalked toward her campsite.

"The blade," Duncan barked.

Whirling to face him, her knuckles whitened as she fisted the dagger, tempted to fight her way back to Orion. After a moment's hesitation, she flipped the knife over, blade now in her palm, and hurled it toward the fallen man. It struck between his legs a few inches below his manhood, pinning his plaide to the ground.

She stormed to her campsite. Fat drops of rain fell, pulling her attention away from the fight. She fixed the waxed cloth overhead on the two poles she'd cut earlier, anchoring the ends to a rock and a couple of stakes, giving it a tug to test its strength. She ambled to the stream and crossed it, not giving her back to the man following her. She washed as much as she dared with MacGregor present, then filled her water skin and a small cooking pot from her pack.

She returned to the fire and inspected her wound. A three-inch-long shallow slash oozed blood below her shoulder. Uttering a curse toward all things male, she wiped the blood away, grateful she'd sustained no greater injury. After boiling the water in the pot, Anna soaked both the needle and thread. She cleaned and stitched the wound, applying the same salve used on the injured men earlier. Fetching bandage material from her pack, she bound the cut.

Adding more wood to the fire, she positioned a number of small twigs around her site to signal her if anyone stepped close. Still seething over her treatment thus far, she sat cross-legged under her small shelter. Eyes closed, body relaxed, Anna forced her mind to still. After an hour of calm, she opened her eyes to the night. The fever from battle, along with most of her anger, had ebbed.

Stretching out, Anna wrapped up in her plaide, trying for as much sleep as possible amongst a group of men who'd proven themselves foes. She hoped her performance against Shamus would discourage any from testing her again this night.

Drowsily, Anna replayed the day's events in her mind and wondered what the next day would bring. Though her actions had resulted in capture, she knew she would rescue those girls again if given the chance. Even if the men possessed no honor, these barbarians would not alter hers. Exhausted both emotionally and physically, she offered no resistance when sleep claimed her.

She rose before dawn and noticed she had a new watchman. She asked for privacy to take care of her early morning needs and walked to the stream. Using a small cloth, she cleaned her teeth and washed her face. After breaking camp, she had nothing to do but wait for instruction. As she finished a slice of bread and an apple, MacGregor the Younger approached with their saddled horses. From his expression, he seemed pleased about something. At least his lighter mood marked a change from the stormy expression he usually wore.

"Ye will ride with me again. We are three full days from home."

Neither answering nor making eye contact, she secured her belongings and climbed aboard her horse. He tied Orion's reins to his saddle, leaving her only along for the ride. All day Anna bore the men's speculative stares, some puzzled, some amused. Though used to such scrutiny as a woman warrior, her skin prickled to have no escape from it. She realized how much she relied on her father's and grandfather's names as a cloak of protection.

"I wondered about yer armor and horse. They are of high quality, which would make ye under the care of a person with means," Duncan said.

She shot him a baleful look. "And yet you insist on kidnapping me. Tell me, sir, how is it you and your father are any different from the barbarians I killed yesterday to rescue your sister and her maid?"

Her question broke his calm demeanor and his angry, brooding manner returned with a vengeance. Judging by the muscles rippling along his jaw and the fire in his eyes, he didn't like the comparison. If he knew the difference, he chose not to explain it.

They stopped once around midday to allow the horses to graze and water. It proved to be the only break of the day. After tending to her personal needs, Anna squatted with her back against a large tree to eat, watching the men. They mostly ignored her. Still, she refused to take any chances by letting her guard down.

"The men willnae harm ye. Ye are under my protection," Duncan remarked, his brows furrowed, hands on hips, feet wide apart as if rebuking a man under his command.

Angling her head to face him, she allowed her gaze to meet his, her features set as if carved from rock. "If your *protection* was demonstrated last night, I will certainly sleep more soundly tonight, sir. Thank you."

The anger on his face shone clear as the water of the loch they'd stopped beside. Springing away without replying, he stalked several paces to finish his meal. After a few minutes, he stomped back to where she sat. Without a glance in his direction, Anna strode to her horse and mounted. Climbing on his horse, he spoke no more as they continued their journey.

The rest of the day unfolded uneventfully. Near nightfall, they finally halted. Without enough light to hunt or fish, Anna ate from the supplies in her pack. She repeated her routine of foraging for wood, creating a fire and camp. Duncan brought her a bowl of something smelling like unwashed feet and cabbage, placing the bowl on the ground in front of her.

She gave him a curt nod, but didn't touch the rancid-smelling concoction, eating only from her dwindling provisions. She'd hunted or fished each day since leaving home to stretch her foodstuffs and would need to replenish her supplies soon.

The next day mirrored the first—the only difference was they began to climb.

"Steady, boy." She patted her horse, murmuring encouragements along the way. Orion, not used to steep, rocky terrain, stumbled a few times until he became accustomed to the trickier footing. His skittish behavior reflected the nearness of unfamiliar men and horses. His muscles flinched occasionally, reacting to her unease.

Once, a group of five men on horseback met them. Duncan and his sire rode to meet them, leaving her in the care of another while they spoke. The conversation was brief and civil and they soon continued their trek. After another hour of travel, the damp chill of elevation replaced the warmer air of the Lowlands.

A slow, steady rain fell, a bitter wind driving the drops before it. Wrapping her braid around her neck for warmth, Anna tucked her cloak in tight with the waxed cloth on top. Though shivering from the cold and damp, she remained mostly dry. She noticed her traveling companions hardly seemed affected by the change in temperature or wind.

Highland barbarians are in their element.

She turned her thoughts from the cold to something more practical. Men surrounded her on all sides when mounted, keeping her closed in. With her reins tied to Duncan's horse, she had no opportunity to escape. Without weapons, she would be helpless against an attack even if she somehow managed to elude them. As much as it pained, she'd have to continue to wait for an opportunity to arise before slipping away from her captors.

MacGregor made no more attempts to talk. To her relief, the stares of the men mostly disappeared. They viewed her simply as baggage at this point—noticed but not regarded.

They stopped by another stream an hour before dark. She didn't see any fish in this one. Unwinding a sling from within her belt, she selected a few smooth stones from the stream, then headed into the woods, Duncan following several paces behind. After stalking the perimeter of their camp, she spotted a hare. She whirled the sling and silently killed the animal, dressing it before returning to her site, ignoring MacGregor.

The chill in the air worsened with nightfall. Anna built the fire a bit closer and larger than the night before to fight off the moist chill threatening to seep into her bones. She was full of rabbit and sitting close to the fire, and the cold remained mostly at bay. She wondered about these men who took her captive, and Duncan in particular. She'd found herself watching him surreptitiously throughout the day. Something about him drew her attention, though it made no sense.

I must be daft! Having any feelings except anger toward this man is folly.

Scraping the rabbit hide after eating gave her something to do other than make and discard plans for escape. If the air grew much colder, she would need to kill several more hares to line her cloak.

Anna remained watchful, sleeping light, waking every two hours or so, though she supposed if someone planned to attack, they would have done so by now. Perhaps Duncan's words of protection rang true. She wasn't willing to risk her life by dropping her guard simply because of his promise of safety. Trusting this group of barbarians could prove a deadly mistake.

After three days of being around this woman, this Anna, Duncan found himself at a loss. Not one complaint, not one request. She'd quietly gone about taking care of her own needs, relying on nothing from the others. What lass, English or Scot, behaved such? How was it possible?

Where would a young noblewoman learn these skills she possessed? Skills that should have taken longer than her apparent years to master? *She accepts our food, yet does not eat it. Her swift kills of both the fish and hare—startling. She slips through the forest like a wraith—more silent than the most skilled warrior.*

He'd come to realize this woman was what she first appeared, an experienced fighter and hunter, though he couldn't fathom the how or why. The numerous scars visible on her, including a rather long one on her neck, confirmed this. The fact that he'd stood by and watched while she added another to her collection tore at his conscience.

The lass is angry—and rightly so. We will not be lulled into complacency around her. She likely would take her first chance to slit our throats and escape. Bonny lass or not, it will not do to drop our guard around this one.

Because of the potential for trouble, he informed his men not to let their attention waver. She required constant watching. This knowledge didn't blunt his protective instincts. On the contrary, they grew stronger with every passing hour. Never one to hide from his feelings, he simply didn't understand them. Nor did he know what to do with his confusion.

The gall of her to compare us to the cursed MacNairns! Upon further reflection, he understood her viewpoint. How indeed were they any different?

For all she knows, she is to be taken to our home and given to a man as wife against her will.

Duncan knew his da did not intend such. However, she did not. Chuckling to himself, he imagined *that* scene playing out. Pity any man who would attempt such a foolish thing. He would wind up with a dagger buried in his heart, or worse.

Her response to his pledge that she would not be harmed seared through him. For some reason she resurrected memories of his brother, Callum, and that terrible day many years ago that had seen the end of his young life. Something about her called to him to protect her, to ensure her safety. She clearly didn't believe him and bore the wound to prove her right. *Barbarians* was the word she'd used. So far, they'd earned the name.

In spite of her manly behavior, Duncan saw her femininity, her loveliness. Like a viper, beautiful but deadly. Best viewed from a distance, treated with respect. She'd been noticeably cold since they left the Lowlands, unaccustomed to the altitude and climate. He considered offering a blanket but thought better of it. She'd want nothing from him but freedom.

Duncan continued to find it difficult to accept a collection of abilities in such a highly unlikely form. The more time he spent around her, the more he wished to know everything about her. He knew he should keep his distance, but for some inexplicable reason he found he could not. His eyes only left her when he closed them to sleep. Her presence consistently pricked at the calm guise he'd carefully crafted for years. Never before had he been more perturbed by a woman. He inwardly cursed his own weakness as he looked forward to seeing her on the morrow.

Chapter Three

$\mathcal{M}$id-afternoon the next day, Anna realized they'd stopped climbing. As the group threaded its way through a forbidding mountain pass, she was unprepared for the breathtaking beauty of the Highlands that unfolded before her. The mountains rose impossibly tall and massive, lush with greenery and sparkling with water. Streams burst from the stones and cascaded over the rocky crags toward the many lakes they'd passed. The majesty of the rugged terrain made her Lowland home pale in comparison.

Earlier in the day, they'd met another group of men from a different clan. Based on the friendly greetings, these men were personally known by clan MacGregor. Once on their way again, she addressed one of the men who consistently rode next to her. A man she'd heard called Iain.

"What are these mountains, sir?"

Surprise crossed each face within hearing distance. She'd not initiated communication with anyone but Duncan or the laird since her captivity.

"The Grampians, milady."

His pleasant tone told her he hoped her question would mark the start of conversation. She knew they wondered about her. *They can remain curious. I will not stir this matter further.* She feared what they might do if they found out she was the daughter of an English baron and granddaughter to the laird of a Lowland clan.

Though, mayhap if I told them about Grandfather, they would exchange coin for my freedom. No, I will not involve clan Elliot. I could not save my English family, but can protect my Scots kin. At least these men provided escort far away from her English enemies. She needed only to find a way to escape. Anna intentionally made no further contact, and eventually the men ignored her again.

As they crested a ridge, a castle loomed in the distance. By early evening, they entered the outskirts of a small town. A cold feeling in the pit of Anna's stomach told her they'd arrived at their destination.

The village sprawled before the castle. The northern wall of the stone fortification sat just short of a sheer cliff making a rear attack impossible. She'd not seen a better site for a stronghold. Its position gave the inhabitants the advantage of seeing great a distance, and enemies could advance only from the front.

The dark gray stone of the keep matched the stone of the surrounding mountains, making it both beautiful and foreboding. An involuntary shiver crept up Anna's spine.

Duncan leaned toward her. "Welcome to *Ciardun.*"

Gray Fortress. The name was apt, though it looked anything but welcoming. The warmth and relief in Duncan's voice made him sound as though he smelled a well-cooked meal after a long hard day. Obviously, he was glad to be home. Her sense of dread increased as she considered the slim chance of escape once they passed through those formidable gates. She shivered again as the coldness in her stomach increased tenfold.

In an effort to take her mind off her new prison, she took in the scene around her. The looks she received from the villagers-a mixture of harsh, curious, and bemused expressions—reminded her of her plight. Not a friendly face among them. She straightened to her full height, chin held high with an expressionless guise.

She suspected the cause for their curiosity was the way she trailed MacGregor, her reins tied to his saddle. Or perhaps a strange woman dressed like a man piqued their curiosity. No one dared attack someone obviously in his charge. At least he'd kept his word about her safety thus far.

Once they rode past the village, the castle's presence demanded attention like flames in the darkness. She found it a truly intimidating structure. Not the largest she'd seen, but daunting none the less. Four stone towers, one at each corner, rose high, with a much larger square tower centered along the back curtain wall. A long, two-level stone and wood building connected the back corner towers to the square one.

I wonder if being female will keep me out of the dungeons. Likely not.

A loud commotion marked the return of the laird and his beloved daughter as they entered the keep.

"Worry not, lass, all will be well. Ye have my word." Duncan leaned closer so his words reached her ears alone.

They dismounted, handing their horses to stable lads, and Duncan led her through the door of the keep and into the main hall. A number of trestle tables and benches stood prepared. Massive hearths at both ends of the hall provided heat for the entire room. A raised dais with a well-appointed table and chairs marked where the laird and family dined.

Continuing toward the back of the room, they strode down a long corridor ending at a thick, locked door. Duncan gently placed his hand on Anna's upper arm, guiding her toward the heavy door. She jerked away as if burned. Something in his touch affected her, though she fought not to acknowledge it. He scrunched his brow, scowling at her. Judging by his reaction, whatever passed between them he experienced as well.

On the other side of the portal stood four cells with stone walls and iron-reinforced doors. Small, barred windows high on the wall allowed the waning sunlight into each cell. Every door had a barred window looking into the hallway. Apparently this would be her home for the foreseeable future. As she entered a cell, Anna glared a challenge at MacGregor which he did not match. In fact, she swore regret lurked in his eyes. It mattered not. It was an unforgivable fact—they held her prisoner after she'd rescued the laird's daughter. *Barbarians.*

Duncan knocked before entering his father's solar.

"Is she secured?" Kenneth asked, briefly glancing up from the parchment on his desk.

"Aye," Duncan replied. Disapproval colored his tone.

Kenneth shook his head, taking a deep breath. "Spit it out."

Duncan shot his father a defiant glare, his body stiff. "Ye dinnae know what ye ask."

"Aye, I have some idea. Say it."

Duncan held his father's gaze as he dropped into the chair across the desk from him, hands gripping the ornately carved arms. "I believe 'tis wrong to imprison the lass. She has earned our trust, not imprisonment."

Kenneth rubbed a hand across his mouth and chin before answering. "We do not know why she is alone. A lass, even as able as she, does not travel alone unless in trouble. I dinnae want her problems brought here. She cannae cause harm if she is locked up."

Duncan sprang to his feet, pacing the floor, his hands boldly punctuating his words. "Then confine her to one of the smaller chambers. She should at least be allowed the same courtesies we would offer a guest."

Kenneth shook his head. "Did ye not see what I saw? She cut through six Highlanders without hesitation. Afterward, she defeated Shamus with very little trouble using *two sticks*. We could claim the MacNairn are not good fighters, but we both know Shamus is a capable warrior. How do ye keep someone like that confined in a guest room?"

Duncan stopped his pacing. He attempted to wrest his temper into control by dropping his eyes, lowering his voice. "Post a guard or two, bar the door from the outside."

"Nae!" Kenneth bellowed, a hand cutting across his body.

Duncan grabbed the back of his chair, using the tension in his grip to launch his next volley. "She saved my sister, *yer* daughter, from rape or murder! 'Tis not right!" Lost to his anger, he rose on his toes, his fingernails biting into the wood of the chair.

"Enough! As long as I am laird my word is law. This discussion is over." His father's voice descended into a growl.

Duncan gritted his teeth, wheeled about and stormed from the room.

Anna shifted her gaze from the fresh straw and blanket in one corner to the well-worn but clean chamber pot in another. The room measured approximately ten by ten with a stone floor. She placed her cloak and plaide on the floor next to the blanket and removed her armor. She quietly considered her fate, realizing she hadn't allowed herself to grieve the loss of her village, home and family. Tears spilled as misery rent a hole in her heart.

I am so sorry, father, Edrick. Misery choked her as surely as a pair of strong hands, leaving her breathless. After some time, her tears ran their course, leaving numbness in their wake.

Later in the evening, someone brought a bowl of more foul-smelling stew, a small piece of bread and pitcher of water.

"Blessed Virgin, how do they stand this fetid fodder?" she muttered crossly. Abandoning the stew, she ate the bread and drank some water, saving the rest for later.

She unwrapped the bandage and checked her wound. It was healing, though the jagged edge interrupted the flowing blue pattern given to her last year by the clan elders. It reflected a symbol of status and coming of age as a warrior, signifying the battles she'd fought. The lines of ink swirled about her shoulders, across her upper back, followed her collarbones and peaked at the back of her neck.

Legend said the intricate swirls and interlocking patterns were unique to ancient Pictish women warriors. The design had taken several sittings to complete and she was proud to wear the blue woad ink, signifying her place among their warriors. The flowing design would be with her as long as she lived, a reminder of who she was—a visible connection to her clan and the past.

By nightfall, cold had crept back again. She coiled her braid around her neck and wrapped up in her cloak and plaide. Burrowing as deeply as she could in the straw, she stared at the deep blue-and-wine pattern of the wool. She closed her eyes, remembering the life left behind at the border, reliving the terrible day of death and fire.

She woke at dawn in a chill. Exercise was the only way to warm herself, and she needed activities to focus on, a schedule to spend her days. She went through conditioning routines to warm her body, then spent a time in meditation. Chilled again, she practiced fighting patterns, routines Master Zhang had drilled into her and Edrick without ceasing. Finally exhausted, she recited Holy Scripture and poetry in English, Gaelic, Latin and French as she drifted off to sleep. She repeated the pattern again that afternoon, ending the day with meditation and reflection.

I did not know I would use this one day, but I thank you, Master Zhang. I will not fall prey to sickness and madness. Though he'd refused to share the particulars of his four years in captivity, Zhang stated his experience taught him that every warrior must be prepared for such a possibility. *For all the games of prisoner Edrick and I played, no matter how uncomfortable, no matter how difficult, I know I will survive, and be strengthened by this.*

The ache in her heart at the loss of her mentor, brother and father would provide the motivation she needed to stay alive, to remain herself. She would not waste her time wondering what plans the barbarians had for her.

Much to her vexation, her thoughts kept returning to her captor, and Anna cursed her lack of self-discipline. She'd managed to live a score of years without a serious thought for any man—why could she not banish thoughts of the barbarian who held her captive? Zhang once spoke of forging a bond of sorts with one of his captors. Mayhap she experienced something similar.

I certainly do not fancy him, she protested, shaking her head at the thought. *Blessed Mother! That would be the height of madness.*

The next day was the same. The stew was unbearable. She wrinkled her nose. *Do they use meat beginning to spoil?* She sighed. *I will make do with the morning's oat porridge and the evening bread and water. Eating this offal would only make me sicken.*

She peered through the small barred window in the door as she placed the foul-smelling bowl of stew on the floor. A guard always stood outside, watching the cells. For what purpose, she knew not, as there were no other prisoners.

What I do know is I have not grown used to this cursed cold, damp air. She rubbed her arms vigorously. *I wake cold, go to sleep cold.* Resolutely, she turned from the door and began her exercises again.

At last warmed and tired, she turned her observations to the behavior of the men guarding the cells. None approached, nor attempted to speak to her. At night, a leering beast of a man kept watch. The way he stared at her left an unsettling feeling. He usually fell asleep around matins, his chair propped against the back wall.

On the second night of her captivity, the guard's snoring jarred Anna from sleep. She tossed a few small pieces of stone into the hall. He didn't stir. She tapped lightly on the heavy wooden door, then louder. The snoring continued. She smiled. He was a deep sleeper.

The midday meal was another bowl of the greasy stew. Anna poked at the chunks of meat floating in the broth, watching the fat congeal on the surface as it cooled. She touched the soft grease thoughtfully. Dipping her fingers in the slippery fat, she slathered it across the hinges of her cell door.

Night fell on the third day. Waiting until the guard fell asleep, Anna took her blanket and pushed it out the barred window of the door until it hung past the lock. Carefully, she withdrew the two steel throwing darts hidden in her bracers, and inserted them in the lock. She worked quickly, one eye on the guard, the wool of the blanket muffling the sounds.

Within minutes, she eased the door open. Creeping into the hall, she stared at the enormous guard, each snore a thunderous boom. Cat-like, she padded to the door leading into the next hallway. Not hesitating, she slowly raised the bar and peered down the hall. Meeting no sign of activity, she moved stealthily along the corridor leading to the great hall. Careful inspection of the large room showed no movement and no sound. The great hall, usually the center of activity, lay as quiet as the bottom of a loch.

At the door to the bailey, she pulled up short, scanning the yard. *The gates are secured for the night. I cannot fetch Orion and leave until dawn and the gates are opened.* She glanced about for a place to hide in the lingering darkness.

The moon loomed overhead, almost full, flooding the vacant bailey with light. Men walked the curtain wall, keeping watch, their attention turned outward rather than into the yard. Sticking to the shadows along the wall, she slipped into the stables without a sound.

Unable to find slumber yet again, Duncan strolled the curtain wall as he had on other sleepless nights. Only a pair of hours till dawn and he'd yet to get the lass out of his mind. 'Twas well beyond frustrating. Never had a woman affected him this swiftly, this absolutely. Each time he thought of her, lust, possessiveness and an overwhelming urge to protect her filled him. She had the body of a *leannan sith* and the heart of a warrior, a mystery constantly prodding his peace. He traveled the same mental paths over and over again, wondering who she was and replaying the arguments with his father, leaving no room for sleep.

A slight movement drew his attention in the yard. *No, it cannot be. Could my thoughts have summoned her?* He squatted in the shadow of a crenel and watched for the movement again. He closed his eyes and scrubbed his face before looking once more to make sure he wasn't seeing things.

The shadow moved again. A cloaked figure made its way around the perimeter of the yard toward the stables. Duncan's lips flexed into a smile as he remained motionless, watching. He wanted to see how much success this hooded padfoot would gain.

Certain of the identity of the brazen sneak, he couldn't fathom how she'd broken out of her cell, past Alain, and then out of the hall without attracting attention. Glancing at the men on watch, he noticed they only scanned the grounds outside the keep. This would be an enlightening experience indeed. His smile curved further in anticipation.

She slipped into the stables as silently as she had out of the keep and around the yard. Duncan abandoned the wall and made his way to the gatehouse to speak with the gate master. Taking up a position atop the barbican, he had full view of the narrow gateway below. He settled in to wait until the portcullis was raised at first light.

As suspected, at the first grating sounds of the windlass, a hooded form atop a now-familiar charger slowly walked toward the fortified outer gate. He chuckled at the pluck of the resourceful woman and shook his head.

St. Filan's teeth! What can she not do?

He considered for a moment that he should be angry, but truly he owed her thanks instead. Clearly their security measures were lax. Also, he couldn't recall enjoying a sleepless night more, thoroughly entertained by Anna's attempt at escape.

On his command, the gate master dropped the outer portal. Kicking her stallion, Anna raced ahead. Duncan's heart hurled itself against his ribs and a sick feeling spread through his gut, fearing she'd be crushed under the gate. At the last possible second, Anna jerked her horse to a halt, pulling him back on his haunches as the iron struck the ground before her with a resounding clang like a broken church bell.

Men stood across the entrance to the bailey, ready to draw swords. Under strict orders not to harm her, they blocked the narrow entryway. Stepping from an inner door of the barbican, Duncan appeared at her side. He grabbed Orion by the bridle and smiled.

Chapter Four

"*T*is a fine morn. Or 'twill be once the sun is up. Out for a ride, then?" Duncan's voice lilted with amusement.

Anna growled in response.

She gave up her mount more easily than he expected, but brushed aside his offer of assistance. Even this momentary touch sent a spark of awareness up his arm. He caught the flash of anger in her green eyes as she spun on a heel and stalked toward the hall, her rapid pace no doubt designed to avoid further contact with him.

Entering the great hall, Anna hesitated as the guard, Alain, strode aggressively toward her, cursing the English as he approached. Duncan immediately intercepted him, shoving him backward.

"Ye willnae talk to the lady thus. Ye owe her an apology."

Alain glared at Anna. Duncan closed the gap between them, fists curled, ready to attack.

"Apologize or I will have ye cleaning privies for a week—after I give ye a lesson on how to speak to a lady." Anger flared as Alain appeared ready to disobey his order, and every sinew in his body tensed in anticipation of the beating he yearned to deliver.

"I apologize, milady," Alain ground out, the muscles on his neck taut from the effort.

Duncan shot the man a glare, refusing to tolerate one word of abuse hurled her way. *Later*, he promised with a hard look. He would find Alain and make sure the man understood hostilities toward her would be met with severe consequences.

Anna nodded once toward Alain, acknowledging his apology. Duncan hesitated, allowing the tension to fade as Alain left the hall.

Anna fairly quivered with futile anger.

"Come break yer fast with me, lady," Duncan said softly, hope saturating his words of invitation.

Ignoring his request, Anna strode toward her cell. Instead of allowing her into the one she'd previously occupied, Duncan opened the door to the one next to it. He turned to one of the men nearby.

"Have a servant fetch the lady and me breakfast." Closing the door to her new cell, he jerked it hard a few times, testing the strength of the lock before reopening it to let her in. He entered the cell she occupied before. She heard him moving around and knew he searched for her means of escape. After a few moments, she heard his laugh.

The guard returned with a woman bearing a tray with two bowls, a pitcher and two cups. Another brought a pair of stools. Stepping into her new cell, Duncan handed Anna a stool and a bowl. Sitting in the open doorway, he glanced at her, a knowing smirk on his face. At a flick of his fingers, the two guards moved down the hall a few steps out of sight, giving them the appearance of privacy.

"I must say, using fat from the meat to grease the hinges was verra clever."

She heard pride in his voice, but why would he be proud she'd escaped his prison? Anna ignored him, tucking into the bowl of porridge he gave her instead.

"What I cannae work out is how ye unlocked the door, and how ye did so without waking yer guard." His voice stretched out, inviting an answer.

If he waited for her to give him one, he would soon be shaking hands with disappointment. Shuttering her expression before looking up, Anna asked with indifference, "Will I be beaten for my attempted escape?"

His smirk softened to a smile before answering. "Nae. Not this time. Indeed, I should thank ye. We are not in the habit of keeping prisoners. It seems yer adventure this morn pointed out certain gaps in our ability to hold captives."

Anna realized she'd never seen him truly smile before. That he was such a handsome man further irritated her. He poured himself a draught from the pitcher and took a drink before pouring hers, demonstrating it hadn't been tampered with. It tempted her to lower her guard, but she must not.

They ate in silence, then he put the items back on the tray and set it in the hallway.

"Ye have been isolated for three days. Would ye like to talk? I would know better the noblewoman my father keeps."

His seductive burr willed her to see him as something other than her gaoler, willed her to see him as a friend—or a protector? No. Until the locks and barred doors were replaced with freedom, she would only see him as a warden.

Handing him back the cup, she responded woodenly, "No, thank you, sir. I am enjoying the solitude you offer and have been using my time productively."

Duncan's eyes danced. "I trust ye willnae attempt escape again?"

Anna nudged the stool over to him with a toe and scrunched her brow. "Why would you think thus? Would you cease if our places were reversed?"

He held her gaze before answering, his smile still roguish. "Nae, I suppose not. 'Tis the duty of every prisoner to escape."

She dipped her head in agreement.

"Should ye change your mind about wishing to speak, inform yer guard. I will come when I can."

The lock on the door snicked closed behind him, and a shudder snaked through her at the sound. The weight of her failed attempt bore down on her, the crush of helplessness replacing the frustration of failure. At least she'd receive no immediate consequence for her actions.

Duncan walked away, shaken by the encounter. Something inexplicable drew him to her. He fought the urge to kiss her, drinking from her full lips until they were both intoxicated. His bright mood dimmed as he recalled the need to tell his father of the morn's adventure. He didn't want to hear the auld man say he was right.

He found both his parents in the great hall, breaking their fast at the high table. When they saw him approach, his mother motioned for an additional bowl to be brought.

"What has ye so ill-tempered this morn, my son?" she asked, curiosity in her voice.

"Good morrow, Mother. I need to speak with Da when he has finished," Duncan replied, staring at his second bowl of porridge of the morning. With appetite already sated, he merely stirred his food, needing something to do with his hands.

"The English lass?" she prodded.

Duncan sighed deeply and nodded with some reluctance. "How did ye know?"

She offered a vivacious smile and placed a hand on his arm. "Ye have been vexed ever since she arrived."

They finished the meal in silence. Mairi rose and kissed them both on the cheek. "Please be civil, gentlemen." With a meaningful glance, she exited the hall, leaving them alone as the servants retreated to the kitchen.

"Very well, what is it this time?" Kenneth leaned back in his chair, his tone exasperated.

On the defensive, Duncan shot his father a flinty look. "Yer prisoner escaped last night."

The news stunned his father into silence, his eyes widening, mouth agape.

With a measure of satisfaction at seeing him so, Duncan continued. "I dinnae know how she opened the lock. She used fat from the stew to grease the hinges and somehow snuck past Alain whilst he slept. I happened to be walking the wall and spotted her creeping about. She made it to the stables undetected. She had her horse saddled and rode amongst a group headed for the fields." Duncan did not bother to hide his admiration.

Kenneth stopped all pretense of eating. "She got away?"

Duncan shook his head, trying not to laugh at the expression on his father's face. "Nae. I alerted the gate master to drop the outer gate. I placed a dozen men at the other end with orders not to harm her. When she entered the gateway, I had the gate lowered. She made a run for it but dinnae make it. Howbeit, 'twas close."

Kenneth stared at him, apparently finding it hard to grasp the tale. "Where is she now?"

"I put her in another cell. I checked to make sure this one locked properly, though I could find no fault with the one holding her before."

"She was not injured?" Kenneth rubbed his brow, his bewilderment plain.

"Nae. Though she did ask if her attempt will earn her a beating."

The laird grimaced. "What did ye tell her?"

"I told her, not this time." Duncan's lips quirked upward.

Kenneth sat quietly, staring at the contents swirling in his mug. "I told ye she needed to be secured." His tone sounded smug with a hint of bluster, as if trying to hide guilt over imprisoning a noblewoman.

"Aye, and I said she wouldnae feel the need to escape if she were treated like a guest—which she has earned." After a few tense moments, Duncan rose to leave before his anger grew worse. He knew there would be no winning this dispute.

Five days. Five days his father forced Anna to sit in that curst cell. For what purpose? He would find out tonight, as a rider had arrived this afternoon bearing news regarding her. Duncan sat by the hearth and waited for his father to broach the subject. After arguing with him several times already, Duncan thought he would try a more passive approach.

"I know my handling of the English lass has been difficult for ye." Kenneth filled his cup and Duncan's with wine.

"'Tis not my place to challenge yer orders, Father." Duncan replied, avoiding eye contact.

Frowning, Kenneth continued, "I could ask for no better son, but ye have done more than challenge my orders on this matter." His voice carried the frustration of their ongoing argument.

Duncan let the well-earned rebuke slip past unchallenged.

"Ye know my priority must be to protect our people. A woman who appears out of nowhere, who has skills equal to our best warriors, who is both Scots and English, 'tis a dangerous problem."

Duncan gave a curt nod in agreement.

"Why is she running?" Kenneth mused. "From whom does she run? And most importantly, could these enemies be brought to our doorstep? I took a risk by bringing her here, but feel a tremendous debt to her for what she did for Nessa."

"Aye, I know, 'tis a difficult situation."

Putting down his cup, Kenneth faced Duncan fully. "Do ye? I see the way ye look at her. I hear the emotion in yer words. I see how ye wish to protect her." He paused between each sentence for effect. "I fear by bringing her here we risk the whole clan. Perhaps even our allies."

"Then why treat her like a prisoner? Do ye know she asked me what makes us different from the men she killed defending Nessa?"

Kenneth closed his eyes, a frown on his face as he leaned back in his chair, fingers rubbing an old battle wound on his shoulder, a familiar gesture when vexed.

"When I told her we would protect her, she thanked me for the protection we had provided thus far, reminding me of the wound Shamus gave her, which she stitched herself." Duncan's aggravation rose, crested, finally softening into surrender. "I trust yer judgment, Father. I just dinnae understand it." Duncan's resolve to remain cordial began to slip.

Kenneth grunted. "I dispatched a rider before ye brought her back to camp that day. I needed to know as much as I could about her. I have found out she is Lady Anna Braxton, daughter of Baron Everard Braxton, a border lord. Her mother was Lady Rossalyn, daughter of the Elliot Laird. Her mother has been dead for several years."

His father shifted his weight in the chair and ran a hand through his graying hair.

"Her father and brother were killed in an attack by a neighboring noble who has been trying to gain Anna in marriage. He wanted to acquire her lands upon Lord Braxton's and his son's death. Apparently, Anna had rebuffed him repeatedly. Lord Braxton would not force her, and it seems the man grew weary of waiting. None within the keep survived the attack." Kenneth's somber voice reflected the harsh reality of her story.

Duncan stood, anger pounding in his skull, demanding he protect her from the schemes of this unknown *Sassenach*.

"From what I have learned, she and her brother were out hunting and came across the attack upon their return. Her brother must have forced her to run, because he met his death in defense of their home."

Duncan settled into the chair, his mind awhirl, absorbing the facts. This explained so many things. The English and Scots blood, the training and regal bearing—though it didn't explain why she was a fighter instead of the wife of a nobleman.

"She sought refuge with her grandda's clan, then?" Duncan still wondered about the circumstances of discovering her alone so far from the border.

As he leaned forward in his chair, Kenneth's face grew harsh. "Nae. She never went near Elliot, never sought aid, nor made contact. They likely fear she is dead or worse. She apparently does not know who attacked her family. She dinnae flee to another barony, but rather deep into Scotland, into the unknown. The heart of a lion, this one."

Duncan finally heard the same admiration he felt mirrored in his father's voice.

"To answer yer question, I have held her prisoner because 'twas possible she committed some sort of crime. I wanted to make sure she had no opportunity to flee. As ye know, there are those who would brutalize her then slit her throat simply because she is English. I captured her as much for her own safety as anything."

This last statement reverberated through the room. Duncan couldn't tell which of them he tried to convince. Duncan laced his fingers together across his chest, pushing deeper into the plush cushions of the chair, his legs stretched out in front of him, crossed at the ankles. Yes, he'd seen her bravery played out several times. This story fit with what he knew of her character.

They sat in silence, considering the situation, considering the options. The truth of her circumstances only proved to intensify Duncan's feelings for her.

"What will ye do?" He shifted position and rubbed his legs, awaiting an answer.

Kenneth strolled to the window overlooking the village. He stood quietly for a long time, staring into the distance, watching night absorb the remaining daylight. "MacGregors never back down from a fight, and we never forget a debt owed. We will harbor her here, hide her if her enemies come looking. Though I cannot think this Englishman will risk war by invading so far into Scotland over one lass."

Duncan carefully chewed over his words before asking the next question. "Considering her experience thus far, is there reason to think she would trust us and accept such an offer?"

A genuine smile crossed Kenneth's face. He seemed amused they were finally able to have a cordial conversation about the matter. His amused expression dissolved into something harder before he answered.

"I had three days to consider life without Nessa. Each day I imagined having to look into yer mother's eyes if we'd failed to find her, or if she had died during the rescue. Lady Anna Braxton is the reason I willnae daily see the pain of Nessa's death on yer mother's face. I will offer her my sincerest apologies and treat her as a daughter if she will allow it. If not, we will provide escort to wherever she wishes to go."

Duncan leaned forward, hands stroking his chin in a lazy manner, pondering his father's plan. He readily agreed it was the right thing to do, however, the thought of her leaving was—unsettling.

"I spoke with her guard. She sits in silent concentration for regular intervals. She recites the Bible and poetry in several languages and performs complex fighting drills daily. She has eaten very little since her arrival. She has not touched the stew we have given her here, nor on the three days' ride here," Duncan said as if offering a crop reporting.

This last bit of knowledge brought a scowl to the laird's face. "She starves herself?"

Duncan paused, considering the question. Fear for her well-being bullied its way into his thoughts. He firmly denied it access. "Nae, I dinnae think so. She hunted and killed on the ride back. She added this to some dried meat and fruit in her pack. I dinnae know why she has chosen to eat naught other than porridge and bread in five days. I do know each of her days is exactly the same. Her pattern is predictable, it doesnae vary. And there's still the wee mystery of how she escaped her cell." Duncan couldn't stop the esteem he held for her, or the accompanying grin when he thought again of her escape.

With his scowl still firmly in place Kenneth asked, "She has been trained to be a captive?"

Duncan uttered a humorless laugh, lowering his head in agreement. "Aye. 'Tis a logical explanation."

"Why the hell would a young woman of noble blood be taught to endure captivity?"

Duncan shared his father's exasperation, but had no ready answer. 'Twas a good question. Perhaps if she accepted his father's offer, if their treatment of her hadn't pushed her too far already, they would find out.

It seemed for every question answered at least one more surfaced. This only served to deepen the mystery of Lady Anna, rousing Duncan's curiosity further. Everything about her seemed a contradiction. Half English, half Scot. An accomplished rider, fighter and hunter, and a remarkably beautiful woman. Bred to live among the highly privileged, but trained to endure imprisonment. He found himself able to think of naught else. He wished he knew what made him desire her so strongly. Blowing out a frustrated breath, Duncan foresaw more sleepless nights.

Chapter Five

*O*n the evening of the fifth day of her captivity, the door to Anna's cell opened. Instead of bringing food, the odious guard glared at her and gestured for her to leave the cell. His clenched fists and constricted face told her his anger toward her hadn't cooled.

Every fiber of her body tensed. Standing at the doorway, she waited for him to move, refusing to turn her back to him. With a grunt of disgust, he walked past the door of the prison, opening the next door, and continued without waiting to see if she followed. He entered the great hall, leading her toward a door at the other end of the large room.

The enormous chamber bubbled with activity. Everyone, from the men and women eating, to those serving, halted their actions and stared as the guard led her through to the next doorway. The experience rattled her, raising the hair on the back of her neck as though she'd been hurled into a room full of predators—with her the blooded prey.

When the guard opened the next door, she saw a smaller, opulent chamber with a table surrounded by high-back chairs. Thick, colorful tapestries covered the walls. The candle stand on the intricately carved table held dozens of candles, the unmistakably sweet smell of beeswax filling the air. Everything about this room bespoke wealth.

This was obviously a private hall where MacGregor entertained guests. The lavishness of its décor aimed to impress or perhaps intimidate. Her guard jerked his head, motioning her forward. As she entered, both Duncan and his father rose from their seats. Raising his cup, the laird spoke. "Lady Anna, join us for a meal."

His tone sounded warm and inviting—in other words, confusing. The guard roughly pulled the chair out at the opposite end of the table, indicating she sit. She did so, then adjusted her chair to keep him in her line of sight.

"Please, help yerself. My son tells me ye have eaten little in five days."

The gentle scold reminded her of her father. She maintained a calm facade, belying the anxiety coursing through her.

"Thank you, Laird." Anna placed a small piece of cheese, a slice of bread, and an apple on the plate in front of her.

"Try the wine," MacGregor urged.

If the lightness of his voice and gesturing were to be believed, he relished the role of host. Gone the harsh warden of the past sennight, and in his place a congenial gentleman.

She ignored his request and reached for a pitcher of water instead. Anna had no intention of fuddling her wits with wine. She'd know if they'd tainted the water. It was easier to drug or poison wine.

After she assembled a small plate of food, the laird encouraged her to eat. Anna took a bite of apple and waited for him to pronounce her sentence. Bringing her into such a room, asking her to join them to sup, went beyond her expectations. As she chewed, she scanned the room for escape, keeping track of the guard. She suspected his movement would forewarn her of any danger.

"Lady Anna, I wish to apologize for taking and holding ye against yer will. Ye must understand I dinnae know who ye were. I did not know what crimes ye might have committed, or what enemies ye might be fleeing."

Crimes! The accusation overrode his conciliatory tone. Anger burned through her blood and it took all the control she possessed to stay seated. She stopped chewing, her fingers gripped the wooden armrests of the chair, and her pulled spine arrow-straight.

He continued. "The day ye assisted us, I sent a rider to follow yer trail, seeking to find out about ye. Since ye were unwilling to talk, I had to know what trouble ye ran from, and mayhap led to us."

"And now you know about me, Laird?" she asked through gritted teeth.

"Aye. Ye are Lady Anna Braxton, daughter of Baron Everard Braxton and Lady Rossalyn of the Elliot clan. Ye fled after yer home was attacked by a rival nobleman, yer family killed, yer home burned. For that I am very sorry."

Having endured eight days of captivity, all for rescuing his daughter, Anna had heard enough. "You are sorry?" she spat as she sprang to her feet. "For what? The death of my family, the loss of my home, or for wrongfully imprisoning an ally for a sennight?"

An unlooked-for blow sent her flying from her chair. The angry scrape of chairs, the furious voices as Duncan and his father shouted at the guard who attacked her, were all a muddle of nonsense as lights danced around her, her head throbbing. She tasted the metallic flavor of blood and felt the warmth of it on her face. A red haze fogged her vision.

Stumbling to her feet, she launched at her attacker. Using every bit of strength she could muster, Anna planted a kick between his legs, gratified to hear his grunt of pain. Grabbing his hair with both hands, she rammed her knee into his face. The satisfying crunch sent a spray of blood across her tunic. She twisted her body and uncoiled, throwing her weight behind an elbow strike, hitting the hinge of his jaw, just below the ear.

As he fell to the floor in a heap, she drew his dagger to finish the job.

"Lady Anna!" Duncan's voice broke the haze of her fury. "Dinnae kill him. I wouldnae wish to see ye hanged for murder."

Glaring at Duncan, Anna grabbed her fallen guard by the scalp and carved a four-inch long gash on his cheek as a reminder. The pain seemed to awaken him and he moaned. Dropping him to the floor, she stalked toward the entry.

"Lady Anna, please stay. We will see to yer wounds. Sit with us, finish yer meal. We wish to speak with ye." The laird gestured toward the table and her empty chair.

Still in a rage, she managed to answer, "Thank you, my laird, but I seem to have lost my appetite. If you will excuse me, I will withdraw to the accommodations you have so graciously provided." She took two steps toward the door when Duncan spoke again.

"Anna, I am sorry, he shouldnae have struck ye. He will be punished."

Realizing she still had his dagger in her hand, she spotted a target board for darts on the wall. She hurled the dagger, hitting near the center.

"Tell your men not to touch me again. The next barbarian who does will die, consequences be damned!"

Slamming the door behind her, she staggered into the main hall. She ignored the stares and the thrum of voices, only making it a few feet before her faltering steps forced her to stop. She leaned against the wall, struggling to clear her head and right her balance. The laird's words about her family, about her home, echoed in her mind. Angry tears burned their way down her cheeks. She wanted to lash out at someone, to scream.

A wave of dizziness swamped her. She gripped the wall. The buzz of conversation filled the hall, though she could not make out the words. As the dizziness eased, she assessed her injuries. A tender knot on the back of her head throbbed, but she detected no broken bones. She wiped the blood from her nose and mouth on her sleeve.

Her left eye began to swell, likely to be closed before morning. Her skin remained hot where his hand had landed, the sting still pulsing. The hammering in the back of her head felt as though a smith had set up shop. Controlling her breathing, Anna focused on letting the dizziness pass. Instead, it folded back, doubling in intensity. She took a ragged breath and slipped to the floor.

Duncan exploded with rage. The urge to protect Anna roared to the fore, stronger than ever. Only his father's intervention kept him from killing Alain with his bare hands. Deaf to reason and dimly aware of Kenneth's shouts, he fought his father's grip as Alain stumbled through the door. The guard gone, Kenneth bade Duncan follow Anna to make sure she wasn't seriously injured, ordering her moved upstairs for Nessa and Isla to tend.

Duncan charged into the main hall to find her and spotted a crowd surrounding something on the floor. Panic bolted through him, and he strode quickly to the crowd, pushing aside those in his way. His gaze fell on the woman kneeling at Anna's side.

"She has fainted, sir."

Duncan nodded his thanks and reached to smooth Anna's hair from her face. He scooped her into his arms, drawing her to his chest, and carried her toward the stairs to Nessa's room. Murmurs of speculation followed, fading as he ascended the stairs.

He took in the blood on her face and clothing and fought back the fury eating away at his control. His murderous rage gave way to an all-consuming need to comfort and safeguard her. Though he knew most of the blood on her clothes belonged to Alain, the knowledge did little to allay his concern.

He shook from the raw emotion of having her in his arms. He had no idea what was happening to him, but knew she belonged there. He hefted her to one side as he opened the door. She weighed more than he thought, her arms and legs surprisingly thick with muscle. This was no delicate lass, but a sturdy woman with a warrior's body.

He laid her gently upon the extra bed in Nessa's room. Feeling helpless, Duncan struggled between his need to seek revenge and his need to hold her again. At his mother's light touch, he pulled out of his conflicting thoughts.

"Da wishes ye to care for her." The gruffness of his voice surprised him. He'd never used such a tone with his mother. He detected the puzzled expression on his mother's face, knowing she caught the swirl of emotion in his eyes.

After a long silence she finally spoke, though barely above a whisper. "Leave her with us. We will see to her."

Inclining his head respectfully, Duncan left Anna in the care of his mother and sister. Skirting the main hall, he tossed a bridle on his stallion and rode to the loch. Stripping, he plunged into the icy depths, teeth gritted against the cold. Lungs near bursting, he surfaced and released a howl, venting the frustration of unfulfilled battle lust. The frigid water washed away the immediate rage coursing through him.

The cold anger remaining would not be slaked until he killed the bastard for hurting her.

The powerful memory of Anna in his arms did not diminish. He thought of the softness of her skin, of the flood of rightness of having her in his arms. Closing his eyes, Duncan vowed to do everything in his power to have her there again.

His instincts to protect her continued to dredge up memories and guilt about his brother, Callum, tormenting him further. Though never far from his thoughts, for some reason Anna's presence brought Callum to the fore of his mind. Perhaps a good night's sleep would help him gain a better view on things in the light of a new day. The knowledge that Anna lay in a proper bed and received care, allowed him some measure of peace.

Alain gathered his belongings, placing them on his horse. He could think of only one place to go—his mother's clan outside of Edinburgh. One uncle and a few cousins still lived, he knew. He faced at least a three-day ride, if not four. 'Twould give him plenty of time to think on his situation. Time to plan his revenge on MacGregor and the English bitch he'd brought back for his son. Based on what MacGregor said earlier this night, there would be people interested in her whereabouts. Interested enough to perhaps pay handsomely.

The trick would be to find out who would offer coin for such information, then be paid without getting killed in the process. If the interested party were to need Scottish allies to kidnap the wench, even better. Though trickier, it would mean a bigger purse, with the opportunity for personal revenge. Yes, 'twould take some planning to be done right. Alain vowed MacGregor and his new whore would pay in blood.

Chapter Six

*P*ain and light leaked through one of Anna's eyelids. As she moved, a wave of nausea swept through her. She rolled over and retched into a conveniently placed bucket. By the condition of the container, she had done so before, but had no memory of it. Giving her stomach a moment to settle, she tried to take stock of her injury and surroundings.

Tentatively raising a hand to her face, she touched swollen, tender flesh. A surge of memory returned. Dry-mouthed, she licked her lips, and the sting of a split lip answered. She tried to rise but gentle hands pushed her down, placing a cool, wet cloth over her damaged eye.

"Shhh, lie still. Ye are safe here."

A feminine voice, one she'd heard before. Turning her head slightly, Anna searched for the source and recognized the young woman she'd rescued a sennight ago. The girl smiled.

"I am Nessa. Ye saved me, remember?"

Taking a deep breath, Anna only managed a whisper, "Yes, of course I remember. How did I get here?"

Nessa patted the blanket in place over her shoulders, and Anna felt instant warmth. "My brother carried ye here last eve after ye passed out. My maid and I undressed ye, and put ye in a sleeping gown. I hope ye dinnae mind. Yer clothes were dirty and needed mending. Father told us to tend to ye until ye are well."

Noticing the brightness of the sun through the window, Anna closed her eyes. "How long have I been asleep?"

"Ye slept through the night and most of the day. 'Tis afternoon. Other than a few times of needin' the bucket, ye have not woken, though yer sleep was disturbed by nightmares. I was never given the chance to thank ye for saving my life. Da wouldnae allow us near ye after the rescue. He said 'twas not safe."

Anna forced a small smile. "He was being protective. He almost lost you."

Nessa frowned, hands on hips in an indignant pose. "But ye saved us from those men. They said they would kill us rather than let us go. I dinnae understand how he could think ye were a danger, after ye saved my life."

"Sometimes a father's protection does not make sense. 'Tis how they tell us they love us." Her voice sounded husky, rough with fatigue, despite her sleep.

"Ye are welcome to rest more. When you are ready, we will help ye bathe. Food and drink await on the table. When ye feel up to it, my da and brother wish to speak with ye."

Anna spotted the tub close to the fireplace, and the food on a small table in the corner. She gave Nessa a frank stare. "The last time your father and brother wanted to speak with me, I almost killed a man."

Nessa immediately dropped her gaze. "Ye should know Alain has been banished. My brother wanted to kill him because of what he did. When Da proclaimed his sentence, he told the clan everyone is to treat ye as if ye were his own daughter. He said if anyone raised a hand against ye, he would kill them himself." Tears sparkled on her cheeks and she wiped them away.

Stunned into silence, Anna closed her eyes again, trying to make sense of Nessa's words. *His own daughter? What does he mean? After treating me as an enemy, he now wants to treat me as family?* Her stomach lurched again, though this time not due to the pain in her head.

As she lay back, gentle hands unbraided her hair.

"Would ye like more sleep, or are ye ready for a bath?"

Anna tried to remember how many days had passed since she'd properly bathed. She couldn't recall. More than a fortnight. Her recent bathing had been confined to rivers and lakes. Even so, she couldn't bring herself to get out of bed.

Unable to open her eyes, she murmured, "Sleep for now."

Only a few hours must have passed, because when she next woke, the sun was still in the sky, though much lower. The pain in her head, a merciless tyrant, had eased a bit. She saw Nessa sitting next to her, reading a book. The girl glanced at her and smiled.

"Are ye ready for a bath?"

Slowly rising, her body stiff and sore, Anna answered, "A bath sounds good."

Nessa motioned to the other young woman with her. "This is Isla, my handmaiden and closest friend. She is the other ye rescued."

Isla took Anna's hand, turned it palm up and kissed it. "Thank ye," she whispered, tears deepening the blue of her eyes.

Anna offered a half smile, half grimace in response as she tried to slide off the edge of the bed. The two girls helped Anna into the tub, then Isla added buckets of water left heating by the fire. Anna groaned at the heavenly touch of hot water on her skin, her sore muscles relaxing one by one.

Nessa produced a bar of soap smelling of lavender and honey and helped her bathe, while Isla washed her hair. Anna tensed as Nessa's fingers traced the blue lines on her shoulders and back. After rinsing with a final bucket, they allowed her to soak, the hot water chasing the chill from her body.

Nessa returned to her book as Anna relaxed in the high-back wooden tub and checked her arm. The wound Shamus had given her continued to heal nicely. *Cursed man.* Pleased to find no swelling or tenderness at the site, she slipped further beneath the steaming water, noting somewhat absently, for the first time since her arrival, she wasn't being watched by guards. However, she was in no condition to escape. Besides, she didn't want to leave the warm bath.

At last the water began to cool, and the girls produced a dressing robe for her and helped her from the tub. Anna sat by the fire and combed her hair, spreading the tresses to help it dry. Nessa offered her a short chemise and thick blue tunic and she pulled them on with slow, deliberate movements, avoiding any quick moves that made the pain in her head worsen, throwing her balance off.

"Here are trews from my brother. I noticed ye dinnae wear dresses."

Stepping into them, Anna noted they fit very well, though they were tight across the seat. "I can wear a dress until my clothes are mended."

Nessa nodded and handed Anna a pale green tunic dress from a large wooden trunk. Unlike the small number of dresses Anna had owned of silk, satin and velvet, the sturdy wool made it a practical garment for everyday use. Anna noticed a lack of judgment in Nessa's voice when she mentioned dresses. Used to being ridiculed for dressing like a man, she was relieved not have to defend her choices.

"I guess I am not like other women you know," she ventured.

Nessa smiled sweetly. "May I ask about yer markings?"

"Does your clan not have something similar?"

Nodding vigorously, Nessa replied, "Aye we do, but only for our experienced warriors."

Anna sat at the table and motioned for Nessa and Isla to sit. Glancing out the window, she winced as the light shot a stab of pain through her head. Turning back to the soothing dimness of the room, she took a piece of bread, hoping her stomach would tolerate it. She'd gone six days with very little food.

"Hundreds of years ago, our people fought the Romans. During that time some women trained in battle along with the men. I am told the pattern I wear is one worn by those women. In my clan, it is a symbol of a warrior."

"Ye are English," Nessa responded, puzzlement on her face and in her voice.

Anna breathed a heavy sigh. "Yes, I am half English, and half Scots. I was raised in my father's keep on the borderlands. My mother's clan is less than half a day's ride away. I spent much time around her people. They taught me their language and customs. I fought in two different battles with my mother's clan and one fighting with my father's men."

After a few bites, Anna's stomach would take no more. Better to eat lightly now, as she had no desire to visit the bucket again. She'd need a week or more before healing enough to attempt another escape. Hopefully they would let their guard down so she could slip out, if she found her horse and possessions. Remembering her last effort, thoughts of escape seemed unlikely anytime soon.

"Please let your father know I will speak with him whenever he wishes."

Eager to help, Nessa hurried from the room on her errand.

Anna glanced around for her pack and spotted it at the foot of the bed where she'd slept, along with her armor. To her surprise, her weapons lay there also. She rose to fetch hot water from the fire and retrieved two types of tree bark from her pack, placing them in a cup to steep.

She sipped the herbal mixture, and a few minutes later her pain eased slightly. Gazing at Nessa's polished reflecting disc, Anna took in her appearance, probing her puffy, bruised flesh. She enjoyed a grim satisfaction knowing she looked as bad as she felt. The entire left side of her face displayed various shades of black and blue marks. She barely recognized herself.

Nessa returned as Anna sipped the medicated brew. "My father and brother would like us to join them for the evening meal at sundown."

Anna nodded her agreement and took her cup to a comfortable chair before the fire. Pulling a small leather roll from her pack, Anna removed a set of needles. She carefully placed the hair-thin steel into her neck and head, inserting them where they would ease the pain and hopefully the nausea. Anna heard a sharp intake of breath. Nessa darted across the floor to her.

"What are ye doing?" Her hand covered her mouth, her eyes wide with alarm.

Anna answered calmly, "'Tis an ancient method of healing from the East called *bian shi*. I am trained in the healing arts of the East, as well as those of my mother's clan."

Nessa watched with trepidation as Anna continued. With a sigh, Anna gingerly reclined into the chair and sat perfectly still.

"Does it not hurt?" Nessa asked anxiously.

"No, it feels like something between a slight ache and a tingle."

Nessa continued to frown, so Anna gave her a simple explanation of internal energy, and their pathways in the body. Though she still wore a stricken look, Nessa seemed somewhat pacified, or at least convinced it didn't inflict more pain.

Anna must have dozed, for the next thing she knew a gentle nudge woke her.

"'Tis time to sup."

Anna removed the needles beneath Nessa's fascinated gaze and replaced them in their cloth, lacing the leather roll.

Nessa waved a hand at the needles. "Did they help?"

"Yes, a bit. It will take a few days, but 'twill help."

Anna followed Nessa out the door. She hadn't resolved Nessa's earlier words. Treated as the laird's own daughter? Her head still ached, and she couldn't think as clearly as she wished despite the tea and *bian shi* treatment. She tried to process the implications of such a declaration, if indeed it had truly been made.

As she wool-gathered, Nessa grabbed her hand. "I always wanted a sister. Having only an older brother to talk to is boring. I wish ye to take Da's offer." She gazed at Anna, hope brightening her eyes. Anna put an arm around Nessa's waist, drawing her close.

"I only had an older brother also. I know what a bother they can be." Anna involuntarily sucked in a breath, feeling sorrow burn her eyes and threaten to spill over. She stopped momentarily and grasped the wall as the image of Edrick being dragged from his saddle haunted her. Closing her eyes, she pushed back the tears.

"Please forgive me," Nessa said. "I forgot ye recently lost yer brother. 'Twas unthinking of me."

Nessa's stricken look touched Anna's heart and she offered a weak smile of reassurance. "No, 'tis all right. Give it no further thought. Having a younger sister would be nice. Though I doubt we will be sharing clothes. "

Nessa glanced sideways at her and giggled. The dress she had loaned Anna fell a few inches too short. They followed the stone corridor, passing doors along the way until arriving at the stairs. Anna kept a firm grip on the rope railing along the wall as she descended, unsteady as a drunkard.

They reached the lower level. A doorway opened into the same well-appointed dining chamber Anna had entered the night before. Immediately vigilant, she scanned the room. The only occupants were the laird, his son, and an older woman who immediately rose and walked briskly to greet them, a welcoming smile on her face. She shared many features with Nessa, including long flaxen hair, though hers bore a few streaks of silver nestled amongst the gold. There was no sign of any guards.

"Lady Anna, I am Nessa's mother, Mairi. My husband and son told me how ye rescued our Nessa. We cannae thank ye enough for what ye have done for us." She gently embraced Anna and kissed her uninjured cheek.

"You are welcome, my lady," Anna muttered, uncertain how to respond to her affectionate display.

Nessa held one of Anna's hands. Mairi took the other and led her to the table. Standing directly across from Duncan, she faced him for the first time. He stiffened visibly, anger washing over his visage.

He tore his gaze away and rose abruptly. "Father, Mother, I ask ye to excuse me from the table."

His father sighed wearily. "Verra well."

Duncan stormed from the room without a second glance at Anna, slamming the door behind him. Everyone seemed embarrassed and the lingering silence created an uncomfortable mood.

Anna lifted her chin. "Forgive me, Laird, if my appearance is so hideous as to ruin your son's appetite. Mayhap I should retire upstairs."

At this, the three of them laughed lightly, and the laird bade her sit between his wife and daughter.

"Lady Anna, I again ask yer pardon." The laird's face softened. "Ye must understand. 'Tis my responsibility to keep our clan safe. For ye to appear from the shadows of the forest, dressed the way ye were, possessing the skills ye do, an English lass—I had to know by aiding ye, we werenae bringing yer troubles to our lands. Ye did much the same by not going to yer grandda. Aye?"

She considered his words then nodded.

"I kept ye prisoner so ye couldnae escape," the laird said. "Both to protect ye from others who would do ye harm, and in case someone had a claim against ye. It rankled to do so, after ye bravely rescued my daughter, but I saw no other choice. The actions of my men since have been unforgivable. Ye are a guest of honor. I offer ye my protection. Ye lost a father and brother. Become as our daughter, and gain a new family with us. I understand if ye dinnae trust me, or dinnae wish to stay. Allow us a few weeks to prove ye have a place here. If ye decide to go, I would only ask ye wait until healed. I will send an escort with ye where ever you decide."

Anna sat in stunned silence. Nessa did not exaggerate.

He pressed on. "Ye dinnae know where ye want to go, aye?"

Absorbing his question, she considered an answer but could think of only an honest one.

"No, Laird, I had no real destination in mind. My brother made me swear I would flee to safety. I could not bear seeing my mother's clan meet the same fate as my home, so I traveled north and west, sticking to the concealment of the forests. I have no place to go." She had not truly admitted this to herself, much less given voice to the thought, and doing so brought an unbearable sense of loss. Tears burned again, seeking release, but pride would not allow her to let emotion betray her in front of this man.

The laird nodded as though satisfied with her answer. "Then ye will stay with us."

How can I agree to stay with the man who imprisoned me this past sennight? What choice do I have? I would not make it a day in my present condition. Even if I were ready to ride, where would I go? Where could I find sanctuary? Not sure what she wanted, Anna replied, "It is a generous offer, Laird. Would you allow me time to consider it?"

Pouring wine into his cup, he waved his hand. "Of course, take as much time as ye wish. Ye will stay with Nessa in the meantime."

Nessa squeezed her hand under the table, beaming her approval.

"And your son? He does not appear too pleased with your offer." She recalled Duncan's face when he saw her tonight.

At this, the laird released a short burst of laughter and shook his head. Nessa giggled. Lady MacGregor merely smiled knowingly.

Laird MacGregor's shrewd eyes met hers. "My son has been verra angry with me. Angry with the way I have treated ye, angry I allowed Shamus to challenge ye, and angry I dinnae let him kill Alain for attacking ye. I cannae say I blame him. Nae, my son wishes ye to stay. He greatly admires ye. I am afraid seeing the damage Alain caused was more than he could bear."

Uncertain what to think, Anna kept her mouth shut. The laird eyed her trencher.

"Please eat. Duncan tells me ye hardly ate this week. Why not?"

She considered an answer so as to not offend. "The stew is not something I am accustomed to eating. I feared if I did, I would become ill, a condition I could not afford with my...current circumstances."

His furrowed brow eased with a look of understanding. She could see he wanted to ask more questions but stayed silent.

The table held fresh bread, cheese, some sort of roasted bird in a thick sauce with vegetables, and fruit. A bowl of soup smelling of peas and leeks sat in front of each trencher. Pitchers of wine, ale, and water awaited. Anna took a few grapes, squeezed them into a cup, then filled it with water. Tearing off a small piece of bread, she sliced a pear and slowly ate the soup. It went down easily and tasted quite good. Glancing around the room, she noticed the others eating from full trenchers, making hers appear almost empty.

"Ye must eat more if ye are to get yer strength back," Lady MacGregor said.

"Thank you, my lady, but I am nauseous from the blow to my head and cannot eat much immediately after fasting a week."

Lady MacGregor placed her hand on Anna's arm, patting it to show her understanding. Anna's response seemed to pique the laird's interest. His face betrayed the questions he wanted to ask. Anna stopped eating and faced him in invitation.

Chapter Seven

"Ye are a baron's daughter, yet ye've been trained to endure imprisonment. Why is this so?" Kenneth MacGregor asked.

One corner of Anna's mouth twitched at the laird's question. She knew of no other noble, especially not a woman, who'd been prepared thus. But she'd grown used to being an oddity.

"My brother and I had a tutor who was very thorough in his instruction."

He cocked his head. "What kind of tutor teaches such?"

"Zhang had been a prisoner, rescued by my father when he fought during the Crusades, before my birth. He served as bodyguard to a wealthy Chinese merchant. They were part of a trade caravan ambushed by the Mamluks. Zhang attached himself to Lord Braxton as payment for his freedom."

A smile crossed MacGregor's lips. "Tutor? He must have begun yer *education* at an early age. How many years do ye have, lass?"

Steeling her body and expression against the grating question, she answered. "A score, Laird."

His smiled turned puzzled. "When did ye become twenty, then?"

"Three days ago."

Nessa quietly gasped, squeezing Anna's hand. Lady MacGregor stiffened next to her. The laird's smile hardened, lips disappearing as they curled into his mouth, his jaw tight. He rubbed the back of his neck. Anna kept her features flat, as unreadable as possible.

Tension seemed to drain the air from the room. Reaching for her cup, Anna drank the fruited water.

"It appears I have more to make amends for than I thought."

His words sounded like pity. She would not allow it. "As laird, you did what you thought was best for your clan. There is no need to dwell on it further. If you will excuse me, I feel unwell. My thanks for the meal." Anna stood to her feet. "Nessa, stay with your family. I need no assistance getting back to the room."

Once upstairs, Anna brewed another tisane for pain. After drinking it, she crawled into bed, exhausted.

Hands gripped her shoulders, pulling her out of a deep sleep. Someone called her name. Startled, she frantically grasped the stranger's wrists and bolted upright, meeting the look of panic on Nessa's face. Anna released her and slumped forward, head in her hands.

Nessa touched her hair. "Ye cried out in yer sleep. Another nightmare?"

She had no memory of it, though her heart raced and her breathing was ragged. She shook her head and watched Nessa rub her wrists. "I am sorry. Did I hurt you?"

Nessa sat on the edge of the bed and wiped the sweat from Anna's brow. "Nae, only frightened me, 'tis all."

Anna took her hand, squeezing it gently. "I am sorry I woke you."

Nessa's lips slipped into a sympathetic smile. "Worry not. Pleasant dreams this time."

With a sigh, Anna curled under the covers and drifted back to sleep.

After three days, the swelling around Anna's eye receded, restoring her vision. Thankfully, the nausea also eased, the headache and dizziness no longer constant companions. The tea and *bian shi* did their work.

Afternoon naps aided her recovery. Nessa read to her at times. Her own eyes struggled to settle on the words, and attempting the task invited an unbearable headache. Nessa possessed a small collection of books she was proud of. Anna thought of all the books, maps, and scrolls in her father's library destroyed by fire. Their loss made her heart hurt as much as her head, teaching her a painful lesson about taking things for granted.

Lady MacGregor visited daily. Anna saw no sign of the laird or his son except at the evening meal. 'Twas just as well. She needed separation from them and had little interest in hearing any more apologies or answering more questions. Whatever his motivation, the laird's decision to imprison his daughter's rescuer remained a bitter taste in her mouth.

She'd considered what her father would have done in his place, and how his men would have treated a noblewoman held captive. There would have been no challenge and certainly no attack due to argument. She would have been well treated and well fed. A maid and bath would have been provided in a guest room. She'd never needed a maid, but a bath and decent food would have been welcome.

Barbarians.

The MacGregor women were a different tale. Anna shared more laughter with the girls than she was accustomed to. She felt strange to be in the company of females, but wonderful as she bathed in the warmth of feminine companionship for the first time in her life. She realized she'd never before known a female she could truly call her friend. Could she walk away so easily?

Conversations often led to speaking of various couples, speculation of who would pair for marriage, the merits of eligible males, and those families expecting children. These conversations typically ended with Nessa and Isla giggling, and Anna feeling oddly left out. *No man wants a woman who can outride, outshoot or outfight him. And I have no interest in becoming a man's property or some dissolute nobleman's breeding stock.*

The thought of never being in love or having children caused a pang of regret, though she brushed it off each time it crept into her mind. It was foolish to think of love as a baron's hoyden daughter, yet even more foolish when trapped in a land whose people resented her very existence.

Something in her expression must have given her away.

"Anna, are ye unwell?" Lady MacGregor's brow furrowed as she stared at her intently.

Banking her emotions as best she could, Anna took a deep breath before answering. "I am fine, milady." The forced smile she offered as proof didn't seem to fool anyone in the room.

Lady MacGregor nodded, but Anna noticed her speculative looks, as if she'd read her very thoughts.

The next afternoon, Lady MacGregor arrived as usual. "Anna, let us take a short walk outside. 'Tis a beautiful day."

A sense of apprehension rippled through her, but Anna could not think of a polite way to say no. "As you wish, milady."

She followed Lady MacGregor out the door. They settled on a bench overlooking the herb and vegetable garden outside the main tower. Anna kept her breathing steady, waiting with trepidation, reminding herself this woman had shown naught but kindness thus far.

"I wished to speak where we willnae be interrupted. I have need to say again how thankful I am ye rescued Nessa. It tore my verra heart out when we found she had been stolen. I have lost one child and couldnae bear to lose another. Ye have my eternal gratitude, and also that of my mutton-brained husband, who held ye in that infernal cell for a sennight."

Anna subdued a smile, realizing the laird had likely experienced almost as difficult a week as she at the hands of this soft-spoken yet firm woman. "You are most welcome. When I heard them cry out, I could not ride away. I am glad all turned out well." Hearing the MacGregors had lost a child created a lingering sympathy. Not knowing how to respond, she let the information pass.

"Anna, I know ye lost yer mother at an age before ye became a young woman."

Anna dropped her head, shame of what those words implied coloring her cheeks.

Mairi continued. "I can only imagine how hard it must have been growing up without an older woman to guide ye. I know I could never replace yer mother, but ye would do me a great honor if ye could perhaps see me as a dear aunt."

Using a finger to gently tilt Anna's chin so their eyes met, she continued. "I am not judging how ye dress or behave, but every lass needs older women in her life for support and counsel. I want yer promise ye will allow me to fill such a role whilst ye are here."

Anna's discomfort rose. While grateful Lady MacGregor would care enough to offer such, she was mortified about her ignorance of what it meant to be a woman.

"I see the conflict in yer eyes." Mairi gave her a look of sadness.

Leaning closer, she put her arms around Anna. The simple motherly gesture led to her undoing, and Anna's tears fell. Slowly at first, then a torrent. She bent over, openly weeping in Lady MacGregor's arms. Feelings of loss, loneliness, of not fitting in poured through her. She cried for the loss of family and the loss of home. As her sobs subsided, she huddled against Mairi's shoulder, inhaling her scent. She smelled of lilacs and heather, reminding her of her own mother, calling forth another wave of grief. At last, her tears were spent.

Mairi leaned her cheek against Anna's head. "I think ye and I shall have regularly scheduled times each week to talk and get to know each other. Aye?"

Her throat too tight to answer, Anna nodded, pulling herself gently from Mairi's embrace. At last, she found her voice. "Thank you for your kindness, Lady MacGregor."

Mairi gave Anna a shooing motion with her hand. "Posh. And Lady MacGregor is the mistress of this manor. When we are alone, ye shall call me Mairi."

Anna found herself thrown off-balance by Mairi's kindness. How could she move on when they continued to undermine her mistrust?

Anna's injuries healed during the next fortnight, both physically and emotionally. Her routine settled into a pleasant one full of stories and dreams with Nessa and Isla, and afternoons with Mairi as often as she could spare them. Anna found herself seamlessly accepted into the women's groups and wondered at her transformation.

A knock on the door midmorning interrupted the girls' lively discussion of English nobles. Glancing up, Anna saw Duncan standing in the doorway.

"Are ye well, Lady Anna?"

A sense of uneasiness stole over her as Duncan's appearance disrupted the one place she'd felt safe since arriving at Ciardun.

"I do not think it wise to use that name, sir. I would prefer Anna, of clan Elliot."

"Very well, Anna, of clan Elliot, how do ye feel today?"

She put on an emotionless mask. "Well enough. To what do we owe the honor of your visit, sir?"

"There is someone who is quite anxious to see ye."

Surprise betrayed her featureless guise. "Who could possibly wish to see me?"

Duncan's grin was smug as he held out a hand for her. "Come see."

Remembering the last time she touched him, Anna ignored his outstretched hand. She walked into the hallway, pausing for him to lead. He led her out the front door of the keep, where her best friend in the world stood waiting.

"Orion," she whispered. He whinnied and ambled over to her, nuzzling his velvet nose against her neck. Closing her eyes, Anna breathed in his smell as his breath warmed her skin, a feeling of pure joy flooding her soul. She stroked his long face, pausing at the white star on his forehead, the inspiration for his name. Duncan shrugged.

"He has been quite unapproachable. I assumed 'twas because he longed for his mistress."

After a few minutes of their comforting exchange, she looked up. "Thank you, sir. Orion is all I have left."

He tilted his head, furrowing his brow as if to argue, then thought better of it. "I wondered if ye felt up to a ride and tour of the village. Ye must be weary of being stuck in my sister's room." They strolled toward the stables near the front gate, Orion lumbering alongside.

Anna frowned. "I doubt I could stand anything more than a gentle walk. I still suffer headaches if jarred."

"Aye, a gentle walk then. Since he has seen ye, I doubt he will allow us to put him away without at least spending some time with ye. I would not put it past him to follow ye upstairs."

She tried unsuccessfully not to chuckle at the image, but his words were too potent. To hide her amusement, she saddled her horse, falling easily into the familiar routine. Duncan tacked a beautiful bay gelding, whistling as he worked. Anna noticed that, while quite lovely, the horses in the laird's stable did not meet Orion's standards. Not surprising, as he cost her father a small fortune a few years ago. They'd spent a sizeable amount of time looking for the right combination of size, temperament and bloodline. Duncan cast Orion more than one look of admiration.

"One of my responsibilities is overseeing the acquisition, training and breeding of our horses. I am quite certain I havenae seen a horse as fine as yers. Would ye be opposed to allowing him to sire on a few choice mares?"

She laughed out loud at his request. "You presume much, sir. I should be fit to ride in a few days. Unless you have a lady ready now, that does not leave much time. Though I doubt Orion would mind overly much."

A scowl settled across Duncan's face. "Call me Duncan, please. Are ye not taking my da up on his offer, then?"

Her humor fled with his question. She remained undecided. Part of her wanted to rage over the treatment she'd received earlier. The other part of her realized she had nowhere else to go. Though still somewhat angry, she'd experienced real contentment these past days.

Nessa looked to her as a hero, the older sister she'd always wanted. Anna had never single-handedly saved someone's life before. They shared a bond not easily broken, their connection strengthened every day. It would be painful not to have Nessa in her life any longer. Soul-weary of loss, she didn't want to face it again so soon.

It was unlike her to waver. She'd always been so resolute in her decision-making. An ache of longing for guidance from her father and Master Zhang swept over her. She would even settle for Edrick's advice, though it would come at the cost of teasing. She'd happily allow him to tease her mercilessly if only she could see him again.

"I see ye are still undecided."

Duncan's voice lifted her from her internal musings. "I am still angry." She cringed to hear the snarl in her voice. She hadn't intended to put so much emotion in her response.

Duncan regarded her as he leaned against the wall, arms crossed, face grim. "I knew ye would be. Ye were right about us. We *have* acted as barbarians. I was told my behavior the last time I saw ye was explained."

"Yes, your father said you were angry with him."

Duncan took a deep breath. "The man who struck ye attacked and injured a guest at my father's table without provocation. I *should* have killed him! Now we share an enemy, one who knows the truth of ye. I fear he could spread this knowledge, bringing enemies here. I have failed to see the wisdom in many of my da's decisions regarding ye. This one was the tipping point. It dinnae occur to me ye would think yer appearance offended me. I apologize for making ye think so."

Fury ripped through Anna. "To hell with apologies and pity from you and your father, Duncan MacGregor! I neither require nor want them! I would prefer respect, and the men of your clan at least to *act* like they possess honor!" Anna closed on him, hands at her sides tightly curled into fists.

Duncan stepped back, hands raised in surrender. Struggling to regain her composure, she spoke through gritted teeth. "I thought we were going for a ride?"

Duncan laughed and boarded his horse, tension eased. "Aye, we were indeed."

She mounted Orion, and looked MacGregor in the eye. "Shall I fetch my weapons?"

"Nae, 'twill not be necessary. I know ye dinnae trust me, but ye are under my protection."

"Mayhap you have not noticed, *sir*, but I do not require your protection." Vestiges of anger colored her voice.

Duncan's cheeks darkened and his eyes flashed, but he clamped his mouth shut and rode out the door, keeping whatever it was he wanted to say behind his teeth.

Neither spoke for several minutes, allowing the tension to ebb once again. As they rode through the village, Anna noticed it was much like her own had been. Viewing the community from a prisoner's viewpoint on the ride in, it had appeared differently.

Duncan pointed out the smithy, butcher, weavers, mason, and the rest. "And once a sennight, there is a market when the villagers buy, sell and barter goods and services."

Anna nodded. "'Tis much as my home was."

As they passed the small mud-and-stone crofts, she noticed each had a small fenced garden as well as chicken houses and pens with pigs. Cattle and sheep stood in the meadows alongside acre after acre of plowed fields. They passed vineyards, orchards, and several storage barns along the way. At the back of one, she spied a large number of beehives. Anna was struck by the beautiful setting. Everything appeared green, lush and growing, with the scent of flowers in the air. The steep hills and rock balanced the ruggedly beautiful land.

Anna stole several sidelong glances at her guide. She watched the play of his muscular body, moving as one with his horse. *Admiring him is surely madness.* She tried to summon the anger she'd felt at the stables as a shield against such foolish thoughts, but found it had waned. Part of her wanted to remain angry, but after being outside in this beautiful setting, she found no appetite for it.

"Your home is beautiful. It is similar to mine, but also very different." Thoughts of home tugged at her heart.

His sky-blue eyes sparkled, and in them she saw pride for his home, his clan. "Aye, I knew ye would like it. Now I need to convince ye to stay."

Furrowing her brow, Anna found herself at a loss for words. She didn't know how to respond to him, nor could she understand what his smile did to her.

I should still be angry, damn him!

They rode beside the small river winding through the village and past a miller's wheel. Following the river downstream, they came to a body of water so large she could barely see the other shore.

"Fadagorm Loch. We share it with the MacFarlane clan, our allies. Their lands are on the far side of the loch, to the west. We trade with them and work together to protect our territories. To the north live the Stewarts, my mother's clan. They are allies, also. North of the Stewarts lies the MacNairn clan. They are the ones who stole Nessa and Isla. We are sworn enemies.

"To the south are the Grahams. We have never had any problems, but do not have an alliance. Father may try to form one with Nessa's marriage in the future. They are friendly enough, and we trade with them a few times a year. We are known for our blend of whisky, which they have a taste for. 'Tis always in demand."

Scrutinizing the area, Anna got a sense of the boundaries he described. "So we were met by the Grahams on the second day of our trip and by the MacFarlanes the third day."

"Aye, ye are a bright one. Nessa tells me ye speak, read and write several languages, and ye have been taught a great number of things."

Clearly he wanted to know more. Instead she offered, "Your sister is wonderful. I have greatly enjoyed my time with her."

"Aye, she is a good lass—my father's joy. Ye have made her very happy by staying. She hopes to keep ye."

His words brought a smile to her lips before she thought to stop it. She hated the conflict churning within. Duncan's consideration today only worsened her confusion. Seeing him as her enemy made things so much easier.

Walking the horses back to the stables, she unsaddled Orion. She grabbed a brush off the wall and set to the task of brushing him. Grooming a horse was always one of her favorite ways to think. The simple, mindless chore freed her to consider solutions to problems or ponder decisions. Today, she found no such respite, acutely aware of the man a few feet from her.

She'd known him less than a month. The early part of that time, he was her enemy. She'd need longer than a few days to think otherwise. They groomed their horses in silence. He finished first and leaned against a stall door. A strange discomfort crept over her, and she slid a glance in his direction. His tilted smile as he watched her work softened his rugged face. She ignored him, attending instead to her horse.

After she finished, Duncan took the reins and led Orion to a large stall. She didn't want to appear rude, but found it difficult to express gratitude. The words seemed to stick in her throat.

"Thank you for the ride today. It was enjoyable. Thank you, also, for taking care of my horse whilst I was unable." She forced a pleasant look on her face, feeling it stretch the limits of plausibility.

He bowed to her. "Of course, milady. 'Twas the least I could do."

There. Though she would not give in to feeling guilty for losing her temper, she could at least be grateful.

With a sigh of relief, Duncan rocked back on his heels and watched Anna climb the stairs. The morning proved to be a success. Kenneth would be pleased to hear it. Maybe a few more outings and she would trust enough to consider staying. Getting Anna to vent a portion of the anger she'd held since her arrival seemed to have brought her some relief. At first, he feared he might have to defend himself. He owed it to her to take anything she threw at him. Words anyway.

She appeared genuinely happy to be outside, and seeing her horse well cared for clearly touched her. Watching her smile when they were reunited filled him to overflowing. Knowing he could be the author of her joy brought a feeling he was hesitant to explore. He only knew he wanted to be the one who made her smile.

Duncan had wondered if not seeing her these past few days would cause his feelings to wane. To his surprise, his attraction toward her had only intensified. The simple ride this afternoon increased his need to be near her. He'd forcibly stopped himself several times from drawing closer during their ride, seeming to have little power over his actions.

Like a stallion with the scent of a mare in season, he found himself inexplicably drawn to her. 'Twas folly to consider she would allow him closer yet. No, he would keep his distance, continuing to invite her to venture out. Doing so would show the clan his intent toward her, as well as give her opportunities to continue to discharge her wrath in a more controlled fashion. This, along with the steady efforts of the women, would surely erode the walls she erected.

He continued to stare wistfully in her direction, long after she left his sight. It seemed she carried away much of the day's beauty with her. Scrubbing his face with his hands, Duncan tried to dismiss the absurd notion.

Where the devil did that come from? Ye are no beardless lad to be taken in by such sentimental foolishness.

'Twould be wiser to attend to the facts of the situation. The blasted woman insists she doesnae need my protection. Shaking his head, he could only imagine what her brother and father must have suffered. Would the lass ever abide direction or care from a man?

He'd finally found a woman who stirred his interests beyond mere physical desires. However, the stubborn lass seemed more interested in fighting with him than anything else. Her rigid independence abraded his patience, leaving behind the polished sheen of frustration. Fine. If she wanted to fight, he would find a way for them to train together. Perhaps that would be the path to gain her trust. He strode toward the gate, anticipating a strenuous bout of sword play with the men, the perfect way to vent his aggravation.

Chapter Eight

Anna found Nessa and Isla grinning widely when she arrived upstairs from the ride. Ignoring them, she sat at the table and poured a cup of cider. Every so often the girls stole a glance in her direction. After a few minutes, she couldn't ignore them any longer.

"Very well, ladies, what is it? Do I have dirt on my face or smell of the stables?"

They both giggled.

Flummoxed by their behavior, Anna turned her chair toward them, arms crossed. "Speak up, what is it?"

Ignoring the question, Nessa sat next to her. "Did ye enjoy the ride?"

Arching a brow, Anna decided to play along. "Yes, it was wonderful to see my horse. Your brother took me riding around the village and the surrounding area. He showed me the loch, explaining the boundaries of your territories and the neighboring clans. 'Tis quite beautiful here."

"So if ye like it here, ye will stay?" Nessa's enthusiasm shone on her face.

Anna smiled. The girl's continued desire for her to stay, to become part of her family, tempted. Perhaps she would stay through winter. She'd have a few months to form a plan for the future.

"I have not made a decision yet, but could not wish for a lovelier place to live. Though I think it will take some time to get used to the cold."

Nessa seemed content with her answer. "How was yer horse?"

"He is quite well, and as glad to see me as I, him."

"Aye, my brother has personally cared for him. He refused to let anyone else near. Duncan treated him as his own."

Anna didn't know what to say, but an odd sensation fluttered in her stomach. "'Twas very kind of him."

Nessa giggled again, and Anna's eyes narrowed in frustration. "Nessa, what am I missing?"

Nessa studied Anna for a moment, her brow furrowed. "Ye really dinnae know, do ye?" Isla stepped to Nessa's side. They looked at each other and giggled.

"Ladies," Anna warned, reaching the end of her patience.

This sent them into another fit of giggles.

"I give up." Finishing the cider, she placed dried chamomile flowers in a cup and walked to the fire, where a kettle hung. Pouring hot water over the petals, she sat in the chair facing the fire, ignoring the two girls.

Nessa placed a hand on Anna's shoulder. "I am sorry to tease. I thought 'twas obvious—that ye knew."

Anna gazed at her over the rim of her cup. "Know what, Nessa?"

"Duncan favors ye." Nessa grinned again.

Anna sputtered. "What?"

Nessa nodded, glee lighting her eyes. "Everyone sees it. I thought ye would, too."

Anna gaped, at a loss for words.

Nessa frowned. "Anna, why are ye so surprised? I would think ye used to the attentions of men by now."

Anna stared at the fire.

When she didn't respond, Nessa started again. "Is it so difficult a thing to think my brother would find ye bonny?"

The odd sensation in Anna's stomach flared again, this time bordering on pain. Men always fit into one of two categories in her life: enemy or ally. Enemies were to be watched, not trusted. Like those idiots who sought to court her. So very obvious. Never really interested in her, but in how much land and coin came with her in marriage. Allies were kin, or comrades in arms, people to rely on not to betray you. She had no room in her life for a third category. A man who, like an enemy, could injure or betray, though posing as the strongest of allies. The very thought chilled her blood.

"I—I am not attractive to men."

Nessa flopped onto the edge of the hearthstone, staring dubiously at her. "Anna, whatever do ye mean?"

With a sweep of her hand she indicated her leather armor hanging from a hook on the wall. "What man wants a woman who dresses or behaves such? Where I am from, men only want women as decoration, servants, or for breeding. I am interested in none of those."

She turned to stare into the flames on the hearth, her voice dropping to a whisper. "When men look at me, they do not see a woman but an aberration. Someone to be ridiculed—or conquered."

They do not understand the cruel jests—from overbearing men and the fairer sex—or how I pretended not to care. The pain of admitting this to another took her by surprise. She'd told herself for many years she was unworthy of the love a man gave a woman, and had hidden from the ache of this knowledge. It was much easier to recall the negatives of relationships she saw, rather than remembering the love and tenderness her parents shared, or other couples she knew who loved each other. Internally shaking her head no, she repeated her oft-spoken words. *I am not meant for love.*

Anna lifted her chin, straightening in the chair. "I am simply a curiosity, an oddity. He is only interested because I am different—because I have defeated a number of men in his presence—nothing more."

Nessa stared at her, the surprise on her face fading to sadness. Reaching for Anna's hand, she drew her near, folding her in a firm embrace. Pulling back, she squeezed Anna's hands, concern filling her eyes. "Anna, truly ye dinnae see yerself. I have admired ye so much, I havenae considered the cost ye paid to become as ye are. Still, it doesnae change the fact ye are bonny."

Kissing Nessa's forehead, Anna whispered, "Thank you. You are always so kind to me."

They supped with the family in the great hall, amongst the rest of the clan, for the first time since her arrival. Anna sat on the ladies' side of the table, furthest away from the laird. Duncan sat next to his father on the other side. Anna kept to herself, not speaking unless spoken to, giving only simple answers.

The rest of the clan seemed to have grown used to her presence. Overt stares and glances from the lower tables became subtle. The weight of their gazes un-balanced her as she sat on display at the high board.

Anna rose from the table when Mairi did, marking her first chance to leave. Duncan took the opportunity to approach.

"Would ye be interested in another ride tomorrow?"

Her stomach churned when he drew near. She chided herself for such an absurd reaction and replied by asking a question first.

"If I were to ride alone in your territory, would I be safe?" From the corner of her eye she watched the laird's belly quiver with silent laughter.

Duncan took her question seriously. "I dare say ye would be safer than anyone fool enough to cross yer path. The laird made it clear. Ye are not to be harmed."

Against her better judgment, and because she grew weary of remaining indoors, Anna acquiesced to his question. "Yes, I would like to ride again tomorrow. When?"

Duncan quirked a roguish smile. "How about after we break our fast? Da and I thought it wise for ye to become more familiar with our lands and to have our people get used to seeing ye about."

"Very well, after the morning meal then. Thank you," she answered in a stiff voice, forcing a fleeting smile, hoping she didn't betray her edginess in his presence. She turned and followed Nessa upstairs.

Nessa bubbled with excitement.

"'Tis just riding," Anna protested.

The girl spun around to look at Anna, her excitement undimmed. "I know."

The next morning, Anna rose before the sun. Dressing quietly to avoid waking Nessa, she slipped out and made her way to the stables. She grabbed a shovel and nearby wooden cart and began clearing out Orion's stall. He watched, occasionally nuzzling her shoulder. Lifting his head, he nickered. Anna turned to see who approached.

"What do ye think ye are doing?" Duncan blustered.

"My horse, my responsibility," she shot back defiantly.

"Noblewomen dinnae muck stalls. We have stable boys for such chores." His voice rolled thick with frustration.

She wiped sweat from her brow, leaned against the shovel and laughed. "I have been responsible for taking care of my own horse since I was old enough to ride, which includes mucking his stall. You must believe me a delicate thing if you think I cannot do a little work."

"Ye, delicate? Nae, I would never make such a foolish mistake." Humor crept into his voice.

Anna had to admit, yet again, he truly was a handsome man when his eyes crinkled with amusement. His smile did things to her insides she'd rather not consider. She could almost see the young boy he must have been. Both cheeks dimpled slightly, easing his appearance. The strangest urge to touch them rose, curious if they were as soft as she imagined, wondering what the stubble on his face would feel like under her fingers.

He wheeled the cart out to dump it into a large pile for the villagers as she put fresh hay in Orion's stall. He leaned against the doorpost. "Why are ye here so early?"

"I feel better, and enjoy time alone tending my horse. 'Tis one of my favorite ways to think."

"Aye, mine as well."

"Sometimes I prefer being around horses to people. Horses do not judge your station, appearance or behavior if you treat them well." Anna frowned, silently chastising herself for disclosing so much. What imp possessed her to allow him a glimpse of her soul?

Duncan tilted his head, drew his brows together and stared at her. "I know exactly what ye mean." He stood silently as she finished her work. "If ye wish, I will fetch breakfast to take with us. We could make an early start."

"That would be fine."

Duncan departed the stables and returned with a small sack. Handing her an apple and a small loaf of sweet bread filled with nuts, seeds and berries, he hung a water skin on Orion's saddle. "Anything in particular ye would like to do today?"

"Yes. I would like to cut a quarter staff, and am interested in gaining skins to line my cloak. I am not accustomed to the cold and damp here. I can only imagine how it will be come winter." An involuntary shiver rippled through her as she thought about snow and the wind, which never ceased to blow.

"We have a man who can fill such a need. He is the village fletcher and cooper. A quarter staff would prove no problem for him. With regard to skins, we could simply purchase them. If not in the village, then from one of our neighbors. Ye hardly have to hunt them down yerself."

"Duncan MacGregor, you confuse me yet again with a delicate noblewoman in need of charity. I am fully capable of cutting my own staff and skinning my own hides. I need only a satisfactory branch or billet and access to tools. With regard to the cloak, I know not what fur-bearing creatures live in your lands, so I will bow to your superior knowledge of where and what I should seek."

Duncan laughed at her reply, and Anna thought it was as pleasing a sound as she'd ever heard. His deep baritone resonated like a distant peal of thunder. His face lit with humor and though his laughter subsided, mirth lingered in his eyes. The sound and sight brought an answering smile she couldn't hold back. *He should laugh more often. His stern look does not suit him. I wonder what causes such a dour guise.*

"Aye, it appears I have made the same mistake again. I am usually a fast learner. I should think we can easily find a billet. Such tools are here in the stables. As far as what animals should have the good fortune to grace yer cloak, I would suggest waiting until Martinmas when their fur is fullest. Summer coats willnae do as good a job ye wish. As for what we would target, I suggest mink, fox or beaver. I dare say ye will find any of those satisfactory."

The thought occurred she would need thicker clothes to stay warm in the meantime. "Very well. I accept your advice. I will have to cope with the cold until then."

"'Twill not be necessary. We can have a set of woolens made for ye. 'Tis a herder in the Graham clan who owns a special breed of sheep. The wool from this breed is very fine and soft indeed. 'Twould be no trouble to obtain enough to have two sets of woolens made if ye wish."

They both mounted and rode toward the village.

"Sounds like a fair solution. I will be happy to pay, of course."

Duncan tilted his head. "My da willnae allow ye to pay for anything. We owe ye Nessa's life. He was quite serious about accepting ye as his daughter. He would no more let ye pay for such a necessity than he would Nessa. Ye are under our care."

Anna's brow furrowed deeply. "Then I will have to engage in some activity to earn my keep. I have no desire to rely upon the laird's generosity, only to have him resent it in the future. Particularly when the memory of his gratitude toward me fades. If I am to consider living here, I must have a role to fill. I will not simply be under anyone's care. Nessa's value as a daughter and future wife to a neighboring clan is obvious. My worth is less so. I refuse to be a burden and will not be married off to form an alliance." Her words rang with determination. She meant every one of them.

Chapter Nine

*T*he thought of Anna married to someone else sent a shudder down Duncan's spine. He hadn't considered the idea his father might arrange a marriage for her or accept an offer from another clan. He was certain she wouldn't accept, but the suggestion disturbed him far more than he expected.

The raw power of his reaction startled him, and he clenched his hands. He would seek out his father to ask exactly what he had in mind for Anna. His horse sidestepped and tossed his head nervously. Duncan guiltily loosened the reins he fisted.

He realized he hadn't answered her question. "I thought this might be the case. We could consider a few roles for ye. Though I should warn ye, my father possesses a rather long memory; he willnae forget. Should the possibility exist, my mother will be happy to remind him."

Anna eyed him curiously. Duncan raised a single finger.

"Fiona, our village healer, is good at tending expectant mothers and delivering babies. She has a passable knowledge of herbal remedies, but she doesnae possess the range of healing skills ye have. Ye would be a highly regarded member of our clan should ye assist her. People who would otherwise die might live because of ye. 'Tis a powerful gift." He nodded, the idea pleasing him. "I could see our allies bringing their more seriously ill and wounded for ye to tend. Having such a healer would make ye very valuable to our ties with neighboring clans."

Anna's lips pursed, thoughtful. "I like this idea very much. Healing is a skill which demands regular use to stay keen."

Duncan held up a second finger. "Ye are also more learned than anyone in the clan. Yer services as a clerk would be useful, reading and writing treaties and trade agreements with other clans. The laird gave me leave to arrange such a contract with a merchant in Stirling. He owns a tavern and inn and has shown an interest in our blend of whisky. 'Twould be a boon for us to have such an agreement, giving us a steady source of coin. Whilst I am confident in my reading and writing skills, I am not as sure with the Latin often used in such pacts. It can be tricky, with one or two words changing the whole meaning of an agreement."

"How do you know I am more accomplished than you in Latin?"

Duncan ducked his head slightly, giving her a smirk. "I must confess, I have heard ye a time or two teaching my sister."

"Eavesdropping? You listened in on our conversations?" Anna's voice rose.

"Aye, when I heard ye speak Latin it stirred my curiosity. I dinnae make a habit of listening at doorways, but hearing ye drew me in. I meant no offense."

Anna eyed him speculatively. Duncan quickly changed the subject, holding up three fingers. "Finally, I see how ye are with yer horse. I assume ye trained him?"

Anna nodded, a confident curve to her mouth. "Yes, I have spent time around the stables since I was old enough to walk and have assisted many foals into the world."

"Ye could have a hand in the care and training of our horses if ye wish. Though beyond yer own, I cannae permit ye to muck stalls. Otherwise, our stable lads would be out of a job," he added with a crooked smile, hoping to make light of their earlier disagreement.

"I like all of these ideas. I agree to your proposal on one condition."

Duncan laughed. "I cannae wait to hear it. No doubt 'twill land me into trouble."

Anna's eyes lit. "My condition is, you agree to train combat with me. I can only do so much alone and my skills will deteriorate if left untended."

"Aye, I would be pleased to train with ye. No doubt 'twould be quite beneficial for both of us. 'Twould probably be wise for us to do so away from prying eyes until the clan grows accustomed to ye."

"May I ask what exactly has been said to the clan about me?"

"Ye have not been told? Ye are from a Lowland clan that had some upheaval, leaving ye seeking a new home. We found ye of course, when ye rescued Nessa. Though people will see and hear the English in ye, 'tis not uncommon for Scots and English to marry close to the border.

"We have not said which clan ye are from, and no one has asked. We suggest Armstrong, as they are many and not too far from yer own on the border. None around here has any ties with them. 'Tis up to ye. We thought ye might desire anonymity, both for yerself and yer remaining kin."

Anna stopped her horse. "I do not care for lies. However, I see the merit in such a tale. I have deliberated on my situation a fair bit and have concluded, as long as I do not reappear, whoever stole my father's lands will have no reason to seek me out. My brother was Father's heir, the true threat. As a woman, I would have no claim on the holding, other than my dower lands, a small estate left in my name. The only thing my appearance would accomplish would be to draw unwanted attention to the manner in which the lands were gained—perhaps even from the crown."

Duncan pressed a bit further. "What would happen if ye decided to draw such scrutiny to the man who killed yer family and stole yer da's lands?"

He could see it in her eyes. She still did not trust him fully. Silence grew, the battle within herself clear. Duncan held his breath.

"Anna, I know I havenae earned yer trust yet—"

She waved him off. "No, I was caught in my anger of the situation. Anger of the injustice, anger of my inability to avenge my family. If I go back I would most likely be forced to marry whomever did this, or into his family, to cover the deed and validate the outcome. Unmarried noblewomen are not allowed to remain such for long. My choice would then be to submit to a husband or be punished. I would be isolated, not trusted, and expected to bear an heir. Going back to England under any circumstances is untenable."

"I can only imagine the rage I would feel were I in yer place. If ye have no other recourse, death seems a more desirable fate."

She slowly rocked in the saddle in agreement.

"What about friends or allies of yer da? Could they not be counted on to right this act of murder and greed?"

Anna grimaced, her knuckles whitening as her hands tightened on the reins. Orion flicked an ear and tossed his head. "If they were going to do something, they would have done it. My presence would not inspire such a response. Moreover, how do I know who was disgusted by such an act and who mayhap assisted in its execution?"

Duncan tensed at her words. "At least in the Highlands a man knows who his friends are, as well as his enemies. I know ye dinnae want my apologies or pity. I am regretful for yer situation. Ye dinnae deserve it. I cannot decide which is the greater tragedy—that someone would get away with this injustice or yer terrible loss."

Anna stared at her hands, clearly uncomfortable. Duncan chided himself. *Idiot for bringing it up again.* Half afraid he'd upset her, he waited for her to speak again.

"Where do you have in mind for our training site?" Her voice was strained but clear, and Duncan relaxed.

"A mile or so from here, a strath is sheltered by the forest on all sides. 'Tis low-lying and off the path, so someone would have to stumble upon us to see. The clearing is not very big, but large enough for our needs. Come. I will show ye." He reined his horse down a nearby path, and Anna followed.

"I would also like to meet Fiona," she told him. "I need to be educated on what plants grow here, what can be cultivated and where others might be obtained. I want to know if she will be threatened by another encroaching on her position."

After showing her his intended training spot, Duncan guided her toward the village to Fiona's home. The stone wall of the one-room croft rose even with Anna's head, the thatched roof supported by several logs protruding past the walls all around. Mud filled the gaps between the stones, making the small dwelling snug against the cold winter winds. An older woman appeared in the doorway, wiping her hands on a well-used apron. Duncan greeted her and made the introductions.

"'Tis good to meet ye, Lady Anna." The pear-shaped woman wore a tunic dress of dark green wool. Her hair, a generous mixture of gray and black, was braided and pulled back into a severe knot. "I have seen yer work. The laird bade me look after the men who were injured recapturin' our Nessa. Ye have a fine touch. The stitches were verra clean, and nae wounds took to festerin'. 'Tis a tribute to yer skills."

Duncan was amused to see Anna's cheeks stain red. Was it the cold, or was she so unused to compliments?

She asked, "You do not mind that I treated the people of your clan?"

The older woman snorted. "Mind? I am the clan midwife. The only reason I treat the sick and injured at all is because 'tis none else. I will gladly hand over the chore if ye are of a mind to take it."

Ushering them into the cottage, Fiona showed Anna the simple remedies she prepared, the herbs she gathered and where to find them. When Anna asked about other plants, Fiona often didn't know. She did know clan Graham had access to herbs she did not, and suggested they attend market there. She generously offered Anna any supplies or assistance needed. Anna did the same.

"Where will ye be workin', milady?"

Duncan caught Anna's questioning glance.

"Out of the keep for now," Duncan replied. "We shall see what the laird says, but I feel certain she can use one of the storage rooms off the great hall until they are needed for harvest."

Bidding Fiona good day, Anna and Duncan continued on their route, stopping by the cooper. They obtained an ash billet, which they lashed to her horse. She stubbornly insisted on paying from her purse with the few coins she possessed. Riding on, they stopped by the weaver's shop. Duncan inquired about commissioning woolens. They would measure Anna and start as soon as he supplied the wool.

They mounted again and started back toward the keep.

With mild trepidation, Anna invited conversation. "Your horse is quite beautiful. What is his name?"

"His name is Lasair. A gift from the Stewart laird, my grandda, when I became a knight. He has been a faithful companion."

"His name fits. His coat is almost red as a flame." *And almost as impressive as his master.* Heat rushed to her cheeks, and she glanced away and resisted allowing the thought further freedom. She eyed Duncan surreptitiously, unable to keep from admiring the way he moved in unison with his mount.

While brushing their horses at the stables, she remembered the question haunting her for some time now. "Duncan, why Nessa? Why did the MacNairns take her, the laird's daughter?"

He gazed at her a moment before answering. "'Tis a long story. Do ye wish to hear the whole?"

Continuing to brush Orion, she nodded.

"There have always been hard feelings between our clans, going back generations, though I dinnae know why. Typically, 'tis naught more than simple raids of a few cattle or sheep. Same was true between the MacNairn and the Stewart clan. For many years both our clan and the MacNairns wanted an alliance with the Stewarts to form a buffer. The Stewarts wished to remain neutral and not choose sides. This way they benefit from trade with both."

Anna snorted. She'd seen this sort of maneuvering between English lords in the past.

"When the MacGregor laird, my grandda, died unexpectedly, Kenneth, my da, became laird in his place, nae more than a score and two summers in age. Shortly after, a MacNairn raid on Stewart land went awry. The men had been in their cups, and a lad was brutally killed. The lad was the Stewart laird's nephew and godson. Da took advantage of the situation and negotiated with the Stewart for my mother's hand, forming a strong alliance between our clans.

"Since then, the MacNairn laird has sought vengeance upon us. We think he stole Nessa to wed his son. Doing so would put my father at a disadvantage in negotiations with them. Taking her would keep him from being able to engage another clan through her marriage. If we were forced to deal with them, the MacNairn would have strengthened their position whilst weakening ours. Nessa would have been treated poorly. The MacNairn is a cruel man." A hard look crossed his face. "One of the men ye killed was Adiar MacNairn. I only wish I had been the one to do it. Ye halted any chance they had of forcing a pact with us. Adiar was the laird's only living son."

Though more brutal, it didn't sound unlike the machinations of English nobility. Anna's chest tightened as she recalled the men who fell under her bow and blade that day. Grabbing a drawknife, she picked up the ash billet, hacking at the length of wood in her hands. Chunks flew as she wondered which of the vermin she laid low had been Adiar. Hearing their intentions for Nessa made her want to kill them all over again.

"Does the MacNairn know I killed his son?" Her voice rumbled low, guttural.

Duncan frowned. "'Tis a good question. I am not sure how he could, since none of their raiding party survived. Da sent a clear message about the consequences of stealing his daughter by killing them all and leaving their bodies unburied on the field for the beasts and carrion crows to devour."

Anna glanced up enough to offer a grunt in response then went back to work on the billet. With each curl of wood dropping to the ground, her anger receded. She mulled over Duncan's story and how she now fit into their clan's history whether she wished it or not.

With a questioning quality to his next words, Duncan continued. "I worried how a woman might deal with having so much blood on her hands. I see by the way ye attack the wood, ye would do so again. Ye are Nessa's champion in truth."

Anna didn't look away from her task or acknowledge his statement.

"If ye will excuse me I have other duties to attend to. I will see ye at supper." Duncan bowed slightly then left.

She raised her head, offering a slight scowl in answer. *How like a man to think a woman could only wield a needle and thread or soup pot effectively, growing faint at the sight of blood.*

Continuing her task, Anna reflected on the morning. She'd noticed the odd looks from the villagers, but nothing suggesting hostility. More like curiosity. Whether due to the laird's declaration or her escort, she wasn't certain. However, she knew everyone, especially the ladies who spun the wool, assessed Duncan's interest in her. Like a filly on the block, she'd been rated all day. She frowned, not liking the sensation one bit.

She worked until she had a smooth, even staff of proper diameter. By the time she finished, darkness had crept past the lanterns into the stables. Having a task for her hands gave her mind the opportunity to take measure of her feelings and she was surprised to discover her anger toward the MacGregors no longer existed.

How did that happen?

Mairi and Nessa had always treated her more than kind. Duncan, if she were to be fair, had also been as kind as allowed, even more so this week. The laird? Though she vehemently disagreed with his handling of her the first week, he'd held true to his word about welcoming her into his family, accepting her as his own.

Could I truly make a home here? Taking her new staff with her, she thought about putting it through its paces first thing on the morrow. The time alone would give her more opportunity to reflect on staying here, about working as a healer and horse trainer. Anna shook her head. She certainly needed more time to think on her strange feelings toward Duncan.

Chapter Ten

Duncan arrived at the stables at first light and noticed Anna's horse missing. Saddling up, he made his way to the strath, knowing she'd arrived, or would soon. Dismounting in the woods, Duncan tied his horse to a tree several yards away and quietly made his way to the edge of the clearing. As he suspected, she'd already reached their site. He chose a tree in the shadows to watch from a distance.

She unwrapped a long, thin rope from her waist. A small knife, or perhaps a spear point, appeared to be attached to the rope. What looked like a small red piece of cloth was tied to the base of the knife. *Odd.*

She started slowly, then swung the blade faster and faster. She twirled with it, wound the rope around her arms, back, legs; then, uncoiling the wraps, launched it toward a tree some fifteen feet away. He was taken aback by how deeply the blade pierced the wood. It didn't take much imagination to envision what this weapon would do to a man, even armored.

Jerking the blade from the tree, she whipped it around again in one deft motion, twirling and dancing, shooting it out again. The red cloth made a whirring sound as it cut through the air, marking the point. Without the red to hold his eye, he'd have had a hard time tracking it. Sometimes she kicked it, firing it into the air, as to a lower target, changing the trajectory. She seemed to be able to let fly this weapon, high or low, in front or behind her at will and with accuracy. Duncan sat in wonder. He'd never witnessed the like before.

After a number of minutes, she coiled the rope around and under her belt, hiding the blade in the waistband of her trews.

Did she have this in her possession her entire captivity? The implication rocked him. *What other weapons did she have hidden?*

Next, she picked up the staff she'd carved the day before. Again she started slowly, as if to become familiar with the heft of the weapon. Soon she whirled, whipping the staff around in circular motions. Her movements were graceful, but to Duncan's trained eye, generated a fair bit of power. Enough for a woman to defeat a man.

Leaping up and squatting low, she struck from all angles. Never before had he witnessed such maneuvers in combat. He'd trained as a warrior since old enough to hold a wooden sword. Sparring had always been conducted in a straightforward matter. Combat never held the grace or fluidity he observed with Anna.

She changed tactics, now treating the staff as a spear.

Her actions mesmerized him. After a longer interval with the staff, she paused and took a drink from her water skin. He thought of her words the day before, about not being able to go back to England, back to her home. He didn't want her going anywhere. His plans certainly didn't involve her languishing in some nobleman's keep, bearing his brats. A wave of strong emotion rolled over him.

Jealousy?

Aye, nothing else could explain the surge of passion he'd experienced these past few days. He vowed to find a way to win her trust, her friendship. Then perhaps he'd have a chance at seduction. With the damage caused by initial distrust, he would have to move slowly. Slow suited him fine. He'd been taught to be a careful hunter, allowing his quarry to come to him. Though a more clever quarry than any he'd hunted before, 'twas hunting all the same.

After catching her breath, she drew her two curved short swords, and the deadly exercise began anew. The intricacies of her footwork, the angles she worked from, demonstrated a style of fighting Duncan had never encountered before. Certainly not English or Scots.

He remembered the two MacNairns she'd taken with ease by sword. He recalled her oblique movements. Unable to contain himself any longer, he rose and strode toward the field. In truth, he felt powerless to resist. Mayhap the blood of a *leannan sith* truly flowed through her veins. Nothing he had ever encountered pulled at him so. Especially not a lass.

"I wondered how long it would take before you mustered the courage to leave the shadows." A wicked gleam danced in her eyes.

Of course she sensed his presence. A warrior always knows.

"I dinnae wish to disturb yer practice." He smiled in return.

"So if not to disturb, participate then?"

He could not mistake her challenging tone. His crooked grin widened. "All I brought is a sword. I have no stave with me."

Anna stepped away, circling him. "Swords it is."

Duncan slowly drew his long sword. "I have yer word then, ye will spare my life if I yield?"

The wicked look returned to her eyes. "Mayhap."

Laughing, Duncan took a high guard.

Anna circled, darting in and out of range, gauging his footwork, trying to bait a reaction. He did not oblige. Eventually, her feints became bolder, trying to draw Duncan into a committed strike, knowing he'd fought many battles and therefore wouldn't be easily tricked into giving up his guard.

Damn. She couldn't lure him into attacking. Each time she offered him an opening, he refused, keeping a high guard and an annoying smirk on his face. Fine. She pushed a bit more to see if he could do more than hold a sword aloft. Unexpectedly, he attacked as she started another advance.

Caught slightly off-balance, she recovered in time to parry his blow. The clang of steel on steel broke the silence of the small meadow. Anna whirled to his side, seeking an angle to attack from. No such luck. He anticipated her move, blocking her strike.

So there is more to his ability than the consistent guard he offers.

Stepping in with another strike, she quickly abandoned it and sought the other side. To her chagrin, he anticipated and countered her again. Blast! Did she give away her intent somehow? Realization hit. He'd watched her practice for some time before joining her. He knew she did not favor straight-line attacks, preferring angles, thus avoiding a direct blow she would be hard-pressed to block because of her disadvantage in strength.

A twisted smile settled on her lips. Time to employ techniques she'd yet to demonstrate. Staggering to the left then right with feints, Anna dropped to the ground, rolling past Duncan on his left, popping up slightly behind him. Before he could pull his guard around to defend her unexpected maneuver, she struck him on the back of the leg above the knee with one sword and at the lower back with the second, turning her blades at the last moment, hitting with the flat rather than the edge.

Duncan dropped to his knees as if the blows had been struck properly, surprised she bested him this round. He faced her as he rose. Anna's smug grin reminded him much of a cat in the cream. Her green eyes sparkled with delight, her chest heaved with breathlessness, her face flushed with exertion. He doubted there had ever been a more beautiful creature on God's earth.

He wanted nothing more than to take her in his arms and kiss her into oblivion.

She must be mine! The thought was so powerful, it echoed in his bones. The hunter in him knew this to be one small step toward his goal. He mustn't let his passion spoil the hunt.

"Again, my lord?" she teased with a toss of her head. She could afford to be playful, having scored first. Chuckling at her taunt, he reset.

They continued until both were spent. Neither could remember who bested overall, though 'twas close. He tossed her his water skin. She tipped the container upward, showing the smooth skin of her throat. The long, thin scar on her neck danced as she drank deeply. Watching her do something as simple as drink stirred his desire. He fought back the vision of having her beneath him, moving as they struggled together to quench a different thirst.

She tossed his water skin back. "My thanks."

He congratulated his good sense in proposing they conduct their training away from the eyes of his kinsmen. He would hardly live down being defeated, even one round, by a woman. Though he wouldn't mind if he were defeated occasionally by *his* woman. A feeling of pride swelled in his chest as he considered the possibility. Perhaps after a few more sessions, he'd bring her to train with his men, and let them see for themselves how well the lass fought.

Those who rode with him to fetch Nessa had already seen her in action twice. Upon consideration, the thought of sharing her in any setting brought forth a feral urge to hide her from those who might catch her eye.

He offered her reins. "To the keep, milady?"

She flashed a smile, striking him as breathless as the strongest whisky.

"As you wish, sir knight."

Neither spoke on the short ride back. Duncan thought about his duties for the day, but his attention kept coming back to the lass next to him. To have a woman so strong, beautiful and learned in healing would be quite a treasure. To include fighting skills to rival his own would be a boon, indeed. A niggling of doubt in his mind made him pause and consider.

Would she find me as dear a prize? He allowed the thought further rein. *What would Anna seek in a man?*

Strength, no doubt. Protection? She clearly believed she could protect herself, continually bucking against the idea she needed such from a man—from him. Her headstrong self-reliance continued to be a source of vexation. She didn't appear to have a submissive bone in her body. If he were to wait for her to ask for his protection, he would be waiting until the whole of Scotland sank into the seas. The usual tactics one employed to catch the eye and heart of a lass would fall woefully short with her. No, he needed another approach.

"I enjoyed our training, Duncan."

"If ye wish, we can set aside time most mornings to do so."

She again flashed him a dazzling smile, and though he'd experienced one moments ago, he was no more prepared for the effect of this one than the first.

"I would like that."

Women spoke regularly about love and passion. He could see the beginnings of one and feel the flames of the other already. To win her, he would need more—what? What did she say a few days ago at the stables? She wanted respect, for them to at least act as if they possessed honor. Chuckling to himself, he thought she had no idea how much of his respect she already commanded.

Anna reflected on how at ease she'd become with Duncan. It reminded her of the years she and Edrick spent training. The same intensity existed, the same competitive fire, but it seemed different somehow. She considered the differences, lost in the comparisons. Belatedly, she realized Nessa spoke to her. She gave her a guilty smile.

"I am sorry. My mind was elsewhere."

Nessa gazed at her, a hand on her hip, a teasing smile on her lips. "I notice ye always seem preoccupied when ye come back from spending time with my brother."

Heat rushed to Anna's face. She wanted to deny it, but knew it to be true. She sought a reasonable explanation to Nessa's observation. "'Tis because he was my enemy for many days," she replied, frowning.

Nessa eyed her thoughtfully. "Is he yer enemy still?"

Is he? No, clearly not. Was he really ever? Anna realized it was much easier to categorize him thus when she didn't understand why they captured her. Now—it was muddled. She didn't know how to make sense of what he meant to her, of how she felt when around him. He provided protection when able, and cared for her horse when she could not. He'd taken time out of each day to acquaint her with his home, to make her feel welcome.

He'd shown understanding of her situation. He'd been gracious, and did not seem to mind overly much when she bested him in training. Anna chuckled. How many men could say the same? She knew from experience male pride could take only so much of a beating. If she were to categorize him? She realized she needed a new category. He didn't fit within any she knew. Remembering Nessa's question brought her thoughts to heel.

"No, he is not."

Anna felt a building excitement as Duncan addressed his father.

"Da, Anna and I have discussed how she might find a role with the clan, and wanted yer opinion." Duncan's statement garnered everyone's attention, including those within earshot from the lower tables.

The laird nodded and glanced at Anna to continue.

"Duncan suggested I might assist in the training and care of the horses at the stables."

The corners of the laird's mouth crept up. "Is that all? Such work, while unusual for a nobly bred woman, doesnae require my permission."

"Duncan also suggested I take on the more serious healing cases, particularly those requiring surgery. We spoke to Fiona. She is eager to relinquish such duties, as she prefers her midwifery tasks." She looked to Duncan.

"If allowed, Anna would need a place to work. I thought she might use one of the store rooms off the main hall until needed for fall."

Glancing over the faces at the table, Anna saw this request pleased everyone. Their approval warmed her.

"What an excellent suggestion," Nessa chimed in, beaming her approval. "'Twould give me the opportunity to continue to learn from her, if ye allow it, Da."

Anna smiled, remembering the questions as Nessa watched her tend her own wounds. Fascinated, she'd begun a journal based on their discussions, listing various herbs, their uses and doses. She was a quick learner, apparently enamored by the topic.

MacGregor frowned at Nessa's declaration. "Yer mother and I will speak about what assistance would be appropriate for a young maiden."

Nessa smiled and nodded obediently. Amused by their exchange, Anna knew with a certainty she would have not been nearly as submissive with her own father.

After the ladies retired from dinner, Duncan sat before the fire with his father to sip whisky and discuss matters of the clan. His da didn't seem to be in a talkative mood, which gave Duncan time to mull over his questions and try to understand why Anna had him so knotted up.

"Da, what are yer plans for Anna?" Duncan stared intently at the flames, not yet ready to meet his father's keen gaze.

Kenneth seemed to carefully consider his question. "Why do ye ask?"

Duncan kept his face toward the hearth, but darted a glance at his da. "Taking her as yer daughter, do ye mean to form an alliance with her marriage?"

An edge of the laird's mouth twitched. "Nae. She is not my blood. I have no authority to do such unless she asks. She still has living kin. Besides, do ye see her marrying against her will? I wouldnae wish such a fate on any man."

"Aye, I have thought the same." Duncan squirmed in his chair, and rubbed the back of his head.

"Has she agreed to stay?"

"Not yet, but I plan to convince her." Duncan's words sounded more confident than he felt.

Kenneth turned slightly toward him, a smile pushing its way onto his mouth. "And how do ye plan to do that?"

"I intend to take her to wife."

Kenneth tossed his head back in laughter. Vexed at his reaction, Duncan waited for his father's mirth to subside.

"Do ye think she would make a good wife?" Duncan faced his father, curious as to his answer.

Kenneth sobered. "I think there isnae much the lass cannae do. She could very well be yer greatest joy and yer greatest frustration.

She willnae submit to any man easily. You might have an easier time fighting dragons."

Duncan frowned, staring into the contents of his cup. "Mayhap the key will be not seeking her submission as if she were a common woman."

The laird studied his son's face for a moment. "Why Anna?"

Duncan exhaled deeply. "'Tis a good question. One I have mulled over since the day I laid eyes on her. Each day the list grows longer as I discover more of her character. I could name her virtues—most ye have seen, the rest ye have heard. There is something there when I look at her. It defies logic, or anything I've encountered before."

He leaned back in his chair and stared at the ceiling. "I cannae get her out of my mind. I think about her scent, her smile, about being around her all the time. I am content to simply watch whilst she grooms her horse. I dinnae have a name for it, but 'tis like a strong thirst. I cannae get enough of her."

"Does the lass feel the same way for ye?"

"I dinnae know what she feels." Duncan sighed and closed his eyes as he considered how to broach such a topic with her.

"So she no longer wishes to run the two of us through?" Kenneth's tone, while teasing, held a measure of sincerity.

Shaking his head, Duncan opened his eyes, his lips turned downward. "Nae. I dinnae think she hates us any longer, but she doesnae trust us, either." He shifted in his chair, ready to change the subject. "We sparred together today."

Kenneth's brow rose to his hairline.

"I found a secluded place to train. We worked with swords for many rounds. She bested me often, though 'twas close."

The laird's grin snapped back into place. "*She* beat *you* in combat?"

"Aye, she did fairly, several times." Duncan found he didn't mind any longer. He wondered if there was a man among them she couldn't defeat in a fair fight. Maybe Duff. "I wondered what ye think of me bringing her to train with the men."

This brought Kenneth's brow back down, furrowing. "Ye may not mind being bested by a woman, but plenty of men will, marked as warrior by her clan or not."

"I know, but she has much to show us. I learned more this morning than I have in a while. Her tactics counter the advantages of strength. Such methods would be useful for the younger lads and older veterans. She also possesses knowledge of weapons I have never encountered before."

The laird arched an eyebrow at this observation. "Have ye asked her where she comes by this knowledge?"

"Nae. I am trying to go slow. I dinnae wish to question yer decisions, nor argue again, but her first days with us have made all of this more difficult." Exasperated, his hands splayed wide. "I am working on earning her confidence and friendship. She spoke at length about why she cannae go back to England."

The laird grunted. "So, ye want a wife who can challenge ye in combat?"

"Aye, it seems I do. But only if 'tis Anna. You care not she has no dowry? That marriage to her would bring no alliance?"

"Ye are a good son and a fine man. At five and twenty ye know yer own mind. In a few years I will take my place on the elder council, and ye will become laird. 'Tis yer duty to marry and produce an heir. In all these years I have yet to see yer head turned by a lass. This one has not merely turned yer head, but has it spinning atop yer shoulders." His chuckle made Duncan squirm like a lad.

"Whether ye recognize it yet or not, ye have lost yer heart to her. Yer mother and I agree on this and will support yer decision to wed Lady Anna, though I dinnae envy ye the task."

Duncan gave a smirk in response, hiding his stunned reaction. *Lost his heart to her?*

They sat in silence, staring at the fire while the whisky flowed. A weight pressed on Duncan's chest as he considered his next question.

"I wish to speak of something painful for both of us, if ye allow it." Duncan looked his father in the eye, waiting for his father to offer a slight nod.

"Anna's presence has disrupted me in more ways than I can count. Each seems to be more challenging than the next. I dinnae understand why she has me thinking of Callum. 'Tis almost as if he has risen from the grave to haunt my thoughts."

Kenneth stiffened at the mention of his dead son's name.

Duncan sighed. "We willnae speak of it if ye wish."

A long silence stretched between them.

"Yer brother's death deeply affected us all, but no one was more profoundly changed than ye. Ye have borne the guilt of it, though 'tis not yer burden to carry." The laird raised a hand to stop the argument Duncan prepared to mount. "Ye became a sober lad afterward with a strong sense of responsibility. Whilst an outwardly admirable trait at a young age, yer mother and I believe the loss robbed ye of yer youth. I cannae pretend to know what it meant to lose a twin. The two of ye were closer than any I have seen. I only know what it was like to lose a son and feared what his death would do to my remaining son.

"Ye developed a keen need to protect all those who are dear to ye. 'Tis a characteristic that will help ye become a strong laird. I believe this fierce connection ye feel with Anna, along with her plight, calls to ye in a powerful way." Kenneth paused then shook his head.

"She has endured significant loss and is adrift," he concluded. "Those things combine to inspire in ye a protectiveness so forceful ye risk scaring her away. With her, ye have found a kindred spirit not unlike the one ye lost. Perhaps she has as much healing to offer ye as ye have to offer her."

Duncan rose and embraced his father. "I am sorry."

Kenneth grabbed him roughly by the shoulders, meeting his eyes with a measured intensity. "'Twas never yer fault."

Duncan turned away. Of course it was his fault.

Chapter Eleven

*A*nna felt Duncan's hand on her shoulder, asking her to wait as she gathered her weapons to leave the practice field. The now-familiar warm tingle from his touch tempted her to distraction. To counter the effect, she grabbed his hand and stepped to the other side of his body, applying downward pressure as she dropped to a knee, twisting away. As swift as a hawk diving for its prey, her action caught Duncan off-guard. He flipped in the air, landing on his back with a satisfying thump, struggling to regain his breath as he flopped about like a landed fish. Unable to help herself, Anna burst into laughter. Duncan clambered to his feet, his eyes wide with shock.

"How did ye do that?" His breathing labored.

She quelled her mirth enough to answer. "'Tis easy. Mayhap I will show ye some time." She mocked the burr of his accent, flashing him a mischievous grin.

Duncan stared at her in disbelief. "Anna. Tell me, how did ye do that?"

Pulling herself under control, she replied, "I will show you another day if you wish. 'Tis not hard. I thought you only wanted to train weapons." She walked toward her horse. Glancing over her shoulder, she faltered at the intensity of his stare.

Duncan closed the distance between them and took one of her hands in his. He rubbed the skin of her palm with his thumb, sending a shiver chasing through her whole body. She grabbed his hand with both of hers, twisting it outward into her favorite wristlock. He dropped to his knees immediately, his face contorting with pain.

"Saint Filan's teeth! Ye are trained in unarmed combat, too?"

Her mischievous grin grew wicked at his acknowledgment. She released his wrist and stepped back. "Of course. Are not you?"

Rubbing his arm as he rose to his feet, Duncan looked at her with awe. "Anna, I am a head taller than ye, and outweigh ye by at least four stone. How are ye able to bring me to my knees with such ease?"

Climbing on her horse, she answered, "Unarmed combat tomorrow if you wish, Sir Duncan." Her teasing tone rang clear. Training with Duncan was much more enjoyable than training with her brother, Edrick. For one thing, she didn't want to kill him all the time.

Though they were plenty competitive with each other, Anna found herself protective of him, as much as Duncan seemed protective of her. She certainly sustained fewer bruises and scars than when she trained with Edrick, though her sparring with Duncan proved as fierce. And there was an odd feeling whenever they drew close, which intensified upon contact. She'd known nothing like it before and didn't know what to do about the sensation. It seemed foolish to mention such a thing to Nessa or anyone else. However, each time they touched, she longed for more.

Spring gave grudging way to summer. Anna met Duncan at the stables early, as they did every morn. His face was rueful.

"Anna, I apologize for missing our sparring, but I need to meet with the smith."

She shrugged. "No bother. I planned on spending time with Fiona after our training."

She watched until he left her sight, then glanced about for a way to fill her time. She ventured outside the stable, slipping her weapons into place, leaving her armor in the keep.

Gazing at the beautiful day, Anna decided to walk. 'Twould do her good. Sore from yesterday's workout, she needed to stretch her legs. After a painful start, Duncan had finally been able to throw her a number of times. He proved slow to learn the subtleties of off-balancing before a throw. She found Duncan to be like most men, thinking physical strength the answer to any obstacle.

Though the thick grass cushioned her landings, Anna's muscles protested from repeated impact. She recalled the look of satisfaction on his face when he finally threw her, his expression that of a little boy, pleased to learn a new trick. A faint smile played about her lips.

Passing the cooper's shop, she saw the man working outside on a new barrel. He waved to her, raising the tool in his hand. She smiled and waved in return. The simple act of friendly recognition made her feel more at home. The *ping* of the smith's hammer on the anvil in the background punctuated the feeling.

A voice she'd heard before stole her peace.

"Look at the English bitch. The laird let ye off yer tether, did he?"

Anna didn't have to see his face to know who spoke. "Good morrow to you, Shamus. I see being home all this time hasn't changed the sweetness of your voice."

A few laughs followed her reply as she kept walking.

"Dinnae walk away from me, whore!"

Anna blew out a breath, and with it her hopes of avoiding confrontation. She considered the many ways she might prove herself to this clan. The one at hand wasn't among them. She'd recently learned that his brother, Alasdair, had met his end on the tusks of a wild boar while hunting. *Surely he does not lay his brother's death at my feet as he did his earlier injury?* She shook her head, remembering the way he'd challenged her for his brother's mistake the first time they met. *Likely.*

Shamus growled. "Ye might be under the laird's protection, but ye still could have an unfortunate accident if ye are not careful."

She spun to face him, hands curling into fists. "Are you threatening me, Shamus? If memory serves, I beat you unconscious the last time we fought. I would think you would have learned your lesson about speaking to your betters."

Shamus's face flushed red, darkening to purple. "How dare ye!" he bellowed, taking a furious step in her direction.

"I dare because if you insult me again, I *will* collect on the debt you owe me. This time, your laird will not be able to save you." She glared at him defiantly, not budging an inch, awaiting his reaction.

Roaring in anger, Shamus drew the claymore strapped to his back. She knew the long, two-handed blade gave him the advantage of reach—and that she would not survive even the slightest of strikes.

His face distorted with malice. "I think I shall add to the scar I gave ye the last time we scrapped and finish what Alain started."

She drew her twin falchions and circled him. "I think I will send you to greet your brother." Her words rang loud, goading him—as she intended. He swung wide, creating an arc of steel meant to decapitate. Stepping under his swing, Anna raised her hand and blew a kiss in his direction.

Further enraged, Shamus changed direction, bringing his blade down at an oblique angle. Anna predicted the arc, parrying the blow by pushing his sword in the same direction with her own. Her parry caused him to stagger as his momentum, paired with hers, carried his strike further than he intended. The clang of steel on steel echoed throughout the village like a thunder strike. A crowd hastily gathered around the combatants, warily beyond the reach of the long blade.

Swinging repeatedly with his whole might, Shamus's breathing labored while Anna parried and danced lightly away. His face bloomed red with exertion, or humiliation, she knew not and cared not. He'd stepped into her snare as predictably as any witless prey.

"For ye, Alasdair!" Shamus roared. He brought his sword high overhead, pushing downward with great force—a blow designed to cleave her in twain.

Anna's sword met his, hilt up, tip down. His blade scraped along hers, sending sparks flying. His strike continued inches past her, piercing deep into the ground with a dull thud. She kicked the flat side of his blade with her boot. The sword twisted in his hands, turning the flat of his blade upward.

Using his sword as a ramp, Anna took a quick step upon his blade, closing the distance between them. Swords crossed in front of her, a blade by each ear, she swung each arm violently across her body as her voice gave cry to her anger. Both blades bit deep into his neck, and Anna straddled him as his life bled out. One spasmodic jerk, and his body stilled forever.

Anna swiveled her head, searching the crowd, her enemy's blood spattered over her.

"I am Anna of the clan Elliot! My grandfather is laird! I am marked as a warrior by my clan!" She ripped her tunic, exposing her shoulder, neck, and arm, her blue markings visible to all.

"Anyone else who takes issue with my presence can face me now!" She turned slowly, her stare defiant.

She saw several expressions of disbelief, and more than a few approving nods. Her gaze met and locked with Duncan's. He held a bow with an arrow notched, pointed toward the ground. He gave her a fierce look and quick bow, apparently well pleased by her actions. She took a deep breath and returned his salute. Wiping the blood off her swords on Shamus's lifeless body, she sheathed them and strode toward the keep, her pounding steps echoing the angry thud of her heart.

Duncan tore his attention away from the smith as Anna and Shamus's verbal exchange rang through the village. It required all his willpower to stand aside and watch, teeth clenched, blood pounding in his veins, as Shamus insulted and provoked Anna. To her credit, she tried to walk away. Realizing a fight was inevitable, Duncan grabbed the smith's longbow, fitting an arrow in case Shamus appeared to gain the upper hand.

Duncan had sworn to protect her, even if she didn't wish it. He hadn't forgotten her scathing remarks about his protection earlier, nor his father's words from their last talk. The instinctive pull to fight in her place proved almost irresistible. Knowing she would be angrier with him than with Shamus was all that kept him from intervening.

Duncan watched the lass who'd bested him many times the morning before, toy with a veteran warrior. Though easily angered, Shamus was no green lad. Never in any real danger, Anna danced him like a puppet at St. Crispin's Festival. She moved and parried, allowing Shamus to over-commit and wind himself. All the while, she pricked his anger, prodding him to be more and more aggressive.

His strikes carried him off-balance, his rage making him reckless.

Her final move was unlike anything he'd ever seen before. Running up the length of a sword to deliver the killing blow? 'Twas the stuff of which the bards sang. Her battle cry and proclamation sent chills up his spine. Her challenge to the entire clan would reverberate for years. No one would contest her now, the laird's protection or not. She would be held in the highest regard—the fact she was female mattered not. Duncan couldn't have been more proud of her, and he made sure she saw it in his eyes when she finally met his gaze.

What started as fear for her life ended in a burning sense of admiration and desire for her he couldn't fathom. He *would* win her or die of the effort. He no longer had any choice in the matter. He vowed to do whatever it took, however long it took.

Anna stood over the watering tub at the stables with no clear recollection of how she'd gotten there. She looked at her tunic, spotted with blood. Removing her sheathed swords, she leaned forward, dunking her body from head to waist in the cold water. She straightened, gripping the edge of the tub, replaying the entire encounter with Shamus in her mind as water sluiced away.

Duncan's voice pulled her from her daze. "Ho, the stables."

Anna spun to face him. A grin lit his face. Gladness seized her, knowing she caused his expression. His approval meant more to her than it should have.

The fact that she had only moments ago killed a man, yet was now warmed by Duncan's approval, created another battle within her. She had no right to feel joy, having taken another's life. Shamus may have deserved to die, but he was a son, a brother, perhaps a husband and father. For certain, a MacGregor.

Duncan grabbed a rag and threw it to her. Wiping off the remainder of the blood and water, she paced the stables, battle lust still coursing through her veins. He gave her a wide berth, leaning against the stable wall, arms crossed, still wearing a heart-shattering grin.

"Duncan," she admonished him. "'Tis no time to smile. I killed a man, your clansman. I could have walked away. I should have walked away." Guilt wrapped its sticky tentacles around her. Surely she could have done something to avoid this.

He grabbed her shoulders, halting her pacing. "Ye tried to walk away, but he wouldnae let ye, aye?"

Anna gaped at him in surprise. "You saw?"

He gave her a reassuring nod. "Aye, I was at the smith's. Half the village saw and heard Shamus. He was not letting ye go without a fight. The men who witnessed his challenge last month have not given him a moment's peace. Mostly because he was a pig-headed arse. His wounded pride is the cause of this. 'Twas not your fault Anna."

Relief poured over her in a giddy rush. Finally, someone on her side. She grabbed Duncan, hugging him with all her might. He returned the fierceness of her hold. Anna became lost in the smell of him, the power of his arms, the feel of his hard body. After a few moments, they eased the strength of their embrace, but held on, reluctant to part.

"Ye were magnificent today. So very bonny. I am proud to be yer friend," Duncan told her, his voice full of sincerity.

"I was beautiful?" Anna heard her own voice, sounding like a little girl to her ears.

"Aye, lass, ye're the bonniest thing I have ever seen." Duncan broke his grip, placing his hands on her cheeks, pulling her face up to look at him. "Make no mistake, ye just won the respect of everyone in clan MacGregor today. They will come to admire and respect ye as much as I do."

Releasing him, she stepped back, shaking her head. "I do not understand."

He let out a short laugh. "What dinnae ye understand?"

She dared to look up at him. "You think I am beautiful, you admire and respect me—are proud to be my friend?"

Duncan moved, but she stepped back. Stopping, he frowned. "Aye, I do. But I dinnae just say ye were beautiful. I said ye are the most beautiful thing I have ever seen. There is a difference."

Anna grabbed her tack and blanket, fleeing the intensity of Duncan's words. Striding to Orion's stall, she saddled him.

"Where are ye going?" The concern in Duncan's voice rang clear.

"I need time to think. I will ride down to the loch. Give me a couple of hours."

Patting Orion on the rump, he grabbed her hand. "Take as much time as ye need. I will be here waiting for ye."

She forced a smile as she mounted and rode away.

"He what?" Kenneth's voice thundered across the room. He sprang from his chair, hands balled into fists, wearing an expression Duncan worried would lead to apoplexy. "My orders were *verra* clear. She is under *my* protection. No one is to harm her."

Duncan watched his father pace the solar. "Ye should have seen it. 'Twas like naught I have witnessed before. She was a cat playing with a mouse. He never came close to striking a blow. After she finished with him, she challenged the whole *bluidy* clan. Asked for anyone who had a problem with her to step forward."

The laird stopped in his tracks and his head swiveled to meet Duncan's gaze.

Seeing the look on his da's face, Duncan answered the unasked question. "Of course, none did. However, I am not sure if it was because of yer order, or because of what they had witnessed. They all know she is Nessa's *Curaidh*."

The laird drew a deep breath and poured a tankard of ale for each of them. "Where is she now?"

Duncan accepted the drink, frowning as he answered. "She felt guilty about killing him and went for a ride. Said she would be back in two hours. I thought ye should hear it from me first."

"Ye explained that 'twas not her fault—she isnae to blame? That there will be no repercussions?"

Duncan took a drink before replying. "Aye. Of course I did."

Shaking his head, the laird placed his tankard on the table, muttering a stream of curses. "Do ye think she will return?"

"Truly, I dinnae know, but I believe so. She said she would. Most of her belongings remain here. I told her I would meet her at the stables when she returns. I am convinced she wouldnae leave without saying goodbye to Nessa and Mother." He and his da exchanged glances, the same thought clear in both their minds.

How in the hell did a noblewoman become such a deadly warrior?

Chapter Twelve

*A*nna gave Orion his head as they raced to the loch. The rush of air over her and the surge of muscled power beneath her always helped clear away confusion. However, Anna found herself as perplexed as before. She no longer felt uncertain about killing Shamus. Duncan was right. The man wouldn't let her walk away. Remembering what he'd said about her 'having an accident' made her recognize the truth of the situation. *Pig-headed arse.*

That settled, she found herself unhinged by her conversation with Duncan in the stables. Recounting each word he'd said, she rolled them around her mind, trying to discern their meaning. To muddle it further, she remembered Nessa and Isla teasing her, saying Duncan favored her. They told her everyone knew but her. How could she not know? *Men do not pursue me. Only idiots playing their games of dominance do, but only for what they might gain from me. I have nothing now.*

Duncan knew she was not a submissive, gently bred woman. She'd not bring wealth or connections. He'd seen her kill a number of men, and still he said those things. A sliver of insight crept in. Perhaps it was *because* of her actions he felt thus? She shook her head. *No, not possible. Men want women who are soft, flirtatious, pleasing to the eye. Not me.* He had said she was the most beautiful thing he'd ever seen. He didn't make sense. She should ride back to the stables and demand to know exactly what he meant, demand to know his intentions.

She wheeled Orion, sending him back down the trail. A shudder ran through her. What if his words were meant merely as reassurances? He knew she was upset for killing Shamus. His actions were likely those of an older brother who sought to comfort her agitation. *Do I fear being spurned?*

She'd not given herself permission to feel for him. Yet she remembered seeing his long, dark brown hair, sky-blue eyes, and rough-hewn body the day they first met. Never had she been so aware of a man before. His presence, as much as anything, moved her, something she had no words to describe.

She understood now. Somehow, she'd allowed this man to breach her heart. How much, she only now discerned. *It matters not. 'Tis folly, and I will not travel further down this path. I will keep my emotions in control.* She squelched the small voice inside her. *It is NOT too late!*

She spotted Duncan at the stable, waiting as promised. Dismounting several yards away, she made a show of cooling Orion, not yet ready to speak. Seeing the man addled her wits. The words she'd formed in her mind now lay tangled on her tongue. He smiled at her. *Damn! How does he reduce me to a hen-brained fool?*

"Was yer ride helpful?"

"Not very. I think Orion got more out of it than me. I did come to the conclusion you are right."

He angled his head. "How so?"

"You were right about Shamus. He would have kept coming until I agreed to fight." She held his gaze firmly, previously unknown feelings eroding her control.

"'Tis the truth. I am sorry 'tis so, but 'tis done. Ye have shown yer mettle to the clan. Ye will be completely accepted now."

"How can that be? He was a clansman. I am a Lowlander, an outsider—*English*." She said the last with a distaste she realized she meant.

Her favorite smile returned, tilting the corners of Duncan's expressive lips. "Everyone knows what ye did for Nessa and Isla. They think 'tis a good omen to have such a hero in our midst. Aye, Shamus was a clansman, but one who was only tolerated. He was a man with few friends."

This reminded her of the guilt of killing him. "What about his family?"

Shaking his head, Duncan replied, "Nae, there will be none. Shamus lived with his brother. Neither married, mostly because no sensible woman would have either of them." He chuckled.

The thought of any woman putting up with Shamus brought the hint of a smile to her lips also. Her quandary about Duncan returned. Her brow furrowed.

"What bothers ye still?" His tone was soft and low.

Taking a deep breath, Anna struggled to answer. She was not possessed of her own mind, and her feelings cascaded out of control. How could she possibly explain it?

"I am confused." It didn't say much, but at least it was the truth.

"May I assist with yer confusion?"

Anna shot him a wary look. "I doubt it."

With a puzzled look, he asked, "Why not?"

Uncertainly roiled through her, the fear of rejection hard on its heels. She took another deep breath and braced herself before answering. "Because I am confused about you."

Understanding swept across his face. He tilted his head back. "Ach. I see. So which part is confusing? Ye embracing me, my words, or how ye feel about it?"

"All of it." Anna kept her attention on brushing Orion, but her stomach fluttered and her heart set a rapid pace, leaving her lightheaded.

"Well, start with the embrace. How did it make ye feel?"

His tone remained calm, as if speaking to a jittery horse. A good analogy, given her present state of mind and half-willingness to bolt without further comment. Could she risk telling him this? He'd not laughed at her yet, nor spurned her. She wrestled with speaking the truth.

"Good. It felt good." Her voice a whisper, Anna stopped the pretense of brushing her horse, and gazed past him, unable to make eye contact.

"Might I try again?" He gently turned her chin to face him.

A burning lump in her throat kept her from answering. She nodded. Slowly, he brought his arms around her waist and embraced her. Anna stiffened. As his heat surrounded her, she softened and returned the hug. He smelled of leather, horses and something unique to him. His breath on her ear created a wave of shivers as he nuzzled her hair. She brought her cheek down upon his shoulder, fully relaxing into his arms, eyes closed.

"How does this feel?"

Anna sighed, considering his question. "Good," she whispered. How *did* it feel? Good seemed an inadequate response. She searched for a better answer. "I feel safe, content."

He shifted one of his hands and cradled the back of her neck. He rubbed the muscles there, easing her tension. He traced the patterns on her shoulders and arms, exposed from the tear in her tunic.

"How about the words I find ye unbelievably beautiful, and am proud to have ye as my friend?"

Chewing her lower lip, Anna considered this more risky than the hug. However, she found courage in his embrace. "Other than my father, no one has ever told me I am beautiful. I do not believe it to be true. Every father thinks his daughter is beautiful. You being proud of me, and considering me a friend, evokes a strong emotion, one I am not sure I can name. I have felt utterly alone for some time." The lump in her throat grew and tears threatened to escape.

"Whether or not ye see it, ye are very bonny. I will be happy to remind ye daily. Ye arenae alone anymore, Anna. Ye are part of us now. Ye have a new home, a new clan."

The remaining apprehension she'd held evaporated with his gentle words. Anna melted into his arms, shifting to draw closer. She reveled in his warmth as they pressed against each other from knee to shoulder. Anna felt the beating of his heart as clearly as her own. Both set a rapid pace. His hand moved upward and caressed her scalp, smoothing her hair. She understood now how her old cat felt when she stroked her fur. If she could, she would purr as loudly as the one-eyed stable cat.

Duncan slowly released her. Cold replaced the heat of his body and an urge surfaced to touch him again. He placed his hands on either side of her face, bringing her eyes to his gaze. She floundered, still confused by the emotions swirling within her.

"Duncan, what does this mean? Why do I feel this way?" She felt so stupid, so ignorant. How could she not know more about this part of life?

His eyes shone with something she didn't recognize. "It means, my sweet Anna, I have offered to court ye, and ye have said aye."

She tilted her head. "It does?"

He smiled warmly at her. "Does it not feel that way to ye?"

Anna searched for an answer. She thought about how she felt both times in his embrace, how much she enjoyed being around him. She considered the words he'd said to her earlier. He thought her to be beautiful, was proud of her.

"Yes it does. What comes next?"

He chuckled lightly. "How can ye be so knowledgeable about so many things and know naught about this?"

Heat raced up her neck and across her cheeks. Self-conscious, she ducked her head.

"Please dinnae be embarrassed. I meant no offense. I mean to say ye are so innocent in this regard. 'Tis hard for me to believe I finally found a subject where I may teach *ye* something." He gently tilted her chin up. "The next step will be for us to spend time with each other, getting to know one another more, developing trust, becoming better friends."

Her brows furrowed. "But Duncan, we already spend time together each day."

"Aye, we will continue to do so, but now we can add closeness to our time together if ye like."

She considered his answer, deciding she liked it indeed.

"Also, we will share kisses."

The flutter in Anna's stomach increased with something akin to fear.

Perking up an eyebrow, Duncan asked, "Have ye not kissed a man before?"

Embarrassment returned unbidden. Unable to speak, she shook her head. Duncan's gaze fell to her mouth. Anna's tongue moistened her lips in anticipation.

Duncan slowly lowered his face and softly touched his lips to hers. The sensation was exquisite. Warmth spread over her body, chasing her fears into a hasty retreat. She rose on the balls of her feet to meet him, changing the soft touch to something firmer, more exciting. All sense of herself fled in the face of this new awareness. A hunger developed and she knew Duncan could answer it. With a sense of desperation, her hands firmly grasped the back of his neck, pulling him against her.

Duncan responded in kind to her bold move. His hand slid to the small of her back, pressing her into him, curving her body around his frame. She grew short of breath, and her lips parted. Duncan's breath and tongue pushed her further and a moan escaped her throat. He toyed with her lips, gently nipping and pulling at them, his tongue drawing lines across them before darting into her mouth to make further contact.

He tasted wonderful, wild, intoxicating. Tentatively, Anna mimicked his motions. With each swirl of their tongues, the kiss deepened. Anna broke away, no longer able to breathe. She stood in his arms, dazed, panting.

Duncan put distance between them. His eyes glowed and she noted he was as out of breath as she.

"Duncan, what *was* that?"

He wrapped her in his arms again. Anna delighted in the sensation. He pressed his lips to her hair above her ear.

"That, my sweet Anna, was passion. I should have guessed ye would approach kissing with the same fervor ye approach all else."

Tilting her head back to see his expression, she asked, "Is that a good or bad thing?"

The rumble of light laughter in his chest teased her nipples.

"'Tis a verra good thing. Howbeit, we need to be careful."

Careful? What did he mean? The realization hit her. She looked down, seeing what she'd felt from him.

"If we had continued, we would have mated?" Having grown up around horses, she knew enough about nature to understand the basics of this part. Besides, her father's men hadn't censored their stories if they thought her out of earshot.

His expression changed to a serious one. "I wouldnae let us go that far. I am not one to tumble a lass in the stables. Ye are a noblewoman, and I will treat you thus. I wish to court ye, not take advantage of yer innocence. Yer response was wonderful, but…unexpected. I half believed ye would take a swing at me." He chuckled again. "I promise to be more careful next time."

She instantly liked the idea of next time. Glancing outside, she noticed the position of the sun in the sky. Morning had given way to afternoon. After a trying few hours, Anna felt emotionally spent.

"My mother wanted me to remind ye 'tis yer afternoon with her."

She'd forgotten.

"She knows about this morn. She said she would wait for ye in the great hall—not to worry about being late."

Still in a daze from Duncan's kisses, Anna walked to Nessa's room. She washed and changed out of her torn, bloodstained clothes. Wandering downstairs, she glanced about for Lady MacGregor. Mairi rose from a chair in front of the main hearth, a look of concern in her eyes as she reached to embrace Anna.

"Anna, I heard about today. Are ye well?"

She wasn't, but not because of what Mairi thought. "I suspect I shall be fine."

Mairi took Anna's hand. "Come, let us walk."

They strolled down the path, reaching their garden bench. Mairi patted the seat, inviting Anna to sit.

"I dinnae pretend to know what 'tis like to take a life, but I will listen if ye wish to speak of it."

Anna smiled, knowing she tried to offer comfort in her way. Killing Shamus wasn't what disturbed her. True enough, taking any life was terrible, but she no longer had a sense of guilt about Shamus.

"No, I have no need to talk about this morning." A look of relief washed over Mairi's face. Anna's smile faded. If Mairi knew what she *did* want to talk about, she might rather speak of killing. *How can I ask Mairi about this? Duncan's own mother?* The very thought of it crippled her tongue, yet her ignorance compelled her to seek information.

She had already decided Nessa was an inappropriate source. At five and ten years, anything she did know, she probably shouldn't.

Further, she wasn't ready to face the certain 'I told you so' looks she would have to endure if Nessa found out. She could either talk with Mairi, or continue along in the dark. As someone who pursued knowledge with zeal, being completely daft on this subject proved intolerable, particularly since it had such a powerful effect on her. She decided to swallow her pride.

Taking a deep breath, she forged ahead. "There is another matter. Something I am terribly embarrassed to admit not understanding."

"Of course, my dear. How may I be of help?" A soft expression reflected Mairi's curious and supportive tone.

Anna closed her eyes and steadied herself. "Do you remember asking me to not think of you as Lady MacGregor during these times, but as my dear aunt?"

Mairi squeezed Anna's hand. "Aye, of course. Ye can ask me anything."

Anna shot her a look of apprehension. "I fear what I wish to speak of may cause my favorite aunt to succumb to convulsions."

Mairi raised an eyebrow, giving a sly smile at her prediction. "Try me."

Forcing out a breath, Anna launched her first question. "Tell me about passion between a man and a woman." Anna scanned her face for signs of her reaction.

The corners of Mairi's mouth tilted up farther.

"Passion is one of the most powerful forces in nature. It can override sound judgment and has been the downfall of good men and women. But 'tis also one of the greatest gifts a man and woman can share. Ye havenae experienced this before?" She sounded surprised.

"No," Anna whispered, heat spreading on her face.

Mairi gave her the same look of disbelief her daughter had a few days before.

Anna felt the need to explain yet again. "Men in my life have either been enemies or allies. Enemies like the neighboring nobles, who were only interested in me bearing their children, or enemies who have wanted to kill me. Allies have been family, clan, or fellow warriors. I have never had any other kind of relationship with a man."

Mairi shifted on the bench, turning to face Anna directly. Emboldened, Anna continued.

"A few sons of noblemen attempted to court me in the past. I refused. They were all selfish, power-hungry fools. They only wanted a wife to stay at home, to produce their heirs whilst they continued their dalliances at court. They cared more about the amount of my dowry than me. I would not accept such a life. To become nothing but a well-kept servant and broodmare, forbidden to do the things I enjoy, and expected to be obedient to the whims of the man who possessed me. The rest saw me as a plaything for their entertainment. How can anyone with a shred of pride agree to such an onerous proposal?"

Mairi's eyes widened in sympathy. "Indeed. Surely not all were so distasteful?"

Anna nodded her head vigorously. "Most were immediately put off by my appearance, behavior and bloodline. I am too tall, too strong and bear too many scars. I helped manage my father's holdings, and know more about farming and livestock than about sewing or cooking. My Scottish blood certainly weighed against me. It is as popular being Scots there as it is being English here. The few times I attended court or social events, my sharp tongue and opinions did the work of pushing most potential suitors away. They saw me as an unbridled hoyden, not worth the trouble, regardless of my dowry." Anna laughed at the remembrance of it.

"So your father dinnae force a match upon ye?"

Looking back, it did seem unusual he didn't. "No, I think he understood how much I abhorred the idea of a forced match, and what kind of trouble I would make. Due to my reputation, I became the target of ridicule among my peers. For these reasons, I ceased attending social events altogether. I found it a relief as I had no desire to play their games. Neither did I find any attraction in their overindulgent lifestyles. Shortly after, any interest in me waned. I find the whole of English nobility repugnant. Having my home burned and my family slaughtered at the order of one only deepens my belief."

"But recently, ye have experienced passion?"

Anna dropped her eyes, grinning broadly. "Yes," she answered quietly.

"What do ye wish to know?"

"How can this emotion completely make reason flee? Nothing

else existed but him and me. Though quite unnerving, it was a most wonderful possession."

Mairi gave Anna a knowing smile, boosting her confidence. "Aye, sounds like passion."

"How do I proceed? How can I know the decisions I make regarding this man are not clouded by these overpowering emotions?"

Mairi patted Anna's hand before answering. "Time. It takes time to be able to see clearly."

"How long did it take for you to know about Laird MacGregor?"

A thin, humorless smile appeared on Mairi's lips and Anna immediately regretted asking the question.

"I am sorry, I did not mean to pry."

Mairi waved her hand. "No, no, 'tis quite alright. My marriage with Kenneth MacGregor was arranged. As ye know, I am originally from the Stewart clan. Our marriage created an alliance between our people where before only neutrality existed. I knew Kenneth from a distance, with time to develop naught more than a friendly acquaintance before we wed."

She must have read the expression on Anna's face. A forced marriage was her worst nightmare, a fact she had thoughtlessly expressed but a few moments ago. Mairi squeezed her hand and smiled.

"'Twas difficult at first, but we have made a good match. We have forged love where none was to start. Passion has played an important role. Marriage has been hard work, but I couldnae ask for a better husband. I believe him to think me a good wife."

They sat in silence while Anna considered her words.

Mairi shifted on the bench. "Passion is a good place to begin, but there must be trust, mutual respect and caring for love to take root. Often times 'tis more an act of will than a feeling fluttering in the stomach."

Anna nodded, not sure she understood.

"Men are often stubborn, prideful creatures, who believe the world should bend to their command. We have to look past this part if we are to love them. Otherwise, we would probably wind up killing them." Mairi chuckled.

Anna giggled. Mairi smoothed a strand of hair from Anna's face. "So, do I know this braw swain of yers?" She gave Anna a sly look.

"*Aunt Mairi,* you are as bad as your daughter!"

They laughed till both were in tears. A somber thought soon ended Anna's merriment. Hesitating to make eye contact, she asked, "Do you think me good enough for your son?"

Mairi pulled Anna into her arms. "If I knew no more than the fact ye risked yer life against six men to save two innocent lasses, I would know enough to say aye. Having gotten to know ye these past few weeks has only deepened my affections for ye. As the daughter of a baron, and the granddaughter of a laird, ye are of noble blood, and a good match for Duncan."

"Even without lands or a dowry?"

Mairi swept her hand in a half circle. "Look about. Do the MacGregors need more wealth? As a mother, I would rather see my son happy than saddled in a marriage without love for more land or coin."

Anna kissed her cheek. "Thank you."

"Ye have the advantage, of course. If my son ever acts in any manner but a gentleman, just tell me. His father and I shall take him to task."

Anna smiled at the image. "I believe I can handle your son, Mairi."

Chapter Thirteen

*A*nna caught Mairi's wink as she filled Kenneth's goblet with ale. "Husband, Duncan and Anna propose a trip to Graham market for supplies. I have sent word to those who would like to offer goods for sale or barter."

The laird tore off a chunk of bread and turned to Duncan. "Who do ye think to take?"

"I thought Liam and Rory in one wagon, Donnan and Ross for the other. Malcolm and Ian plus me and Anna should be enough."

"Very well. When do ye leave?"

"Mayhap five days. Does it suit ye?"

The laird nodded as he took another slice of venison from the platter. "Aye. See if they have some of the wine ye fetched last trip."

While discussion of the trip continued, Anna realized she was more aware of Duncan than ever. The current seating arrangement always put Anna furthest away from him. Her gaze frequently sought him out, often catching him staring at her. She felt the memory of his lips on hers and hungered to have them there again.

She saw Lady MacGregor's serene smile and the laird's half-scowl, and blushed to think they understood the shared glances between her and Duncan. Nessa chattered away, oblivious to the actions of those around her.

"Did anyone hear me?" Nessa asked impatiently, hand on her hip as she stared at Anna and Duncan. The two of them exchanged quick glances, and Mairi smiled indulgently. The laird shook his head and called for more ale.

"I want to know if Anna can bring back velvet to make new gowns."

"Of course, Nessa. I will be happy to purchase any fabric you ladies might require." With a last look at Duncan, she listened attentively as Nessa discussed various dress styles.

After the meal, they rose from the table. Rather than joining his father at the hearth, Duncan chatted with the women. Mairi smiled at his behavior, while Nessa gaped at him like he had grown an additional head. Though uncertain why he stayed near them, Anna found herself glad for the additional time in his presence.

As soon as Mairi excused herself to retire for the evening, Duncan spoke. "Anna, would ye like to go for a walk?"

Nessa whipped her head around, waiting to hear Anna's response.

"Yes, I would."

A grin split Nessa's face, lighting her features with joy. A blush heated Anna at Nessa's reaction. She accepted the arm Duncan offered, and they headed out the door. As they strolled toward the gardens outside the keep, Duncan lifted her hand to his lips, his breath warm on her skin as he kissed her fingers. Moonlight filtered through the clouds, bathing their path in silver light.

Stopping beneath a large oak tree, Duncan leaned against the trunk, pulling Anna into his embrace. She placed her hands on his chest and settled her cheek on his shoulder. Taking a deep breath, she savored his touch and scent. He no longer smelled like horses and leather. The heady, masculine scent belonging only to him filled her senses. They stood several minutes in silence, soaking up each other's presence.

"Ye are less confused tonight."

She was glad he sensed the difference. "Yes. I had a discussion with my favorite aunt this afternoon."

Drawing back slightly, Duncan scrunched his brow, waiting for the rest.

Anna saw the question on his face. Cocking a smile, she laid her head back on his shoulder. "Your mother has asked to be my female counsel."

His body shook with a mild laugh. "That must have been difficult."

She shrugged. "What choice do I have? I have experienced nothing like this before and refuse to remain in the dark."

"I am glad ye have someone to talk to. I cannae think how it has been for ye not to have an older woman to rely on all these years."

His voice rumbled in his chest and the vibration enticed her to draw closer.

"Your mother has been wonderful. I needed to be sure she approves of me. I want to understand what is happening to me, and do my part…"

Duncan waited for her to finish her thought. She didn't. "Do your part?" He firmed his embrace, prompting her to explain.

She didn't answer right away. Her lungs filled deeply before she exhaled with force. "To do my part if you decide to keep me."

Duncan couldn't believe his ears. She sought out information from his own mother so she could better understand how to become his *what*? His friend, his lover, his mistress? No, he couldn't dishonor her by using her that way. He knew they'd already progressed well beyond companionship, past friendship. Marriage was his intent.

Placing his hands on either side of her face, he gazed at her. Anna's confession merited one from him in return.

"I have felt this pull since the first day I saw ye. I thought 'twas simply desire, as when a man sees a lass who pleases him. I have learned what I feel for ye surpasses simple desire. I've never wanted to court anyone before. 'Tis new to me as well."

His words made her smile. Gazing into his eyes, she asked, "I wondered…"

Meeting her gaze, he mirrored her smile. "What is it, my Anna?"

"Might we kiss again? I promise to be more careful this time."

Before he could answer, Anna reached both hands around his neck and pulled his mouth to hers. Though she knew better what to expect this time, she found herself swept away as quickly and as thoroughly as before. Hungrily, she kissed him, savoring his taste. How was it possible to want someone this intensely?

Anna molded around his body, needing to get closer. Warmth spread through her, heating every nerve. Her hands found their way under his tunic to his back, craving contact with his skin. She reveled in running her hands over the sculpted muscles quivering under her touch. It empowered her to know she affected him so. His hands did the same to her, accelerating her heart rate, her breathing. With each touch, he set small fires crackling across her skin. It was not enough. Needing his hands everywhere, she ached for skin-on-skin contact.

Duncan broke contact, muttering a low oath. "*Bluidy* hell woman! Ye will be the death of me."

She fixed her gaze on him. Both out of breath, they teetered on the edge of control.

"Aye, 'twill be a sweet death, no doubt," she answered, imitating his burr.

He enclosed her in his arms again, and she felt his lips smile when he kissed her forehead and whispered, "Nae doubt."

In a stupor, she leaned against him as he escorted her back to the keep. His parting kiss landed light as the fall of snowflakes. What it lacked in ardor it made up with tenderness. Anna staggered upstairs, clinging to the rope rail along the wall. Nessa ambushed her the instant she opened the door.

"I *knew* it! Ye and Duncan!" Nessa erupted, dancing with excitement.

Anna realized there'd be no denying it. She knew she had to look different. Her cheeks warmed with remembrance of their passion, and her lips felt swollen from kissing. She simply smiled at Nessa, remembering her teasing from a few weeks ago. Was it only weeks? It seemed much longer. Anna calmly sat down and prepared for bed.

"Ye *must* tell me."

Anna ignored her plea, refusing to meet her gaze. "Whatever do you mean?" she drawled lazily, her voice as innocent as she could muster. With a squeal of indignation, Nessa launched herself at Anna, catching her off guard and tumbling them both to the bed.

The absurdity of her behavior sent Anna into peals of uncontrolled laughter. Unable to resist, Nessa followed suit, and they found themselves entwined in a fit of uncontained hysterics. Once their mirth faded, Anna rolled to her feet and resumed dressing for bed.

"Tell me." The whining in Nessa's voice threatened to start the giggles again.

"Tell you what, Nessa?"

Impatient, Nessa huffed, rattling off a string of questions. "Are ye courting? Do ye love him? Does this mean ye shall stay forever? Are ye planning to marry? When will I become an aunt?"

Anna plopped onto the bed, stunned by the directness of Nessa's questions. She still searched to find her bearings, not sort things out for her nosey adopted sister. Love? She wasn't sure what love was. At least not between a man and woman. Mairi said love needed passion, trust, respect and caring to form. They had all of these, so perhaps love would develop. It was too new to her, too early in their relationship to claim love. As for the rest, she couldn't think that far ahead. Turning at last to Nessa's eager face, Anna answered carefully.

"Yes, we are courting. He asked today, so you haven't missed anything. 'Tis too soon to speak of love, but I do care for your brother. There is something powerful between us. As for the rest, only time will tell."

Clasping her hands to either side of Anna's face, Nessa gave her an elated smile. "We shall truly be sisters! It has been my dearest wish." Unable to contain her joy, Nessa crawled under the bedclothes with Anna, extolling the virtues of love until they both fell asleep.

The next few days flew swiftly by. Each morning she trained with Duncan in both armed and unarmed combat. He readily saw the logic behind each technique they covered and regularly praised her abilities. Often, their sparring led to heated embraces and kisses. She relished them as much as the fighting, perhaps more.

Duncan's prediction she'd won over clan MacGregor proved accurate. Setting bones, stitching cuts, tending burns, soothing fevers, and treating a number of other maladies kept Anna busy for several hours most afternoons.

The laird grudgingly allowed Nessa to assist Anna on most cases, after Anna suggested the future wife of a laird, skilled in healing the sick and wounded, would be quite valued. Not in the least put off by the sight of blood, Nessa showed signs of a true gift, and her kind, gentle nature put people at ease.

The gratitude of the people whom Anna assisted warmed her heart. She'd turned down a pig, sacks of grain, and some vegetables she didn't recognize as payment for services. Duncan explained to everyone that the laird provided for her, and in turn her services were part of his care for them. She'd never received compensation before for doing what she viewed as Christian charity, and felt uncomfortable doing so now.

In spite of the laird's words, she noticed her favorite things continued to crop up anonymously. The jam she enjoyed so much at breakfast always seemed to be on the table. Loaves of the dark, sweet bread with nuts and berries she favored was regularly served. A never-ending supply of lavender soap appeared for her bath. Two thicker tunics and a new pair of deerskin breeches found their way into her possession. Anna never knew who was responsible for these things, but her heart filled each time she saw them.

The laird set boundaries on the types of cases Nessa attended. Again, Anna was surprised by the lack of protest the girl offered. It also made her feel guilty she wasn't as obedient a daughter as Nessa. Watching father and daughter together made Anna grasp the depth of love her own father had possessed to allow his only daughter to pursue the unconventional interests she did.

Isla attended also. She and Nessa kept a running log of treatments, tracking details for each case. Anna used this opportunity to teach the girls Latin, English and mathematics. They kept various remedies cataloged in another book.

Though Nessa shied from any use of acupuncture, Isla allowed

Anna to treat her, as she experienced difficult pain the week leading up to her monthly courses. This, along with an herbal tea, eased her suffering considerably.

Two days after Isla's first session, Anna received requests from a number of women in the village for the same tea. A few even allowed acupuncture. While she had envisioned healing more grievous wounds and illnesses, she experienced satisfaction knowing she brought comfort to other women.

Anna cherished her time at the stables working with the horses. She found joy in training the unruly young steeds to take the bit and saddle and prepare the already-trained horses for the demands of combat. Working there proved the perfect way to end a day, though she always came to the evening meal smelling of horses.

Duncan placed a MacGregor plaide on her bed. On top lay a *sgian dubh* with the MacGregor crest. The lion's head with crown was a powerful symbol, as was the slogan; "*'S Rioghal Mo Dhream,* Royal is my race." Touched deeply by the gesture, Anna smiled through tears.

Duncan escorted her to the seat next to him at the table that evening. So close they frequently brushed hands, arms and legs, each random touch sent a jolt of awareness through her. It was a delicious torture to sit close to him yet not get carried away. This arrangement allowed them to enjoy both mealtime and the company of family, while being acutely mindful of each other. Family? At some point, she realized indeed the MacGregors had become like family.

Chapter Fourteen

*A*nna met Duncan at the stables to depart for Graham Village at first light. Two large carts loaded with crates of produce, casks of mead and whisky, jars of honey, bundles of woven goods, sacks of grain and other goods were packed and ready. In addition, four horses they had trained stood tied to the back of the wagon, intended for sale. Two men on horseback and two in each wagon accompanied them. One man in each wagon drove, while the other wielded a large crossbow.

"'Twill take a day to reach the MacFarlane lands, then another to Graham territory. The main village is a half-day ride from their border," Duncan explained.

He nodded toward the plaide she had draped around her shoulders. "It suits ye."

"Aye, 'tis growing on me," she answered in her best burr. His smile lit his whole face, and her heart stirred to know she brought him happiness. Wrapped in the same tartan he always wore created a tangible connection between them, making her feel as though she belonged.

She considered what it would be like to belong to him and he to her. Simply thinking about their kisses and caresses produced a warm, tingling sensation deep inside. She considered what it would be like to share his bed, to bear his children. Such thoughts had once brought a sense of dread and fear, but the thought of being tied to Duncan in such a way fostered a sense of longing.

The beautiful, lush green of the Highlands had definitely gotten into her blood, even if her blood hadn't thickened enough to fully embrace them yet. She fingered the soft wool about her shoulders, grateful for its warmth. "Duncan, why do we need eight swords to protect two wagons? Are we not traveling through ally territories?"

"Aye, we are. Even though we stick to friendly lands, bandits sometimes waylay unprotected travelers."

She shrugged. Their numbers afforded an opportunity to get to know some of his men better. However, it did reduce opportunities to be alone with him. Probably for the best, as she found it a challenge to ignore him riding just a few feet away, while she needed to concentrate on staying watchful.

The first day's journey proved uneventful. The men set up camp near a stream while Duncan and Anna hunted for the evening meal. A brace of hares and three grouses later, they headed back to camp, lingering as they took advantage of their time alone before rejoining the men. A mournful whine interrupted their kiss. Pulling out of Duncan's arms, Anna listened for it again.

"Did you hear that?"

"Aye, but 'twas so faint, I am not sure from where it came."

They waited for the cry to repeat. The whine came again. They followed the sound to a rock overhang and a small cave. In the cave lay a litter of wolf pups. All were dead save one. The pup opened its mouth and keened again. Anna scanned the area for signs of an adult wolf. None were about.

"What has happened to the mother?" she wondered.

"She must have been killed. She wouldnae leave her pups to die were she alive."

Cooing soothingly to the remaining pup, Anna scooped him up, holding him to her. He nestled into her tunic and whimpered. Her heart twisted, as she knew the pain and helplessness of losing family. Reaching for Duncan's water skin, she poured a few drops into the pup's mouth and he lapped greedily. She wrapped him in her tunic.

"Ye mean to keep him, then?" Duncan arched a brow.

"Let us see if he survives, but yes, I think so." She glanced at the ball of fur huddled in her arms and smiled.

Duncan frowned. "I admire yer charity, but how can we keep a wolf around our horses and livestock?"

"If he grows up in the stables with the other dogs, why would he become a problem? I shall train him and he can hunt with me."

He looked at her skeptically. Anna tilted her head in challenge.

"I have trained dogs before to track and hunt. Why should he be any different?"

"Ye think ye can train away his wolf instincts?"

She wasn't sure, but relished the challenge. "If his nature wins over training and causes harm, I will kill him myself. Agreed?"

Duncan's lips quirked. "I have seen the effect ye have on me, horses and others. I look forward to seeing if ye can charm the wolf as easily."

As they returned to the fire, curiosity rose among the men regarding the newest member of the party.

"Lady Anna, what have ye found?" Liam asked.

"We found a wolf's den. The litter had been deserted. 'Tis the only survivor. I thought some goat's milk butter would be a good start."

Rory, Liam's younger brother, hopped up and searched for it in the cart.

"Aye, 'tis a good idea. We might see if he'll take a wee bit o' meat also, though he may be too young."

Scooping some of the butter into a bowl, Anna put it and the pup on the ground and sat next to him. He sniffed the bowl once, then lapped at the butter hungrily. He licked the bowl clean, then stumbled back to her and curled up on her lap.

"He is smart for such a wee one. He already kens who his mistress is." Liam smiled and winked at her. "Have ye thought of a name fer him?"

"Trean, since he was the strongest of his litter."

"Aye, strong. 'Tis a good name," Liam replied. "Let us see if he is strong enough to last the next couple o' days."

Anna stroked the pup's ears and back as he dozed. He rolled over in her lap, offering his bulging tummy for petting. She glanced at Duncan and smiled as she obliged Trean's silent request. The pup gave a whimper of pleasure at her touch. Duncan rolled his eyes.

"Seems the charming has begun." Anna grinned broadly.

Duncan chuckled and shook his head.

Malcolm and Iain, two of the warriors who rode with them, dressed and skewered the game on a spit. When it was ready, she roused Trean and offered him some of the bird. He ate a small amount, then licked the grease off her fingers.

The men took turns on watch in two-hour shifts. Duncan took the first shift. Anna lay awake watching the stars, Trean cuddled next to her, waiting until he returned. Though his bedroll lay a few feet from hers, she felt his presence like the heat rolling from an oven.

She marveled at the changes he'd inspired in her. Never before had she dreamed of anything like this. The approval in his eyes when he saw her wrapped in the plaide he'd given her warmed her more than the blanket ever would. Sleeping only a short distance from him under the stars made her want to close the space, to lie in his arms. Only the presence of his men kept her from doing so. The look on his face in the glow of the fire told her he desired the same and more.

They broke camp before dawn. Trean rode with Anna, perched on the front of her saddle, content to ride. He was more active when they stopped, and his increase in appetite gave her hope he would survive.

By the end of the second day, they stopped on the edge of Graham lands to camp. Sitting with the men gave her the opportunity to ask questions about their families and backgrounds. Liam told stories of Duncan as a boy, and the trouble he caused, along with Malcolm, Iain, Donnan and others. There were more than a few tales of Duncan and a lad called Colin MacKay who had fostered with the MacGregors for a few years. It sounded like Colin did his best to get Duncan into trouble, while Duncan attempted to keep Colin reined in.

Liam belched and leaned forward, gaining attention. "I remember when Callum…"

The mood changed immediately. He cleared his throat, shot an uncomfortable look at Duncan, then swiftly moved on to other stories. Though puzzled with the reaction to Callum's name, Anna enjoyed hearing them laughing so easily once the awkward moment passed.

Anna observed how they treated Duncan with respect, even in the stories they told. It was obvious they recognized him as their captain and future laird. The history and loyalty they shared brought a sting of envy. Anna missed the deep connection of family. Though she laughed along with them at the more outrageous exploits, laughter did not stave off the acute feeling of loss. Though they accepted her, Anna's own history now lay buried in ruins many days' ride away.

Duncan bumped his shoulder against hers. "Anna, ye have heard some of our most embarrassing moments growing up. 'Tis only fair ye tell a few tales of yer childhood."

Smiling, she thought of the myriad ways she'd caused mischief while growing up. She recounted how many nursemaids she'd gone through, and the terrible tricks she played on them to escape outside so she could watch the men training.

She pointed out several scars on her arms, head, and one in particular on her neck, describing the circumstances behind them. Most were earned training in combat, sparring with both Edrick and Master Zhang. Or gained from headstrong behavior typically involving a horse, weapons and youthful foolishness.

Anna noticed the mood around the fire changed. Instead of enjoying the escapades of a reckless youth, the men now stared at her with grim expressions. Self-conscious, she fell silent.

Iain recovered first. "Forgive us, milady, we are not used to a lass being treated thus. 'Tis more than a little unsettling to hear of ye being wounded so and seeing the scars."

Nodding her understanding, she forced a smile of reassurance. What little camaraderie she'd felt earlier evaporated. Silence and discomfort wove together, creating a tension demanding resolution. The bitterness of loneliness formed in her mouth that neither wine nor ale could wash away.

Taking Trean with her, Anna rose to take the first watch. The new moon offered very little light. Putting aside the mixed emotions of the evening, she slipped into the role of sentry. Opening her senses, she relished hearing and quickly assessing every noise, every movement in the woods around her. The aroma of moist earth and heather rode on the slight breeze. With a clear sky, the stars shone so bright they seemed almost close enough to grasp.

Rory came by for his watch, surprising her at how quickly the two hours passed. Not yet sleepy, she chose instead to quietly walk the perimeter of camp, Trean at her heels.

Halting beneath a broad-branched tree, she slid her back down the trunk to sit on the ground. Anna hugged her knees, laying her head on an arm. Alone with her thoughts, Trean curled at her feet, she considered the night's events. She had been lulled into thinking she belonged with the MacGregors, but she didn't. Thoughts and feelings from yesterday, of wondering what it would be like to belong with Duncan, seemed far away. A few scraps of plaide wouldn't change reality.

She felt her time with him was fleeting. Tonight served as a painful reminder. Through his loving words and amorous encounters, Duncan had awakened a woman in her she'd never suspected existed. His recognition and nurturing of this part served to make her care for him even more. This caring was too potent to be anything else but love. It was, wasn't it? Their time together daily had steadily allowed it to grow.

Sadly, Anna found his loving words could not erase her lingering doubts. Too long had she been the subject of ridicule and scorn. Part of her believed it to be only a matter of time before Duncan truly saw her for what she was—a destitute hoyden of noble blood. On that day, he would turn away and break her heart. Was risking the pain of a broken heart worth experiencing the passion and tenderness he offered now? When it came to an end, she would at least have memories of this time to cherish. It would have to be enough.

When the time came, she would accept the laird's offer of escort elsewhere. She might be familiar with pain, but she knew she couldn't bear to stay and watch Duncan marry another. Perhaps she could fulfill the role of healer with one of the neighboring clans, giving her the ability to visit Nessa and Mairi from time to time. She pushed those thoughts aside, fearing they would demand her attention soon enough.

Deciding not to give into despair, she crossed her legs and settled into meditation. She heard Duncan's step before he arrived.

He sat next to her and scratched Trean's ears. "Yer watch finished a half hour ago." His voice was calm, but laced with concern.

"I am not sleepy."

Silence. A small nocturnal animal rustled nearby in the leaves.

"Do ye want to talk about tonight?"

Did she? What was there to say?

"I saw the faraway look in yer eyes when we talked of our youth. Then I saw the despair. Sometimes I forget how much ye have lost."

More silence. Exhaling her lingering self-pity, she finally said, "There is nothing to be done about it."

Duncan cupped her cheek with his palm. "Nae, we cannae change the past, but we can do something about the future. Ye think ye have no place in this world, but I would make a place for ye, if ye would allow it."

Anna closed her eyes and leaned into his hand. His words soothed her ragged sense of sorrow like a balm.

"I know ye are not ready, but when ye are, I will be here. Know I willnae be able to sleep until ye return to the fire."

As he walked away, her thoughts wove into a tangled mess once again. The old doubts crept in, but she refused to allow them sway. His presence, no matter how brief, proved her undoing. She felt safer, at peace by his side. She did not know what the future held for them, but right now she longed to be near Duncan. Gathering Trean, she made her way back to the fire.

Anna caught the relief on his face as he watched her approach.

Returning his smile, she grabbed the edge of her pallet and dragged it next to his. The surprise on his face became something else. Anna lay down next to him, pulling the plaide over her. She shifted her back toward him until flush against him. Trean curled against her stomach with a sigh.

"That was bold," Duncan whispered into her neck.

"Am I to belong with you, Duncan MacGregor?" she whispered in return.

He stiffened slightly. "Aye. There is naught in this life I want more." He lightly kissed her cheek, put an arm around her waist and drew her tighter. She responded with a contented sigh and gave in to sleep.

She woke the next morning before dawn. Duncan lay on his back with an arm around her. She curled into his side, her cheek on his chest and an arm across his middle, Trean at her feet. She didn't want to move and disrupt the warm serenity, but thought to rouse before the men noticed them. Smiling, she realized she didn't care if they saw.

She watched Duncan as he slept. The brooding look he often wore had fled, making him look much younger, almost boyish. Anna leaned up and placed light kisses along the stubble of his chin. His breathing hitched and he squeezed her shoulders as he woke.

"Is this what you had in mind when you said you would make a place for me?" she whispered, her voice raspy with sleep and passion. She gazed at him with teasing eyes. He rewarded her with a look of raw desire.

"Aye, though what I had in mind included fewer clothes and a softer bed."

The image made her involuntarily clutch his chest, causing her to move closer. Her breathing accelerated. Only the thought of the men across the fire from them kept her from demanding the kiss she longed for. She had to settle for the knowledge he twisted as much with longing as she.

Chapter Fifteen

*A*nna rose from Duncan's side. After adding more wood to the banked fire, she boiled water for a quick breakfast of chamomile tea and oatcakes, passing out the simple breakfast as the men finished their morning tasks.

"Many thanks, milady." Iain said.

Malcolm's brow bunched after his first bite.

"What's the matter, Malcolm? Does it not suit your taste?" Anna asked playfully. She had eaten enough of their bland version to expect a reaction to her variation.

He glanced at her as if caught stealing sweets from the kitchen. "Not at all, Lady Anna, 'tis just I have never eaten bannocks like this before. They are usually less...tasty."

She smiled and kicked at the apple cores on the ground. "I added apple and a bit of the honey we carry to market. I did not think they would be missed."

Hearty agreements came from bannock-filled mouths, along with muffled suggestions she make breakfast each day. Listening to the men's comments, she thought to address something on her mind.

"Gentlemen, as much as I appreciate the respect, I would request you not address me as Lady Anna, but merely Anna. I am not a titled noblewoman here. Doing so brings attention I would rather not have."

By the shocked looks on their faces, one would have thought the oatcakes they ate suddenly turned sour. To a man, they all looked at Duncan for confirmation.

He shrugged his shoulders. "As she wishes. I can see her point."

Uneasily, the men returned to their food, finishing quickly.

By midday, they arrived at Graham village. The Graham keep was a third again larger than the MacGregor stronghold. The market stood in the center of town, more than a furlong away from the walls of the large castle. The lanes were crowded with tents of every color and many permanent stalls with people barking out their goods.

Within a few hours, Duncan had a price on the horses, secured more wool than anticipated and sold or traded everything else. The barrels of wine requested by his father replaced the barrels of whisky and mead. New fabrics and spices, along with grains and other produce not grown by the MacGregors, were added to the wagons.

The village was much larger than the MacGregor village, but then the Lowlands were more populous. It made Anna wonder if an alliance with the Grahams involving Nessa was truly being considered. She recognized creating a bond was a good idea, if for no other reason than to bolster the border between the Lowlands and Highlands, and securing future trade. It also made sense from a strategic viewpoint.

Anna decided to hold her judgment until she got to know the Grahams better. The thought of Nessa marrying into a clan where she was treated less than she should raised her ire. She chuckled at her strong feelings of protectiveness. After a little more than a month, they truly were sisters.

After watching Duncan barter and trade goods, she was ready to explore. Handing Trean and Orion to Rory to be taken to the stable, she presented Duncan with her intent. He reached into his sporran.

"Here, take these coins. Find my mother and sister something ye think they would favor. I will be flayed alive if we dinnae come back with gifts for them." The twinkle in his eyes hinted he only partially jested. "And if you see something ye fancy, buy it."

She immediately frowned at his offer of money and opened her mouth to argue. He put a finger to her lips.

"Consider it payment for providing guard duty. I will be paying the others, so anything ye like, consider it payment, aye?" With a slight nod, he motioned Iain to accompany her.

Irritation immediately flared within. "Iain, you know I do not need tending like some child."

"Aye, lass ye dinnae, but the laird's orders are we never travel alone on another's lands. 'Tis the same for any of us. The fact the laird calls ye daughter doubles the order. Plus, there's the wee bit o' value Duncan places on ye." He gave her a teasing wink.

Knowing none were allowed to venture alone pacified her. Since they were stuck together, Anna enlisted Iain's help securing gifts.

"Iain, does a lady wait for you back home?" she teased.

"Aye, there is a bonny lass I have spent time with the past couple o' months," he replied cautiously.

"And does this bonny lass have a name?"

Quirking an eyebrow, he answered, "Her name is Colina."

Anna smiled sweetly. "Duncan has charged me with finding gifts for Nessa and Lady MacGregor. Perhaps we could find something for Colina while we are about. Unless you do not wish her to think more of your affections than she should."

Anna knew she was terrible at such flirting, but it was fun watching Iain squirm. She would know soon enough if Colina was important to him or not. She recalled Nessa and Isla discussing them and knew Colina's heart was engaged. She could at least investigate Iain's intentions. She would thrill the girls if she contributed to their gossip. The smile creeping across his face suggested he held more than a passing fancy for the woman.

"Tis a good suggestion, Lady...er, Anna, but I am at a loss what to seek."

She considered for a moment what Nessa enjoyed. "What do you like most about her, Iain?"

He looked slightly away before answering, a witless smile on his face.

"I like the way her soft body feels in my hands." His hands came up to chest level, as if she was there to embrace. He immediately stopped himself, a look of embarrassment on his face. "My apologies, lass. Duncan would have my head if he knew I spoke to ye thus."

Anna laughed and replied, "Not to worry, Iain, it will stay between us. Think about what else you appreciate about her, besides her...physical charms." Anna couldn't keep the grin off her face. Reassured, Iain considered her question for a moment.

"Her smell. I love the way she smells."

"Now we are getting somewhere. Let us seek fragrant soaps and bath oils. No doubt she would use them if she knew she would see you afterward."

"Aye, 'tis just the thing. Do ye think Nessa and Lady MacGregor would appreciate such gifts?"

"I doubt very many ladies' would think poorly about such thoughtfulness. The trick will be to try to closely match fragrances they already use."

Iain nodded in agreement and they made their way to the soap-makers. Finding a selection of soaps, oils and sea sponges, they made their purchases and wandered around before returning to the cart. Anna procured a number of dried herbs she hadn't seen growing in their area and a few growing in pots to add to their collection. She was eager to see if she could get them to flourish in the Highland climate.

Vendors of all kinds lined the road. Anna bought the ladies colorful beaded necklaces, bracelets and earrings, along with two more bound tomes of blank pages for Nessa to record their healing studies. As luck would have it, she found a few books for sale. With an eye on teaching Nessa, she purchased a haggard copy of *Beowulf,* along with well-made versions of *Vita Columbi,* and *Historia Regum Britanniae.*

They were all written in English, useful for their studies of her native language. Nessa would enjoy the stories, particularly the romance in many of them. If nothing else, she could share the stories with others during the dull winter months indoors.

They passed a booth of exquisitely embroidered linen goods. Anna begged Iain to wait out front while she searched for something very specific.

"How may I assist ye, milady?" asked a middle-aged woman dressed in black.

"I am looking for something to ignite a man's...appetite."

The woman shot a glance at Iain. Anna ignored the implications of her assumption and watched the woman pull a very soft and sheer night rail from one of the chests in the back.

It was a frothy thing with lace and delicately embroidered flowers, the lace and embellishments strategically placed to provide minimal cover. The narrow satin ribbons looked inadequate to the task of holding it on, and appeared designed to be taken off rather hastily. The woman gave Anna a knowing wink.

Anna stared at the garment. *Scandalous. Wanton. Brazen. Perfect.* Heat rose to her cheeks as she imagined herself in such a thing.

She bought the gift for Mairi in appreciation of their discussion on passion. Anna giggled when she imagined Mairi explaining to her husband how she came to possess such a garment. The woman bundled it discretely. Anna wrote "Lady MacGregor" on one corner so there would be no mistake if it were accidentally grabbed.

At a leather smith, she purchased two finely crafted leather belts with matching sporrans. They featured beautifully tooled interlocking designs she'd frequently seen on tapestries and other artistic objects since her arrival. She hoped Duncan and his father would appreciate them. Each sporran had an ornate, silver cantle on top, with the center left blank to carve one's clan crest.

"How long will it take to carve two, sir?"

The leather smith stroked the stubble on his chin and clicked his tongue between his missing front teeth before answering. "'Twill take a sennight, m'lady."

Anna placed twice as many coins on the counter. "I need them ready first thing on the morrow."

The man smiled, flashing his remaining teeth. He nodded and pointed to her waist. "I will need yer dirk for the design."

From the huge grin on Iain's face, she knew she'd made a good choice. "Iain, you must promise 'tis our secret, and you will have to be the one to come fetch them."

With a look of mischief on his face, he replied, "Aye. Ye will make the MacGregor men verra happy. I am glad to play conspirator, particularly since ye assisted me with purchases for my Colina."

Anna took his arm and laughed in response. "So 'tis *yer* Colina now is it?" Giving him a sly smile, she mimicked his accent.

He looked sheepishly at her. "Aye."

A commotion erupted not far from them. Barking and snarling rose above the noise of the crowd, and a whinny of terror pierced the melee. Shouts of warning echoed as an empty horse-drawn cart sped by, carving a wake through the unsuspecting crowd. Iain and Anna bolted to the spot where the shouts originated, and found four men and a boy, no more than ten summers old, lying on the ground wounded.

Anna wasted few words. "Fetch my pack and find a cart to carry the injured." Taking their packages, Iain nodded and raced back to their wagon.

Graham guards stood around, uncertain what to do, so Anna took charge. "Clear this area and keep the people back. I am a healer, and have sent for my supplies and a cart."

Two of the injured men were members of the Graham guard, while the others were either merchants or unfortunate victims in the way. The largest guard lay unconscious, bleeding from a nasty head wound stretching across his forehead. The other appeared to have broken ribs, clutching his side in pain. Of the rest, one man obviously had a broken leg, the other a long cut on his back. The boy also lay unconscious, though other than a simple cut on his arm, Anna spotted no other injuries.

She tended the head wound first, tearing off part of her tunic to staunch the bleeding. Based on how much blood he'd lost thus far, she feared for his life. She glanced up in relief to see Liam and Iain approaching with a horse and cart.

"Careful. That man has a broken leg, and we don't want the bleeding to start again on this soldier." As they loaded the boy, a cry rose from the crowd.

"Shaw, Shaw! What happened? Where are ye taking my boy?" A woman not much older than Anna stepped from the crowd, terror etched on her face. Anna turned to one of the guards for an answer. He rested a hand on the woman's shoulder.

"Yer son was injured by a runaway wagon. We are taking all the injured into the keep for this woman to tend."

She clutched Anna's arm in fear, her eyes wide. "Please save my boy. He is all I have."

Anna assisted her onto the bench beside Liam, then hopped on the back of the wagon as they drove toward the main gate. At the hall, Anna asked for boiling water, whisky and linens for bandages as the injured were laid on tables.

"If you have a healer, send for her," she ordered the closest guard. "I will need help."

He nodded and hurried out the door. Anna assessed the injuries again. The guard with the injured ribs struggled to breathe, but was not issuing blood. The broken leg appeared a simple break and easily set. The man with the long cut on his back lay on his side, conscious but grim. His wound had mostly stopped bleeding. The head injury and the boy remained her greatest concerns. She looked over the boy again. His heartbeat sounded strong, as did his breathing.

"Ma'am, your son appears to be only rendered unconscious. He has no other serious injury I can discern. Place this cloth over his wound. I will stitch him when finished with the other men."

Nodding, the woman bent over her son, singing to him in a low whisper.

Anna fetched the needle and thread from her pack, and then used the whisky someone brought to clean the head wound. Glad the man lay unconscious, she stitched the jagged cut closed. Iain stayed by her side. At her direction, he dispensed whisky to the other wounded men.

Moving on to the injured ribs, she counted three broken but not displaced. She bound them carefully as the man paled, sweat on his brow. Though he winced with every touch, he remained silent.

"You must stay idle the next three weeks, breathing deeply several times a day to stave off fluid on the lungs."

He nodded his understanding with a grimace and a whisper of thanks.

With the help of several swallows of whisky, Iain and two guards, Anna set the broken leg. Securing it in place with two boards, she bound it with strips of cloth.

The man with the deep cut on his back also benefited from liberal amounts of whisky. Anna offered a piece of leather for him to bite upon as her needle pierced the skin on each side of the gash. While she closed the gaping wound, the Graham healer arrived. Anna talked her through what she knew and what she'd done. As she did, family members of some of the men came and took them home.

The Graham healer checked Anna's work and made poultices to ward off infection. Finishing at last, Anna moved to Shaw. She glanced at the mother's tear-stained cheeks as she bent over her son in prayer. Her heart lurched with pity for this young mother and child.

Used to treating grown men after battle, Anna found the sight of a boy on the table more difficult to stomach. Shoving aside such feelings, Anna cleaned her needle and thread and closed the cut on his arm. When finished, she conducted a more thorough examination, feeling for any bruises or hardening of the body in the soft areas. She discovered a small knot on the back of his head, but nothing of a more serious nature.

"Shaw has a small lump on his head. His heartbeat and breathing remain strong. He appears to be healthy. I see no reason why he should not come around soon."

At this news, the woman burst into tears. "Thank ye, milady, how can I ever thank ye enough?"

Uncomfortable with the woman's praise, especially since her son had not woken yet, Anna replied, "Thank me when Shaw is awake and well again. You may stay until he rouses." She glanced at a guard, who nodded agreement.

Walking over to a basin, she cleaned the blood from her hands and arms. A serving woman brought several mugs and a pitcher of ale. Anna filled a cup and drank deeply, dropping onto a bench closest to the guard with the head wound. A tray with a loaf of bread and round of cheese arrived for them to eat while they waited. She glanced at Iain. He gave her a nod and a smile.

Shaw stirred first. "Mam?" he called out softly.

"I am here, Shaw, I am here," his mother answered with tears of relief.

Anna rose to check on her young charge. Certain he suffered no more than the bump on his head and the cut, she made him drink a cup of willow bark tea. His grimace from the bitter drink reassured her, so she released him into his mother's care.

With only the unconscious guard left, she sat and waited. For the first time she noticed the four other guards standing around him. "Who is this man to your clan?"

"He is one of our commanders, milady. Our captain will thank ye personally for yer timely treatment and care."

"What is your name, and his?"

"He is Ronald, and I am Neil, milady." He bowed slightly, his smile warm.

"I will tell you, Neil, as I told Shaw's mother. You can thank me when your commander is awake and out of danger."

His face turned serious. "'Tis in God's hands now, whether he lives or dies. His chances would be naught if ye hadnae arrived to take charge an' stop the bleeding. Our healer wouldnae have gotten here in time. If he lives, 'twill be because of yer efforts."

Anna smiled in return, knowing better than to argue with a soldier. Fatigue settled in.

"Are the commander's quarters close, or is there perhaps a bed nearby we can move him to?" She knew it would probably be several hours, perhaps days, before he woke, if ever.

"His quarters are in the guard tower, but there are small guest rooms just off this hall."

Fetching a litter, the guards moved their commander up one floor to a small but cozy room with a fireplace, single bed and table. Once he was settled, Anna addressed Neil. "There is nothing more I can do for him at the moment. I would like to find my clansmen."

"I was ordered to bring yer group to the laird's hall when ye finished tending the commander. The laird has requested ye dine with him this eve."

Motioning for him to lead the way, she followed him into the bailey and toward the stables where Duncan and the men awaited with their carts and horses.

"Ach, there ye are. Liam told us what happened. Is everyone well?" Duncan asked. His voice echoed with possessiveness, his face a partial scowl.

Anna quirked a brow but took his offered hand. "All will be, but for the commander. He suffered a hard blow to the head and a vicious cut. I think he will live, but know not when he will awaken."

Neil led them through the double oak doors and into the great hall. A score or so men sat on stools and benches around trestle tables, eating. As their group walked past the seated men, a deep voice bellowed, "Wench, why are ye dressed like a man? Come here, and I will teach ye what it means to be a woman."

He followed his taunt with a stinging swat to Anna's backside, hard enough to propel her forward. Anger ignited Anna's blood, accelerated by the accompanying laughter of his companions. She shot a warning look to Duncan to stay out of it, shoving his chest for emphasis.

She took a quick side step toward the man who'd hit her, bringing her knee up high to her chest. Using the momentum of the step toward this oaf, Anna released a sidekick, driving her booted heel into the center of his chest. Her stepping kick knocked the breath from his lungs with an exaggerated grunt, and sent him sprawling backward onto the floor, his head bouncing off the flagstones.

Not allowing him time to recover, Anna grasped his left hand, twisting it away from his body, locking both his wrist and elbow. Bringing one foot down on his neck and jaw, she stretched his arm out further.

"You will apologize, mongrel, or lose the use of these fingers," she snarled.

He struggled against her hold, but she had the lock cinched tight and his struggling only caused him additional pain.

"I willnae apologize to a wench who plays at being a man!" he ground out between clenched teeth.

"As you please," she answered. An audible snap sounded as Anna pulled his smallest finger out of socket at the second knuckle, causing it to protrude at an odd angle.

A loud yelp and an anatomically impossible curse flew from his mouth.

"Apologize!" she yelled at him.

"Nae, never!"

She responded by displacing his third finger, creating a louder snap. This time, his fellows groaned in sympathy with him, but none dared come to his aid.

Anna glanced at Duncan, who leaned against an empty table, arms folded across his chest, a smirk on his face. Only the taut muscles of his jaw belied his calm expression. He warned off the MacGregor men with a glance and slight hand gesture. Before she could demand another apology, Duncan spoke up. "What is yer name, Graham?"

The man on the floor continued to hurl curses, each more creative and colorful than the last, as he struggled uselessly against her hold.

"What is his name?" Duncan calmly asked the man seated nearest to him.

"Angus."

"Angus, I would like ye to meet Anna of clan MacGregor. She has been adopted by our laird, my father, as a daughter, and is my future wife if she will have me."

Anna shot Duncan a look of astonishment. The expression on his face showed no emotion except the silent fury he barely contained.

"I have seen her defeat six Highlanders in battle unassisted and another two warriors from my own clan. She saved yer commander's life this afternoon. Ye might want to reconsider yer position on that apology."

The men seated at the table stared at her with disbelief. Anna scowled. She was not letting this cur up without an apology. Otherwise, some other man from this clan would take issue with her appearance and try the same or worse. No, she would set an example here and now. Not caring to ask again, Anna jerked his second finger out of joint, the accompanying snap the loudest yet.

The doors to the inner hall slammed open and a large man, dressed in a laird's finery, barreled in.

"What the hell is going on?"

Chapter Sixteen

The man glanced from Anna to the man she had trapped.
"Angus, what trouble are ye causing my guests?" he demanded, his
face an indignant shade of red.

Angus's manner changed. "No trouble, m'laird. This lady offered
a lesson in weaponless combat." Glancing up at her he gritted his
teeth "I apologize for me earlier actions and doubts of yer ability."

Anna was not deceived by the apparent sincerity of his
apology. Releasing his neck, she used the wrist she held to haul him
to his feet.

"No offense taken, I am sure, Angus. Allow me to *assist* you with
your hand," she said with a smile and sarcasm sharp enough to cut.
Taking each finger individually, Anna repositioned them into place as
sweat ran from Angus' brow.

"Be sure and wrap those tightly. They should be fine within a
fortnight." She leaned in so only Angus could hear her. "If you ever
touch me again, I will gut you like the pig you are."

He flinched, eyes wide, as the point of her small dagger prodded
him below the belt. Turning toward her host, Anna hid the dagger and
bowed to the Graham laird.

The Graham responded with an assessing glance and wry smile.
"Come, the servants have prepared food and drink."

The laird led them into the inner hall, smaller but luxurious,
designed for entertaining important guests. Motioning for them to sit,

the laird directed two women to serve the group, and each MacGregor was quickly given a *quaich* of ale.

A twinkle in his eye, the Graham laird asked, "How is it one of my strongest men, though more than a wee bit daft, was bested by a woman?"

Anna glanced at Duncan, the gleam of anger in his eyes telling her he still seethed over the encounter. She chose a diplomatic answer. "It was an opportunity for a demonstration of unarmed tactics, is all, Laird," she answered, trying to keep her irritation with Duncan out of her voice. She could handle herself and did not need him running to her rescue at every turn.

Graham gave her an odd look and a smile, but left her explanation alone. He moved his attention to Duncan. "I heard about the accident in the market today—how yer group assisted my men, especially ye," he said as he spared a glance at Anna. "Ronald has been one of my most reliable men. I would be hard pressed without him. Neil believes yer timely efforts gave him a chance to survive. For that I thank ye, milady."

"Iain and I were close when it happened and glad to offer assistance. All involved are recovering. Your commander has not awakened. I know not if he will, but your healer watches over him."

The laird changed topics again as servants plied the tables with meats, vegetables and bread. "Though yer use of our language and plaide says ye are a MacGregor, yer accent, cuirass, and the way ye carry yerself tells me ye are English. There is a very entertaining story here. I wish to hear it."

Anna nodded to Duncan, prompting him to respond. "'Tis an interesting story. I will tell most of it. There are details we withhold to protect Anna."

Smiling, the laird motioned for him to continue. Leaving out the details of her family's name and fate, he told the same story they'd related to the MacGregor clan. The laird seemed satisfied with the telling, and their conversation drifted to clan politics, alliances, and common enemies, which of course included the English.

Anna took no offense, having seen the horrors the English were capable of firsthand. After living in the Highlands only a matter of a few months, she had no desire to return to England. She *was* Scots. Since her father and brother had followed her mother in death, she'd considered her English heritage at an end. Another revelation to ruminate over.

After the meal, they retired to chairs by the large stone hearth, where conversations continued. The laird made a point to ask Anna questions about the unsteady peace along the border. He asked what she thought about the likelihood of war and where it might start. Offering her insight about the most power-hungry English nobles in the area, he seemed pleased with the information and agreed with her assessments. She sensed he tested where her loyalties lay. They certainly did not lie with Edward Longshanks or his corrupt group of nobles.

As the evening grew late, a messenger entered and spoke quietly to the laird. He stood. "It seems my commander has regained consciousness. Lady Anna, would ye be willing to see to him before ye retire or wait until morn?"

"I would gladly check on him now."

At Duncan's nod, Iain rose to accompany her. Following the guard who escorted them, Iain leaned into Anna and whispered, "Though I have seen ye fight before, I am astonished by yer abilities and am proud ye joined our clan."

Self-conscious at his overt praise, she smiled at him. "Thank you, Iain."

"Ye should know every man in our group would lay down his life for ye."

Unsettled by the depth of his pledge, Anna made light of the moment. "So all I had to do is defeat the largest, most obnoxious man in the clan to earn your respect? Had I known, I would have called out Duff my first day at Ciardun." She gave him a sideways glance and he laughed loudly in reply.

When they arrived at their destination, the guard told Iain to wait outside the door. Iain bristled at the command, but Anna nodded her acceptance.

"Commander, the woman who tended ye is here."

He struggled to sit up in the bed. "Come in, milady, and let me thank ye." His voice, while strong, sounded immeasurably tired.

She stepped into the room and his eyes narrowed as he took in her appearance. "The men tell me I have ye to thank for my life."

Remembering Neil's claims, she merely nodded. "'Tis true I tended your wound, Commander. However, the men insisted your survival is due to the hardness of your head rather than my efforts." Anna gave him a grin, ignoring the surprised looks on the guards' faces at her words.

The commander's face broke into something likely intended to be a smile, though it arrived as a grimace. "Och, now I see ye and a wee bit of yer character, 'tis easier to believe ye able to best Angus. How I would have loved to have seen that great lug lowered a peg or two. I owe ye a debt of thanks for saving me life, and for humbling one of me more difficult men."

Anna offered a brief bow. "Glad to be of service, Commander. You no doubt have a concussion, and will need to stay away from your duties a sennight or more. Watch for blurred vision, nausea, light sensitivity and headaches. You should not go back to your post until these subside. Resuming duty too soon will make these effects linger longer than they should. Your healer can give you poppy tea if the pain becomes too severe, otherwise bark tea will ease the pain enough to be tolerable."

"Aye, I have seen my share of head injuries and understand. My thanks again for yer care."

Anna nodded. "Your men and laird speak highly of you. 'Tis my pleasure to serve clan Graham." She started to leave the room, then turned back with a smile. "I kept the stitches as fine as possible so your scar doesn't scare the lasses over-much."

The commander stifled a laugh, though the other two men in the room guffawed loudly.

"Duncan has told some of us about yer sparring together," Iain said as they walked back to the hall. "I hope ye consider joining the rest of us in the future. Though some would refuse to train with a woman, many of us would welcome the opportunity to test our skill against ye. Mayhap learn a wee bit as well. I have never seen anyone do to a man what ye did to the Graham today, and he twice your size."

"I would be happy to demonstrate, Iain, as I get bored besting Duncan all the time."

Iain shook his head and chuckled. Anna grinned.

"Mayhap when we stop to camp tomorrow night we can work a bit. As far as training with the rest of the men, that is the laird's decision. I would welcome it but do not want to create more conflict with my presence than I already have. If I cannot train with the main group, perhaps the laird will permit a smaller group. I will ask Duncan."

They reported to the laird his commander's condition, then were shown guest chambers for the night. Anna's room had a fire already lit, and a maid escorted her to the bathing chamber near the kitchen. Having slept on the ground the past two nights, a bath and bed sounded welcoming.

After her bath, Anna dressed and returned to her room. She spotted Duncan leaning against the wall outside her door. She gave him a quizzing glance, trying to gauge his mood.

"May I speak with ye?" he asked.

"Of course. I would ask you in, but 'twould not be proper."

He nodded, motioning to the stairs. They headed through the hall and outside. She wondered what he had in mind. The thought of kissing him rose to the surface as it always did of late, and her body tingled with anticipation. Stopping beside the well in the center of the bailey, he turned to face her. From his stern look, kisses were not what he had in mind. Anna assumed a defensive posture, waiting for the scold she knew to be forthcoming.

"Anna, I would speak with ye about this afternoon."

She raised her eyebrows and leaned her head slightly toward him in invitation.

"Ye took on a man twice yer size, surrounded by his lads." Frustration crept into his voice.

"And what would you have me do, Duncan? Take his abuse and insults?" She crossed both arms over her chest.

Duncan scrubbed his face twice before answering. "Nae, ye should have let me handle him. Ye are adopted by our clan. We are courting. Both those things mean ye are under my protection."

Anna narrowed her gaze. "You watched closely today. You saw I did not require assistance. A man like Angus needed a lesson on how to treat women. Which do you think would present the more effective lesson, *my lord*, a thrashing from you, or one from the very woman he offended?" Anger surged through her. *He* was telling *her* not to defend herself?

"Arrrghh!" Duncan pushed away from the well. His body tensed, his hands opening and closing tightly. He scrubbed his face again and took a deep breath before facing her. "Aye, the more effective lesson was for him to be humbled by the verra lass he handled roughly. Dinnae expect me to like it."

At his confession, Anna immediately softened. Anger bled away and she walked straight into his chest and placed her arms around him. He returned her embrace fiercely. Leaning her head back, she peered at his face. Seeing his scowl still present, she kissed him on the chin. She looked up again, but his remained expression unchanged. She pressed light kisses on his cheeks, his nose, his neck, until he relaxed. Sensing his acceptance, she pulled back slightly to gaze into his eyes.

"It is hard for you to accept I am not a weak woman always in need of your protection, even though we train together daily and you know what I am capable of," she whispered.

"Aye," he grumbled.

"You were there to protect me if I did not succeed in the lesson." She punctuated her statement with a kiss on his cheek. "You were there to protect me if any of the others joined the fray." Another kiss touched his jaw. "You did protect me. But like you, I do not back down from a challenge. I would not ask you to do so, and would guard your life as if it were my own. I only ask the same."

He shook his head. "What am I to do with ye, Anna Braxton?" A corner of his lips quirked upward in question.

Her eyes sparkled with invitation. "Kiss me, I hope, sir knight."

The next morning, Anna rose and descended the stairs to the hall to eat, meeting Liam, Donnan, and Rory along the way. The rest of their group followed shortly after. Bowls of oat porridge with fresh fruit, cream, and honey awaited. She saved a bit of cream for Trean, who bedded down in the stall with Orion.

"The laird wishes to see us off this morn," Duncan announced.

They lingered in the hall while the wagons were readied. Duncan caught Anna's hand, leaning into her so no one else could hear.

"Da wanted me to wait and assess the Graham laird's reaction to ye before proceeding. He has written a missive to yer grandda, briefly explaining where ye are."

All the air left Anna's body, and her stomach clenched as though she'd been punched. Fear clouded the edges of her vision as she gave Duncan an apprehensive look.

"He left it in my hands, but said not to carry on without yer consent. The message is coded so if read by anyone else, they willnae understand it. We think yer family should know ye are alive and well. Do ye agree?"

She couldn't find her voice so she nodded, her eyes wide. Putting his arm around her comfortingly, he gave her a tender smile.

"It seems everywhere ye go, ye inspire strong feelings. The Grahams are amused by the way ye handled Angus. The laird feels a debt to ye for yer care of his commander and people. I have nae doubt we can trust him to deliver our message with the strictest confidence as thanks for yer services."

Anna fought to push back her distress, moisture welling in her eyes. "I—I trust your judgment, Duncan. I would like nothing more than to allay the sorrows of my remaining family."

Placing a kiss on her forehead, he gave her shoulders another squeeze.

The Graham appeared with a dark-haired young man at his side. He introduced him as his son Blaine, of one-and-twenty years. His merry eyes matched the color of his short, dark brown hair, his smile quick and infectious. The laird turned the discussion to a possible marriage between his son and Nessa. Her sense of protectiveness instantly aroused, Anna assessed the young man. He seemed bright and respectful to both Duncan and his father. His eyes met hers more than once, no doubt having heard the news of her encounter with Angus. He smiled when their eyes met, though she merely nodded in acknowledgement. Anna knew Nessa would pester her with questions, so she wanted to see the things Duncan would not think to notice.

Nessa, he is broad of shoulder, has a strong jaw, and stands as tall as Duncan. He is a youth, but moves with confidence and strength. I see kindness in his eyes, and when he speaks, he is thoughtful and gives sound answers. He looks to be a good man. Mayhap good enough for you.

Blaine pulled her into the conversation. "Ye must be the lass I have heard so much of since last night." He bowed politely.

Duncan nodded. "Aye. This is Anna of clan MacGregor, my sister's *Curaidh*, her champion."

Blaine's eyebrows rose at the title, his smile growing wider. Duncan quickly explained her relationship with the clan and with Nessa.

To his credit, Blaine responded, "I look forward to the opportunity to earn yer respect in the future, milady."

She smiled, hearing both the sincerity and playfulness in his tone. "As do I, Sir Blaine."

Blaine took his leave, clasping Duncan's arm and bowing to her with a smile. Duncan took the opportunity to pull the laird aside and ask about a rider for the missive. As he explained the details, the laird's face grew hard, then softened into understanding. The laird motioned for Anna to come closer.

"The least I can offer is to see this important message delivered. I am honored to have the opportunity to repay some of what ye have done for us. Whether ye wear the MacGregor plaide or nae, ye will always be welcomed here."

She bowed her head. "Thank you for your generosity, Laird." She moved to where Iain and Malcolm waited, a gamboling Trean waiting impatiently for her in the wagon. Iain quietly slipped her *sgian dubh* into place on her belt. She quirked a brow in question. He gave a brief nod.

After a few more minutes of conversation, they bid the Grahams farewell. Anna endured the wolf pup's enthusiastic greeting with a grin, scarcely able to keep his round body from spilling from her arms as he licked her face. She tucked him in front of her in the saddle and he settled in to his accustomed spot, watching the surrounding scenery go by.

They left the village in silence, Liam's soft singing to the horses the only sound. Anna broached the subject most on her mind. "Is Blaine to be wed to Nessa?"

"What did ye think of him?" Duncan countered.

She gave him her opinion based on her slight observation.

"Aye, 'tis how I see it also. 'Tis something Da considers. Strengthen existing alliances or form a new one. There are strategic benefits. Ye saw the size of their clan. There are mutual benefits regular trade would provide. They have a large number of warriors and would be a powerful ally. If the laird were to ask for yer counsel, what would ye advise?"

"I would not offer advice beyond getting to know Blaine and his clan better. Perhaps an invitation to host him a month or more would be in order. I would need firm evidence Nessa would be happy and well cared for before I agreed to any marriage for her."

"Exactly what I would have expected from Nessa's *Curaidh*," Duncan replied. Several of the men nodded agreement.

She smiled at the title. "Among other things, Duncan MacGregor, I am most assuredly that. Any man who would not treat her in the manner she deserves would welcome death before I finished with him." Anna surprised herself with the passion of her words.

"I pity the man who would invite such," Iain added with a grin stretching across his face.

The men laughed at Iain's declaration, and a peaceful camaraderie settled over the group. Anna glanced at Trean's small, furry form tucked before her. She hadn't spent much time with him the past two days, though Liam assured her the stable boys had taken turns feeding and playing with the young wolf, winning his affection. The pup seemed happy to be back with her, continually nuzzling and licking her hands.

Anna sighed, watching the others as they exchanged stories and laughter, their moods light as they anticipated their arrival home. She canted an eye toward the clear sky. Was it too much to ask for an uneventful trip home?

Chapter Seventeen

*T*oward the end of the day, the MacGregor party stopped to camp by a stream. Anna and Duncan made a fish trap out of tree limbs with Donnan's assistance, and caught enough trout for supper. While supper was readied, Anna demonstrated a few joint locks and throws to the men, explaining each. Every time she executed a throw or dropped them to their knees with a joint lock, the men's eyes rounded with disbelief.

Knowing they would be sore the next day, Anna called a halt in time to eat. She shot Duncan a smiling glance, noticing his brooding scowl had returned. Scrunching her brow in confusion, she let it pass. Like the night before, he would tell her what was on his mind if he wished.

As they all tucked into their meal, Malcolm spoke up. "Forgive me, Anna, if I am ill-mannered, but my curiosity has gotten the best of me. Where did ye get yer fighting knowledge? Ye have a collection of skills none of us 'ave seen before."

Anna glanced at Duncan sitting next to her, mild surprise on his face. She knew he had the same questions, as did every MacGregor who'd ever witnessed her fight, though he'd not pressed for information. Considering how to answer, she glanced around the fire at the faces, all anticipating her response.

Taking a deep breath, she explained about Master Zhang and how he came to be in her father's service. She described his teachings in great detail, from the healing arts to the armed and unarmed combat. She described the weapons and the games of strategy he'd taught, including chess and Yi. There had been long discussions of historical battles on this land and his own, analyzing the wisdom and folly of each using maps and drawings to explain the details, showing how each decision affected the outcomes.

Anna spoke of the continual questions designed to make her consider all angles of any situation, without emotion, seeing past ruses, seeking possibilities and solutions where none seemed apparent. She recounted the mental disciplines, through meditation, difficult physical conditioning and imprisonment, elaborating on the benefits of these disciplines with a zeal that would have made Zhang proud.

She compressed almost two decades of experiences and training, ceasing when her mouth finally became dry and she reached for a wineskin. A long silence stretched before anyone spoke.

"Yer father allowed his only daughter to be imprisoned for days at a time?" Malcolm asked in disbelief.

"Yes, and it served me well when I first came here." She motioned for Duncan to respond. He hesitantly told the men of her behavior during the five days of captivity with them. To a man, they were all shocked to hear of her treatment. They all knew she was held, but were unaware of the conditions. Iain rose with a jerk and strode away from the fire. The grimace on Duncan's face told her he still held strong feelings about her imprisonment. Upon reflection, the anger she'd harbored had faded into a distant memory.

Anna thought about her responsibility to pass on the knowledge she had been entrusted with. Master Zhang always spoke of himself as merely another link in a long chain spanning the centuries. He said one day it would be her turn to be such a link. Before her lay the opportunity to both pass on these skills and protect her new clan.

She resolved to ask the laird's permission to train whomever would be willing. She would contribute to the strength of clan MacGregor as best she could. Perhaps she could even convince him to allow her to teach Nessa a few skills. Just knowing she could handle a dagger would ease some of Anna's worry once Nessa married and moved to her new home.

Wanting to change the subject and lighten the mood, Anna rose. She took a dagger and carved a rough circle at head height on a large nearby tree, with a smaller circle in the center. Uncoiling the rope dart around her waist, she began a demonstration. Anna explained its use, repeatedly hitting the target. She then put it away and showed them the throwing knife she kept hidden in her bracers, along with the steel throwing spikes.

When Duncan saw the spikes, he smiled and shook his head. Anna knew he recognized yet another weapon she'd held in her possession while captive. She quickly launched them into the target on the tree. "How about a friendly bout of knife throwing? The winner gets their pick of the watch." Anna turned to Duncan for his permission. His smile-dimpled cheeks said yes.

The men greeted the challenge with enthusiasm. Each lined up for a turn, placing bets on the outcome. Having not seen a knife like hers before, each wanted a chance to use it.

Duncan slipped behind her and whispered in her ear. "These spikes, ye used them to open the lock on yer cell?"

She kissed him on the cheek. "You catch on quickly, sir."

He chuckled. "What other weapons were hidden on ye?"

Anna gave him a sly grin. "I shall never tell—in case you get the foolish notion to imprison me again."

His smile faded. "'Twas never my idea to imprison ye in the first place."

She had always wondered about this, but knew not what to say, so she turned back to the contest.

Liam was declared the winner. Darkness had fallen, and watches were assigned. Iain approached Duncan and Anna, a pained expression on his face, and motioned for them to follow him outside earshot of the others.

"I wish to apologize to both ye and Anna for my disrespect earlier."

Duncan offered his hand and Iain hesitantly took it. "Fear not, my friend." Duncan said. "My reaction was much like yer own. I argued off and on for days with the laird, trying to understand his wisdom. Though I did not agree with him at the time, I have come to realize I would have done something similar, though with better accommodations." Duncan glanced at Anna for her response.

"'Tis in the past, Iain, and it does not serve to dwell on it. Things have changed considerably. Whilst I thank you for your concern, let us not reflect on it further." Anna patted his arm and offered a smile.

Mollified, Iain took the first watch.

Anna faced Duncan. "You argued with your father for *days* about how he treated me?"

He gazed at her intently. "Aye, though *argued* might be too polite a word. I have never been so angry at my da in all my life. I railed at him. Looking back, I am surprised he dinnae do me harm."

She was taken aback by the emotion in his voice. "Why would you, for a stranger?"

He grabbed her with such force the surprise of it stole her breath.

Whispering near her ear, he said, "I have loved ye from the moment I saw ye, though I dinna know it at the time. I suspect the only reason Da gave me leeway was because he recognized how I felt about ye long before I did. Anna, I love ye and cannae imagine going a single day without ye with me. I want ye to be my wife, and the mother of my bairns. I have withheld the strength of my feelings, hoping to earn yer trust and heart. I am prepared to give ye as much time as ye need, but know I am willing to do anything to have ye belong to me."

The power of his declaration stunned her. Anna had sensed he felt strongly, but did not understand the depth of his feeling, nor when it had begun. She recalled his words to the barbarian, Angus, about her being his future wife if she would have him.

His words flowed over her like the warmth of the sun as they melted away her lingering doubts. As the words *wife and mother* settled, she discovered they did not conjure fear and loathing as before. Coming from this man, they inspired a sense of peace and rightness. As she reveled in his love, his hold loosened and she realized the time for her to respond had passed.

Gripping him around the waist, Anna pulled him back into her with as much force as she could muster.

"Do not pull away from me, Duncan MacGregor—ever. I have never looked at another man as I do you." Taking a breath, she continued. "You know this is all new to me. I know not my own heart well, but do know I love you with a fierceness that frightens me."

Duncan's eyes glittered. Anna eased her grip.

"The thought of marrying and having children was always the worst future I could imagine, because I knew it would be to a man I would not want, one who would not truly want me. I do wish to be your wife, and mother to our children. Howbeit, you need to understand what you ask, because I am not like your mother or sister. I am a warrior, and will continue to be after I become your wife and bear our children."

He shuddered at her words, and she wondered why.

Duncan thought he'd pushed too hard, scaring her into retreat. He inwardly cursed his stupidity. He needed to move away, give her space, but she surprised him by grabbing and drawing him roughly to her. Her threat to him about not pulling away ever, brought a smile to his face he was certain would never leave. Then he heard the sweetest words to ever reach his ears. She loved him so much it frightened her. Her confession put him in such a state of elation he shook.

But her next words doused his joy like tossing it into a loch in the dead of winter. *I will always be a warrior.* Duncan immediately heard his da's words echo in his head. *I think there is not much the lass cannae do. She could very well be yer greatest joy, and yer greatest frustration. She willnae submit to any man easily. Ye might have an easier time fighting dragons.*

The calm part of him reminded him this was still a hunt. Though much was accomplished between them tonight, there was plenty yet to fathom, to untangle. Wisdom advised him to savor her love, to continue to nurture the trust they had developed and save future battles for the days ahead. Let the fact she reflected the same love and passion be enough—for now.

"Ye cannae possibly know how happy yer words make me, my love."

Anna drew back. "All of them?" The familiar rumbling in his chest returned, as he laughed at her question, lighting the flame within.

"We dinnae have to decide our entire future tonight. I am more than content to know ye love me as I love ye, and recognize we belong together. The rest we will negotiate as we go, aye?"

She smiled, spotting the evasive tactic as he spoke it. He was right, there would be plenty of time to work out their relationship. He now knew she would not become a submissive lady of the keep if they wed. A sudden thought leapt to her mind. She needed to make sure there were no misunderstandings.

"Duncan, I was brought up in the church. I am aware of the differences between Scottish and English traditions. I will not agree to merely a handfast. If we join, 'twill be a permanent marriage, agreed?"

The warmth of his smile allayed her fears. "'Twould be an insult to offer such to ye, my heart. When we marry, 'twill be in the kirk, in front of God and our clan for life. I will be faithful and committed to only ye. Ye have my word. Besides, I have no intention of giving ye an opportunity to leave me."

Anna grabbed his shirt and smiled. "I match your pledge of fidelity with my own. You should know I would maim any woman who tried to come between us." She rose on her toes to kiss him. "I am not a biddable woman, Duncan MacGregor."

"'Tis one of the reasons I love ye."

This kiss started like others they shared, but quickly became more. It was as if he had earlier held back both his words and expressions of love. His kiss claimed, possessed and branded her as his. Anna backed him away from the camp, out of sight of the men. Her hands found their way under his leine and struggled to take it off. She assailed his mouth with hers, taking what she wanted, what she needed. He gripped her wrists and broke off their kiss.

"We cannae. If we continue, I willnae be able to stop. I wish to protect yer virtue until our wedding night." His voice darkened.

"I did not mean—I am sorry," Anna murmured, shocked at her wanton behavior.

"Dinnae apologize. One of the greatest gifts a woman can give her man is to match him passion for passion. 'Tis too soon to release it, but I dinnae want ye to have the misunderstanding I wish anything less than the fire ye demonstrate when we are alone."

Once again, his words soothed her fears, helping her regain her confidence. "You know not what you ask for. After we are wed, I fully intend to burn you night after night with the very fire you speak of."

He spun her about, embracing her from behind.

"Do I have permission to announce our betrothal?" he breathed into her ear.

She leaned into him, feeling his arousal prodding her bottom.

"If you do, Duncan MacGregor, there is no turning back."

"Ye have no idea how I have longed to hear ye say those words." He kissed her on the cheek and led her back to camp. "I must warn ye, the men will refer to ye as 'Lady' again, now we are to be wed."

Her head giddily in the clouds, she chose to ignore this information. As they approached the camp, the men glanced their way, trying not to stare. Duncan squeezed her hand, and a thrill skittered up her arm, across her chest and into her heart. He waited. One by one, he captured the gaze of each man. When he had their full attention, he stepped forward.

"I declare my betrothal to Anna of the clans Elliot and MacGregor."

The men surged around them, slapping Duncan on the back and voicing their congratulations. After a round of teasing for Duncan and well-wishes for Anna, the men faded away to their posts.

Setting their pallets next to each other, Anna lay in Duncan's arms and tried to rest. Too excited to sleep, she played with Trean until he tired and curled against her. She lay quietly, listening to Duncan's even breathing. At last she dozed, but woke when he rose for his turn at watch. When she followed him, he tried to convince her to stay, but she would not be dissuaded.

He sat on the ground against a tree, her back against his chest, his hands caressing her scalp, neck and shoulders. They listened to the sounds of early morning in the forest. Though they spoke no words, something mystical passed between them in the quiet.

Time flew by, and as they made their way back to camp, she

could not resist the urge to tease. "If you were pledged to a gentle woman, you would not have her company during your watch, nor would you have a second pair of trained ears and eyes to rely on."

He captured her around her waist, dragging her back to him. "Och, nor would I be fighting my body to behave when I should be watching and listening."

"Oh yes you would, though instead of having me near, your thoughts would be of me in our bed."

She earned a chuckle and a squeeze before he released her. Fingers entwined, they entered camp where Iain prodded the cook fire.

Using pears purchased at the Graham village and honey from their own supplies, Anna made a batch of oatcakes for breakfast. The men quickly dispatched them, and at dawn they were on their way. Trean was still sleepy, so she put him in the wagon.

Clouds threatened rain, and a chill hung in the air. Anna shivered, thankful for the wool they'd purchased. She looked forward to seeing the whole of their inventory once they arrived back home. Home. They were almost home.

Chapter Eighteen

By midmorning, a light rain fell on the MacGregor party, the sky the dull gray of tarnished metal. The men seemed oblivious to the damp inconvenience, but Anna was glad for Trean's small, warm form tucked against her once again beneath her plaide. She draped her oiled cloth over them and found some relief from the rain as they wound along the edge of the forest. Their track followed close to the river, the trees thick on one side, the river on the other.

A prickling sensation darted up the back of Anna's neck, alerting her to the presence of others. Noticing the tense line of Duncan's body, she knew he sensed the same. Pushing Trean into a saddlebag, Anna loosened the ties on her bow strapped to Orion's saddle.

A crossbow bolt struck Duncan in the thigh. He grunted and stared blankly at the feathered shaft.

"In the trees to the northwest!" Anna cried. Quickly drawing her bow, she struck the first man she spotted.

A second bolt struck Duncan, this time in the shoulder, spinning him in the saddle from the force. Kneeing Orion between Duncan and the attackers, Anna sent another arrow into an enemy.

With a shout, Liam and Ross stopped the carts. Donnan and Rory fired their crossbows, hitting another of their unknown foes. The man pitched from a tree to the ground, writhing in pain. Iain and Malcolm lowered Duncan from his horse and set him on his feet beside the cart. Steel scraped against leather as they drew swords to protect their captain.

Turning Orion to make another pass at the concealed men, Anna found another target, and he, too, fell under her bow.

A shout sounded from the trees. "Dinnae attack the woman, she is worth double unharmed."

Shock nearly doubled her as she realized she was the reason for the attack, the reason Duncan fell injured. She rode between the wagons and their attackers, scanning for a target. More than a dozen men broke from cover. They ran toward the wagons, swords and axes drawn. She felled the first one with an arrow. Rory and Donnan fired another volley from their crossbows, killing two more.

Re-slinging her bow, Anna stripped the saddlebags from Orion's rump and slid them beneath the nearest wagon seat. She quickly drew her swords and kneed her horse forward, charging the oncoming attackers. Two more men met their death as she struck them down with a slash of her blades.

"Bluidy hell, woman, get back here!" Duncan bellowed from across the field.

Ignoring his command, Anna scanned the area for bowmen. Finding none, she wheeled Orion around and raced to the group now attacking the wagons. With a start, she recognized Alain leading the charge. It was *his* voice shouting orders! Though the attackers' numbers were reduced, ten to their eight, Duncan was in no condition to fight. He barely remained upright, sword in hand as he fended off an attacker.

Dropping from Orion's back, Anna flanked the enemy. She evened the odds by cutting down one of the two men engaging Liam. The bulk of the group crowded Iain and Malcolm, who still protected Duncan.

Sheathing a sword, she threw her knife, piercing the back of the man closest to Iain, leaving him two to deal with. She then cast her steel spikes into the next two men, wounding them, which allowed Ross the opportunity to finish one, Malcolm the other. Iain slew another. Anna redrew her sword and took her place at Duncan's side.

"Alain!" Anna yelled.

He faced her. She'd forgotten how large he was, but things had changed. No longer an unarmed prisoner under his watch, she stood ready for the confrontation. Behind her, a high-pitched growl and yip told her Trean had slipped from his bag. She put him from her mind and considered the man before her.

He wielded a lochaber axe, the hook winking evilly at her from the end of the heavy blade. She sheathed her swords and swiftly uncoiled her rope dart. With his longer weapon, she could not let him get too close. As she began her dance, Alain's sneering contempt changed to confusion. He made ready to charge, but stuttered, hesitating at the distracting buzz of the red cloth cutting through the air as she brought the swinging blade close to him.

She wrapped the line around her shoulders and arms, shortening its reach, and he restarted his charge. With a sharp jerk, she propelled the dart forward, embedding it deep in his thigh. Yanking hard on the rope, she dislodged the blade, sending him staggering. She swung the dart around, back and forth. The last two surviving men in his company fled, leaving him behind. Alain growled.

"Why, Alain? Why have you attacked?" she demanded.

He spat on the ground. "Because MacGregor chose an English bitch over the loyalty of a clansman!"

"Ye great fool, she was a guest at our table, under my father's protection!" Duncan snarled. Iain and Malcolm advanced. A volley of yips burst through the tableau.

"No! He is mine!" Anna shouted. The men halted, hands flexing on their weapons. She gave her attention to the oaf before her. "That does not explain it all, Alain. You had a score of men with you. This is larger than your petty vengeance against MacGregor. I heard you cry out I am worth more alive than dead. To whom?"

He limped toward her, blood flowing freely from the wound in his leg. He tracked the red flag as it hummed its unceasing path through the air. "Ye will find out soon enough. Though I may not live to see ye to yer new home and husband, I have nae doubt others will be sent to finish the task."

Anna kicked the blade toward his heart, a killing blow. Not quick enough to deflect it with his heavy axe, Alain moved to avoid her weapon. Her blade missed its mark, opening a gash on his upper arm. Twirling and wrapping the rope around her, she kept him at bay, shooting the blade out unpredictably. Within a few moments, he stopped advancing. Bleeding from a multitude of wounds, he seemed to no longer possess the strength to charge. Holding his axe in front of him with both hands, Alain struggled to evade her weapon.

She launched her dart toward him, centerline. As expected, he deflected it with the handle of his axe. Quickly spinning the handle, he trapped her rope between his long axe head and handle. Another two turns secured her weapon to his axe. Anna allowed herself to be pulled toward him.

Using the momentum he provided, she spun around and drew her swords. He dropped his now-tangled axe, drawing a long bladed dirk. Before he could reach her, she completed her spin and drove both swords into his chest.

Anna lingered only a moment before racing to Duncan's side. Though still conscious, he had lost a lot of blood—*too much*. Quickly assessing the others, she discovered Liam had a deep gash on his thigh, and Rory a gash across his chest. Ross bled from a number of small head and leg wounds. Iain and Malcolm, though nicked up, remained mostly uninjured.

Then she saw Donnan, a bolt protruding from his chest, his eyes unseeing. She closed her eyes briefly then turned back to Duncan.

The bolt in his leg did not go all the way through, but the one in his shoulder did. She snapped off the tip and pushed it through as Malcolm put pressure on the front and back of his shoulder with bandages retrieved from the wagon. With Iain holding Duncan's leg firmly, Malcolm removed the bolt. Anna pressed the wound to staunch the bleeding, earning a growl of pain from Duncan. A warm, furry body pressed against her and Anna glanced up in surprise. Trean flattened himself on the ground at her side, muzzle on his paws, eyes intent.

"Keep out of the way, Trean," she warned. Seeming to understand her, he wiggled his body once, then was still, though his eyes followed her every move.

Hands shaking, Anna made a poultice of yarrow and rose bark to stop the bleeding, mixing in clove and plantain to ward off infection. She allowed her healing skills to take over, pushing her emotions away. She told herself she treated a fallen warrior, not her future husband. Cleaning both wounds with the whisky Iain produced, she then applied the compound to the wounds, binding them tightly.

Moving to Liam and Rory, she stitched them both. Liam flinched each time her rounded needle darted in and out of his torn flesh, and he pulled hard on the flask of whisky. Rory lay unconscious, a blessing, as his chest wound went to the bone. Ross's wounds proved shallow and easiest to treat.

Iain, Malcolm and Anna discussed their options. They agreed the men should not be moved for at least a day. They dared not risk further reducing their numbers by sending someone for help. Home remained roughly a day's ride away.

Iain and Malcolm allowed Anna to treat a couple of smaller wounds she did not initially detect, needing only a few stitches between them. The fact she bore no wound only infuriated her further, creating a deeper sense of guilt. She started a cook fire while Iain and Malcolm searched the fallen. They collected what could be of use, then piled the bodies a furlong away downwind to burn.

A heap of retrieved weapons lay stacked in the wagon when they finished. Included in the haul were eighteen saddled horses picketed a few yards from the ambush site.

Iain approached. "I found these on Alain. Thought ye might know where they came from."

He dropped a bag of silver coins, along with a note allowing safe passage for the bearer, in her lap. The seal on the note was unmistakable. *The Earl of Northumberland.* Her gut clenched to have her suspicions confirmed. The man had made several attempts in the past on behalf of his son for her hand. Now he offered payment for her capture. With this information, Anna knew in her bones he was the one who ordered the attack on her home, the one who had ordered her family killed. She stowed the items away for further consideration, pushing her thoughts only to the health of Duncan and his men.

Duncan was in obvious pain. Trean had moved his allegiance to Duncan, his small body tucked tight against the man's side, Duncan's hand fisted in the plush coat. Anna checked the dressings. The bleeding had halted in both wounds, though she knew movement could tear them open again. The real threat would be infection and fever. The men needed time to heal, but sitting here left them exposed.

As the men completed their chores, Iain stood by Anna's side while she stirred a pot of stew and brewed a large batch of medicated tea for the wounded.

No tea could ease her pain. Restless, she checked on Rory, still lying unconscious on the back of the wagon, and made Duncan as comfortable as possible. Malcolm took the first watch while Anna stayed by Duncan's side, absently stroking Trean's soft fur. She placed her swords on the ground within easy reach, in case of another attack. Staring at the glow of the fire on the hillside where their enemies burned, her thoughts turned several days south.

"Who was it, Anna?"

She inhaled a deep breath, drawing strength from the love and concern she heard in Duncan's voice. "The Earl of Northumberland," she replied. "His son chased me for years. He pursued me to the point where his father offered to buy me, as if I was so much livestock at market." With an involuntary shudder, she handed Duncan the bag of coins and the letter of safe passage. "I heard Alain yell I was worth double unharmed. This man is reaching across Scotland for me, hurting people I care about. What am I to do?" Despair choked her voice.

Duncan took a shallow breath. "I have known Alain all my life. He was overly prideful and misguided, but he wasnae stupid. He wouldnae have told the earl where ye are. If he did, the earl would have sent agents of his own to do the job. Then Alain would be out a purse, and possibly his life. The earl now knows ye live in Scotland, but not with yer grandda's people. Any man this determined would have made sure of that by now."

Anna mulled over his logic, her fingers stroking Trean's tummy as he slept, paws in the air. She smiled to see the pup so relaxed.

Duncan touched her hand. "The question I need answered is, will he still pursue ye if he knows ye are wed?"

The thought shook her. Would he? She truly did not know.

"Men like the earl take what they want, regardless of the law. I would no longer have my virtue, but if his son still desired me, I doubt it would matter. Who could stand up to him if he did? He rules the northern part of England for the crown. It is not beyond him to seek an annulment from the Church on my behalf."

Duncan frowned. "Who is this son of his who would take another man's wife as his own?"

Anna's lip curled at the thought of him. "Henry is a slimy, despicable man whom I could easily defeat in a fair fight. He has been taught to take what he wants regardless of the consequences. Though he lacks his father's cunning, he is a vile creature. He is one of the reasons I avoided any interest from men. I would fight to the death rather than submit to him."

Hauling himself jerkily to one elbow, Duncan stared at her. "Anna ye *will* be my wife, and I *will* keep ye safe. I cannae lose ye, too."

Blinking against tears, she nodded in agreement, though somewhat confused by his words. *Lose me, too?*

Duncan shook his head, forestalling her question. "Please promise me ye willnae do something so foolish again. Ye charged the cursed lot of them on yer own."

Anna heard the pleading in his voice, and she couldn't be angry with him for questioning her abilities. "I only charged when I heard Alain shout I was not to be harmed. I would not have done so otherwise."

Judging from the scowl on his face, her words didn't have the placating effect she hoped for, but he did not press further.

She curled next to him, one arm around his good shoulder as she sifted her fingers through his hair. He calmed, settling under her touch, until he slipped into a troubled sleep. She continued to stroke him, watching as he slept, until Malcolm tapped her shoulder, letting her know of her guard shift. Guilt and fear for Duncan filled her as she listened for signs of another attack. Like him, she could not bear the thought of losing him, too.

What if the earl had sent men to follow Alain?

Chapter Nineteen

*A*fter waking Iain for his watch, Anna returned to her bedroll. Before she knew it, light broke over the horizon, signaling a new day. Groggy, she rose to check on the wounded. Only Liam was awake, looking much improved. Color returned to his cheeks, and his wound appeared healthy.

"We would 'ave been done without ye, lass. Ye killed more than your share o' those men yesterday, then patched us all up."

She shook her head. "Liam, you do not understand. If it was not for me, you would be home this day. Those men were sent to capture me. 'Tis my fault we were attacked, that you are all injured and Donnan lies dead."

"Wheesht now, lass. Alain was daft. He would be seekin' his revenge one way or the other. We all saw what ye done. Ye are part of us now. Anyone who attacks one MacGregor attacks us all. Because of yer skill with a bow and sword, we live. Because of yer hand with a needle and thread, I will soon be dancin' again. And because of yer bravery and generous heart, Duncan will 'ave himself a bonny bride who will be one of the clan's best defenders. Donnan's blood is on Alain's head, not yorn."

"Thank you, Liam." Overwhelmed by his declaration, Anna kissed his cheek.

He winked and hobbled over to check on Rory, who'd still not regained consciousness. Scooting gingerly onto the back of the wagon next to Rory, Liam quietly talked to him, though none knew if the man heard or not. Unwilling to interrupt an intimate moment between brothers, Anna busied herself preparing breakfast.

She tossed out the remnants of last night's kettle, then brewed more tea while oatcakes cooked. Motioning to Iain, she walked to the front of the wagon where they would not be overheard.

"I worry we are too exposed here. Two of Alain's men escaped. I cannot help but feel vulnerable here with the forest to hide them, and the river at our back."

Iain's easy smile turned grim. "Aye, Malcolm and I believe the same. We thought one of us should ride ahead to find a more secluded spot to camp." He jerked his head toward the injured men. "How far do ye think they can travel without risking further harm?"

"If they lie down in the wagons, I do not think an hour of slow travel would bring them harm."

Iain nodded and turned to go. Remembering a question she had forgotten to ask yesterday, Anna grabbed his arm. "Did you recognize the men with Alain?"

Iain shook his head. "Nae, none of us did, but Alain's mother was a Hamilton, a clan south of Edinburgh. We suspect 'tis them. We put a dirk with a clan badge in the cart to ask when we return home."

Anna stared into the distance as she considered his words. Iain saddled one of the horses and galloped down the trail.

An hour later, Iain returned, having found a better place to camp three furlongs away. He'd scouted the area thoroughly and reported no sign of activity. Anna allowed herself a sigh of relief.

By this time, Rory had regained consciousness. Still shaky, he painfully sat and ate the last of the oatcakes, letting Trean lick the crumbs from his fingers.

Iain and Malcolm rearranged the carts, transferring some of the lighter bundles to the captured horses, creating enough room for Rory and Duncan to lay in the wagon, a pile of hay between them for Trean. They wrapped Donnan's body in his plaide and draped him over one of the horses, tying him securely.

At the new campsite, Anna inspected the wounded and added fresh dressings, thankful the ride did not start any new bleeding. They settled in for the day, restless and alert.

Later in the afternoon, four riders approached. Iain, Malcolm and Anna greeted them cautiously at the perimeter of their site.

"We saw the smoke last night, and our laird sent us to investigate." Their leader identified himself as Dougal MacFarlane.

Iain described the events of the previous day. An angry murmur rose among the MacFarlanes to hear a group of allies were attacked on their lands. They'd not run across any sign of those who escaped and did not recognize the clan crest when Iain showed it to them. Anna suspected the men had returned to the Lowlands. If they were Hamiltons, where else would they go?

Dougal walked to where Duncan lay in the cart and greeted him as an old friend. Trean's youthful growl brought a smile to his face. "I see ye have a wee guardian." Keeping his fingers well away from the sharp baby teeth, he halted a pace from the wagon. "I will send a man to report the situation to our laird. When ready, we will escort ye home."

They agreed to resume their journey at first light. Anna stayed with Duncan through the night while the others shared the watch. At daybreak, they loaded the wounded onto the wagons, tethered the captured horses, and continued their trek. Whether because of their new escort, or lack of enemies, the trip proved uneventful. By evening, they arrived at Ciardun.

They were greeted by the guards at the gate, and word spread quickly of their arrival. The laird accompanied Duncan's litter inside, Mairi and Nessa following worriedly behind. Rory was placed in the small room Anna used for healing. A small wooden box was placed in Nessa's room for Trean. After seeing to his comfort, Anna left the drowsy pup in his new bed and dashed to Duncan's room on the third level of the north tower, where she found the laird speaking with his son in private.

Waiting impatiently, Anna briefly related the story of the trip to the women, leaving out many details for Nessa's benefit. Eyes wide, Lady MacGregor put her servants into motion as she hurried to her son's side.

Pulling two chairs next to Duncan's bed, Mairi took one. She doted over Duncan while Anna and Nessa prepared fresh poultices and dressings. Keeping their minds busy and away from the reality of their patient, Anna used it as a teaching opportunity, describing what she'd done thus far, and why. The laird glanced her way briefly, then left the room.

Duncan appeared better, but Anna knew infection from such wounds killed as often as the wound itself. Unable to stem her deep sense of blame to see him injured, Anna avoided eye contact, quickly glancing away when his gaze tried to catch hers. She knew he attempted to comfort her, but his need to make her feel better did nothing to assuage her guilt. With Mairi and Nessa present, there was no opportunity for private words between them.

A gentle knock sounded, and Mairi rose to answer the summons. Malcolm peeked in.

"Lady Anna, the laird bids ye join him downstairs."

As she arrived at the lard's solar, MacGregor rose from his chair in front of the fire.

He waved to the seat next to his. "Please sit. Can I offer ye wine?" His voice and expression gave her no clue as to his mood.

She nodded, wordlessly accepting the goblet. Taking a long drink, she allowed the dark liquid to warm her insides as the libation coursed its way through her blood.

"Ye had quite an adventure. I would hear yer version of it."

Though his voice sounded gentle, the command rang clear. Taking a deep breath, Anna set her goblet aside and began from the day they left until they returned. When she reached the part of the attack, she handed him the bag of coins along with the note from the Earl of Northumberland.

They both stared into the fire for a long time. Fear of the laird's anger for her responsibility, and the possibility of being asked to leave, gnawed at her gut. His prediction of her presence bringing enemies to his clan echoed in her ears.

"I understand ye are to become my daughter-by-marriage." Kenneth still stared at the fire, his voice calm.

Of all the things she expected to hear from him, this was not among them, and it took a moment for her to recover. "Duncan asked me to marry him two days ago." Anna held her breath, waiting for his reaction, wondering if recent events made their betrothal unacceptable.

The laird must have read her discomfort, for he smiled. "Duncan spoke to me a few weeks ago about his intentions. I am pleased the two of ye have come to an accord."

She was surprised by this news, but upon reflection, she shouldn't have been. She knew Duncan was close to his father and would seek his advice and approval.

"Is there no other match you wish him to make, then?"

"Nae. There are no daughters of marrying age among our allies at this time, nor among those with whom we might forge a new bond. Besides, I doubt it would make a whit of difference if there were." His smile deepened, but the lines of worry still creased his forehead.

Anna wanted to return his smile, but her guilt shoved like a dagger in her chest.

Duncan's father shrugged. "He is quite determined to have ye. My son has always been quiet, thinking through a situation before acting. I have never seen him so resolute and passionate about anyone or anything before."

Knowing how important alliances were to the safety and well-being of the clans, Anna's stomach twisted with guilt, realizing she brought nothing to this marriage. "I regret I bring no benefit to your clan, though I promise to serve faithfully."

The laird's eyes narrowed and his face folded into a frown. "Ye are mistaken. Already, ye have saved both my son's and daughter's lives, along with several of my men."

Holding up his hand to halt her argument, he continued. "I understand ye think this ordeal is yer fault, but as with Shamus, ye dinnae instigate the attack. Alain would have found another way to get himself into trouble. Had I allowed Duncan to kill him when he wanted, this never would have happened. So ye see, Anna, I too feel guilty my son lies upstairs seriously wounded, and a good man I have known since his birth is dead."

Anna squirmed uncomfortably in her chair. She was not ready to relinquish her sense of responsibility and the remorse accompanying it. Kenneth sighed.

"Duncan is right, you dinnae see yer own value. Ye won us favor with the Graham, which is not easily done. An alliance would be a boon for our clan. Ye saw how large and prosperous they are. They field almost twice as many men, and their location is advantageous. Ye witnessed the benefits from trade, from having friends who live where the Highlands meet the Lowlands."

Anna jerked her head in agreement.

"The information gained by having an ally to the south, plus having a buffer between our home and the English, is quite valuable. In addition, the Graham laird seeks a match for his son. Yer actions helped make Nessa a bride he considers. Tell me what you think of Blaine Graham."

Relieved to find MacGregor still firmly supporting her, much of the tension she carried faded. Agreeable to the change in their conversation, she related her observations about Blaine, proposing they host him before negotiations grew serious.

"Thank you for sending the missive to my family," she added.

A grin broke out on his face. "Ah, the other alliance. Ye think you bring naught to our clan, but in one sennight, I predict ye have prepared the ground for not one, but two treaties. Though Elliot lies too far south for regular contact, any pact strengthens our position. Graham and Elliot allies potentially become MacGregor allies. A united Scotland benefits us all. 'Tis only a matter of time before war comes with the English again. Longshanks is too greedy. When it does, Elliot and other border clans will be the tip of the spear."

"You think Elliot will want to enter into an agreement through my marriage to Duncan?" Anna hadn't considered the possibility.

"I can assure ye, as a father, yer grandda will be verra glad to hear his granddaughter is well. He will use the opportunity of yer marriage to forge a relationship with us. Ye are all he has left of his beloved daughter. I can only think of what it would be like to lose Nessa, and have only her child left to care for. She would be a priceless jewel to us, as Nessa is now. I will be surprised if we dinnae see an Elliot representative within a fortnight."

The thought of hearing from her grandfather raised Anna's spirits. She mulled over other possibilities until the laird's voice broke through her musings.

"I am told ye have begun training Iain and Malcolm."

Anna looked at him tentatively, hearing no rebuke in his voice.

"Yes, Laird. With your permission, Iain suggests a small group might be willing to allow me to instruct them."

Refilling their goblets, he gave her a hard look. "With my permission? First Duncan, now Iain and Malcolm. Before long, I will discover every man under my command will have found a way to train with ye. Starting in two days, ye will take over the morning session with my guard. With Duncan out, Tavish is in charge. Ye will report to him on the training grounds. Split the time evenly between sword work and unarmed combat."

Anna couldn't believe her ears. She was to be responsible for training the laird's guard? This went well beyond what she had hoped. Her throat constricted, tears of gratitude burning her eyes.

Kenneth's eyebrows arched. "Why so surprised? Only a fool doesnae accept the gifts he is given. That they are borne by a woman matters not. Or are you hesitant to accept this assignment? Did I not hear your pledge of loyalty a few moments ago?"

Wordlessly, Anna nodded her assent.

With a grunt of satisfaction, Kenneth queried, "It dinnae bother you these men may be called upon to fight the English in the future?"

She found her voice. "No, Laird. My living family is Scots, my future husband and family are Scots. As far as I am concerned, the English side of me died along with my father and brother. Other than getting used to the cold, I could not ask for a better home. I will gladly offer my knowledge and sword to train and defend clan MacGregor."

Kenneth gave her a satisfied smile. "Ye must be tired and hungry. Go, I will see a tray is brought to ye in Nessa's room."

She met his eyes. "I would stay by Duncan's side to watch for sign of fever, or in case he needs something, Laird."

Kenneth gazed at her for a moment before answering. "Aye. I will have the tray brought to Duncan's room. Get some rest."

"Thank you, Laird."

As she rose to leave, he said, "We have come a long way, ye and I."

Her gaze met his. "Aye."

She found Nessa curled in one of the chairs near Duncan's bed. Mairi rose from the other to greet her, grasping both of Anna's hands and giving them a gentle squeeze before releasing her.

"Welcome home, my soon-to-be daughter. I had a bath drawn for ye. We have seen to Duncan, and now 'tis yer turn. Come. Nessa can keep watch for a few moments whilst ye wash away the grime from battle and yer travels. Ye need clean clothes."

Glancing down, Anna realized her clothes were stained with blood and other things she was too tired to contemplate. Without the strength to argue, she followed Mairi to Nessa's room, where Isla readied her bath. Trean rose from his bed and slipped to her side. Anna bent and scratched his ears.

Isla looked at him in surprise. "I dinnae see him when I came in the room. What a quiet puppy!"

"'Tis a wolf and bonded to me. He is very young and likely watched you carefully." Anna gave Isla an apologetic smile. "He is not a pet."

The girl eyed the pup doubtfully as Anna stripped her stained clothing away and stepped into the tub. The hot water immediately relaxed her muscles and she sighed deeply.

Mairi sat next to her. "Duncan explained more about what happened."

Responsibility for his plight flooded back, and she fought off tears. "He would be uninjured if not for me," she managed. Though she remembered the laird's words, a terrible sense of responsibility remained.

Mairi didn't argue, allowing silence to pass while Isla washed Anna's hair. "Has Duncan told ye about Callum?"

Anna glanced at her, remembering the name from that night at camp. She shook her head.

"Duncan had a twin brother. 'Twas difficult even for me to tell them apart. They were inseparable, so close I often wondered if they shared the same soul. Whilst good lads, they were very active, always into mischief. One day, when they were two and ten summers, they were sparring with wooden swords, as they did every day. Their play brought them close to the burn. 'Twas early spring, and the waters ran high, swollen from melted snows. Callum lost his footing, fell in and drowned." Mairi's voice trembled and tears fell.

Anna grasped her hand, feeling her own heart lurch at the woman's words.

Mairi smiled feebly, breathed deeply to regain her composure, and continued. "After that day, the lighthearted boy I knew, who delighted in the world around him, became serious and withdrawn. He no longer engaged in the playful antics of his age, but instead assumed more responsibilities around the keep, especially at the stables. Tending the horses seemed to bring him solace.

"His father and I were encouraged as he threw himself into useful tasks. Whilst we grieved the loss of one son, we grieved the loss of innocence in the other. He became quiet, thoughtful, always considering his words and actions. He has been highly responsible and protective, though distant, since. I havenae seen anyone engage his affections or emotions until ye arrived."

In spite of the tragedy of the story, Anna's heart warmed at Mairi's words.

"Ye havenae been here long enough to know how much ye sparked a change in my son. He is resolved to marry ye. Part of being married means bearing each other's burdens. If not for us, Alain wouldnae have notified the earl of yer presence here, nor attacked you. So the argument of who is to blame cuts both ways." Mairi smiled wryly. "Believe me, ye will carry yer fair share of the load as the wife of the MacGregor laird. Running the castle can drive one mad."

Anna felt an easing in her chest. Along with the laird's words, the truth of Mairi's argument did much to lessen her guilt. Perhaps it wasn't her fault. Mairi's comment about assuming the role of chatelaine reminded Anna of her discussion with Duncan on the same topic.

"Aunt Mairi, fear not, for you will not be out of a job anytime soon. Who will watch our children? Or make sure Ciardun runs smoothly whilst I am riding with Duncan, seeing to the needs of our clan and defending our borders?" Anna asked.

"Dear God, ye cannae be serious?" Mairi asked, a stricken look on her face.

"I am quite serious. I explained to your son that simply because we marry doesn't mean I will cease doing what I have done all my life. I will gladly make compromises, particularly whilst breeding, but being wed will not change who I am."

Mairi laughed. "I can see ye and I will have plenty to discuss during our afternoon talks. I may yet surrender to those convulsions ye spoke of, if this indeed is what the future holds."

Chapter Twenty

*O*nce finished with her bath, Anna fed Trean from the tray brought up from the kitchen, then returned to Duncan's bedside, the wolf pup at her heels. Nessa gasped, her eyes wide as Anna and Trean entered the room. Slipping from her chair, she knelt on the floor, patting the rug with her hand. Trean eyed her, but showed no signs of accepting her invitation.

"Trean is a wolf, Nessa. He may grow to trust you, but he is not likely to want to cuddle."

Nessa tilted her head, her lips pursed in a moue of disappointment. "I think he is adorable!"

Anna chuckled. "I do not think he will be adorable when he loses his baby fat."

"Come, Nessa. 'Tis time we took our leave." Mairi grasped Nessa's hand and helped her to her feet. Breaking free at the door, Nessa ran to Anna, gripping her in a fierce hug.

"Thank ye for saving my brother's life. I couldnae ask for a better sister."

"On the morrow, if you fetch breakfast, I will tell you all about the handsome Blaine Graham," Anna teased, hugging her firmly.

Nessa pulled away, a huge smile on her face as she kissed Anna's cheek and followed her mother from the room.

Duncan slept soundly. Resisting the urge to crawl into bed with him, Anna poured a cup of chamomile tea and banked the fire while

Trean created a cave beneath Duncan's bed. Satisfied her betrothed was comfortable, Anna settled into the cushioned chair next to his bed, staring into the coals until sleep found her.

The next morning, she woke at first light. She stroked Duncan's hair, feeling his cool forehead. He stirred at her touch and pulled her into bed with his uninjured arm. She feathered soft kisses over his face, neck and lips, careful to not place any pressure on his wounds.

"I love ye, Anna Braxton," he whispered.

"As I love you, Duncan MacGregor." Anna realized saying the words echoed the truth of them in her heart. She checked the skin around his dressings. Satisfied to find no swelling, she settled into his embrace, vibrantly aware of every point their bodies touched. "May I do something for you?"

"Touch me. I love it when ye touch me."

Smiling, Anna stroked his face and neck, using light touches to caress. She moved her hand through the opening of his shirt, skimming across his shoulders. Tracing the lines of his collarbones, her fingers brushed the muscles of his chest. He closed his eyes with a contented sigh. She continued her path, stopping at his nipples, which hardened under her touch. Curious, she circled first one, then the other with her fingers. His breath hitched and his face hardened.

"Do you like that?" Anna asked softly.

"Very much," he whispered.

Emboldened by her ability to affect him so, she continued her slow exploration down his ribs to his smooth stomach. At her touch, his muscles rippled beneath her hand and his hips moved slightly, his breathing labored.

Feeling brave and delighted she pleased him, Anna slowly slid her hand lower and felt the firm tip of his manhood. Curious, her fingers trailed further. Duncan's eyes flew open and his body stiffened. She sucked in a startled breath as his hand covered hers.

"Anna, please." He inhaled sharply.

"Did I hurt you?"

He gave her a tight smile of assurance. "Nae, just the opposite. Ye have no idea how good it feels."

Buoyed by his words and her discovery, she shifted her position over him and splayed her free hand over his chest. His grip tightened. She dragged his leine upward, leaving his body to her view. Her belly tightened as she perused him, her fingers following her slow gaze. A low murmur of approval from Duncan, as his cock strained upward, urged her on.

Her touch grew bolder and she wrapped her fingers around his rigid staff, squeezing gently at first, then tighter. Moisture beaded at the tip and she lightly ran her thumb around it, spreading the glistening wetness. His hips bucked upward.

"Anna." Duncan's voice cracked.

She froze. "Did I do something wrong?"

"Nae." A soft chuckle rumbled in his chest.

Anna considered the wry grin on his face and squeezed his cock again. "What happens if I do not stop?"

His face darkened. "I will spill myself in yer hand."

"Do you want me to stop?"

A choked laugh burst from his lips. "Nae."

Tentatively, she stroked his cock and it pulsed beneath her fingers. She bent closer and ran the tip of her tongue around the tip. His cock jerked convulsively. Taking him in her mouth, she continued to stroke him, increasing her pressure and rhythm.

Duncan gripped the bedclothes, a moan drawing from his throat, his breathing labored. Suddenly, his body hardened and shuddered, her name a constricted whisper from his throat. He grabbed her shoulders and tried to pull her away, but she easily resisted and felt his warmth spill forth. She lightly kissed and caressed him as he softened in her hand.

His breathing evened and he reached for her. Fascinated and elated to have pleasured him so fully, she placed a final kiss on the tip of his retreating cock and allowed him to reposition her under his arm.

Peering at him from beneath her lashes, she idly trailed a fingertip down his chest. "Did you enjoy that as much as I did?" A tingling sensation, much like the one created by his kisses, lingered low in her belly.

"Ye enjoyed that?"

"Very much," Anna purred. "Did you?" She knew he did, but wanted to hear him say it.

"My angel, ye just took me to heaven and back. How could I not enjoy such a trip?"

She nibbled his ear, then whispered, "Good, because I like the way you taste, and want to do it again."

Winding his fingers through her hair, he answered, "The next time 'twill be my turn to do the same for ye, my love."

Anna propped on an elbow and looked at him askance. "Duncan, be serious. I do not have a cock."

Hugging her tightly, he chuckled. "Nae, ye do not, thank the saints, but ye have something better, and I shall look forward to showing it to ye."

Anna nestled onto his shoulder, making lazy circles with her fingertips in the coarse hair covering his chest. Her body hummed with the need to be close to him.

"I find myself wondering what I did to deserve ye," he murmured.

She leaned over and kissed him, tugging his lower lip with her teeth. "Remember, we have yet to address my role as your wife. I fear you may be getting more than you bargained for, my dearest Duncan."

"Oh, I havenae forgotten, *boidheach laoch,* my beautiful warrior—she who is able to send a man straight to heaven or hell, depending on her mood."

Anna liked that very much, and was about to playfully reply when a tap at the portal ended their privacy. Hopping off the bed, she straightened the bed clothes before opening the door to admit Nessa.

She greeted them with a tray of Anna's favorite breakfast foods and a hot bowl of porridge for Duncan. "Good morrow, brother, good morrow, sister. When is the wedding?" Her youthful face glowed with happiness. Duncan and Anna both chuckled at her question.

"Good morrow, Nessa," Anna replied. "We have yet to discuss a wedding day, but you will be the first to know when we decide. What have we here? I see you took my parting words quite seriously."

Nessa grinned as she put the tray down on a side table and plopped into one of the chairs. "Aye, I did. I have been looking forward to hearing what ye have to tell me."

Anna helped Duncan sit, supporting his injured shoulder with a pillow. Grabbing the porridge, she dipped the spoon and raised the bite to his lips.

"I am able to feed myself, woman. Place the bowl and spoon here. My sister demands an audience with ye." His voice was gruff, but his eyes sparkled with humor.

After settling the bowl on his lap, Anna watched him take in the first spoonful before she spoke. She started by telling Nessa a slightly watered-down version of her conversation with Iain at the market—minus Colina's physical attributes. Delighted to hear about Iain and Colina, Nessa quickly grew impatient to hear about Blaine Graham. Wickedly teasing the girl, Anna dragged out her story until Nessa whined and bounced in her chair with agitation.

Duncan and Anna told of their meeting with the young man. As suspected, Duncan glossed over the specifics Anna knew Nessa would want to know. Anna happily supplied them, enduring a litany of questions going well beyond her ability to answer. Nessa at last seemed satisfied.

"Dinnae get yer hopes up too much, little sister. 'Tis no sure thing," Duncan warned.

Nessa waved him off. "I know, but it gives me something to dream about."

Anna smiled at the sight of this beautiful, budding young woman. Almost ready to become a wife, Nessa's remnants of childhood demonstrated her need to fantasize about love. Finishing their meal, Anna and Nessa removed Duncan's dressings and examined his wounds. With a series of questions, Anna led her through the steps to ensure proper healing, keeping infection at bay.

Duncan grew sleepy, so Anna suggested they leave him for a while. Nessa took the tray down to the kitchen. Anna leaned over and kissed him lightly on the lips.

"If you wish to continue our earlier discussion, my lord, I will be delighted to oblige."

Smiling, he caressed her cheek. "I look forward to carrying our discussion further, love, when we can be assured of a bit of privacy. Believe me, there is much to discuss."

A tremor slid low through Anna's belly at his words. With reluctance, she brushed the hair from his face then left, pulling the door closed behind her.

Several packages waited on her bed, one of which she didn't

recognize. Curiosity getting the best of her, she opened it and discovered a stack of books bound together with twine. On top lay a copy of Plato's *Dialogues*, and a volume each of Aristotle's logic and physics treatises beneath.

In addition, a book of poetry and prose, along with one each on mathematics and astronomy. All were battered, but in good enough shape. A new book she had not seen before lay at the bottom of the stack. *Inventarium Sive Chirurgia Magna.* To her great surprise and delight, this book was a comprehensive manual on surgery and medical treatments. Written in Latin, many of the subjects covered held new knowledge for her. Anna knew Nessa would be as excited as she to explore it.

Another stack held three new, leather-bound volumes filled with blank pages. A wooden tube full of blank scrolls, several quills, a bottle of ink and a trimming tool lay nearby. Anna knew instinctively Duncan had purchased the items for her and saw them as a clear invitation to write out things she had learned. Grabbing the gifts she'd obtained for Nessa and Lady MacGregor, she delivered them. Anna placed Mairi's special present under her pillow with a note of thanks. She left the package with the laird's belt and sporran on top of the bed.

Anna then strode to the stables, eager to get a good look at the new stock they'd captured. At the paddock, she met Ross.

"Your stitches look good. We will leave them in another few days. It appears as though there will be little scarring."

"Yer work is verra fine, milady, but a man needs a few scars. They are evidence of his worth in battle. The next time ye have occasion to stitch me, dinnae be so careful." Ross grinned at her.

Anna laughed, remembering their talk of wounds and scars over the campfire. "I will bear it in mind. How are the horses we brought back?"

"I was told to wait for ye to inspect them."

They examined each horse thoroughly. The animals were all in good health, though two needed new shoes. Almost half were mares and would make decent breeding stock. The geldings were acceptable, though two were short and stocky, better suited to working the fields or pulling carts.

From there, she walked to the spinner and weaver's shop, where the new wool had been delivered. After being measured, they assured her two pairs of woolens would be ready within a few days. Nessa and Lady MacGregor were also to be measured for a set. After thanking them, Anna made her way back to the keep.

She gathered her new scrolls and quills and checked on Duncan, finding him still asleep. His color appeared improved, though the trip had taken a toll on him. She settled at his desk and organized lessons for the training sessions beginning on the morrow. Since she'd never taught before, she wanted to be well prepared. Her sex would be a hindrance for many, in spite of the laird's order. She vowed to prove his decision a sound one.

The afternoon faded into evening before Duncan woke. "Ye are here," he observed, his voice thick with sleep.

"Yes. I have been to the stables and checked over the new horses with Ross. They all appear fine, and he has them well in hand. I thought to organize the lessons I am scheduled to teach on the morrow. Thank you for the generous gifts." Anna nuzzled his neck, placing a soft, lush kiss on his lips.

"Who knew the way to a lady's heart was through her mind?" Duncan replied with a chuckle.

Anna thumped his chest playfully with her fingertips. "This lady's heart at least." Her mood changed from playful to mournful in an instant.

"What is it?" His voice was like a silken caress.

She forced back the melancholy and gave Duncan a sad smile. "I was thinking of my father's library. It resided in an expansive, circular room atop a tower in our home. It was one of my favorite places—a truly magical place with large maps and charts adorning the walls that showed all the places in the world men have traveled. When I was a little girl, I would read about such places, then find them on the map. Many nights, I would dream of traveling to them, and having all sorts of adventures along the way. It is so painful to think it all lost."

Duncan took her hand. "Grief has an odd way of raising its head when we least expect it. We will devote a room to a new library. In the meantime, we can make a lark of collecting books and maps when we travel. Ye can tell me about these places and show them to me.

Tonight, ye can read to me one of these adventurous tales."

She kissed him again, soft as goose down, but lingered, lightly running her tongue along his bottom lip. When she rose, her smile returned and she handed him a package, a twinkle in her eye.

"What is this?" Duncan asked, shaking the package next to his ear, listening for clues.

"'Tis a gift from one of your sweethearts, I believe," she replied mischievously.

Duncan frowned. "I only have one sweetheart."

He unwrapped the rough material and binding. When he saw the tooled belt and sporran, his eyes widened with surprise. He fingered the MacGregor crest etched in the decorative silver and lifted his gaze to hers.

"Anna, how did ye get this made?"

"Do you like it?" Giddiness lightened her heart to have found a gift he obviously liked.

"How can I not like it? How did ye get this carved so quickly? We werenae there long enough to have this done." His eyes rounded with wonder.

"I paid extra and left my *sgian dubh* to carve the crest from. Iain fetched it for me the morning we left."

Anna gave him a brief hug, then settled in the chair next to the bed to discuss her plans for training the men. He had very little input and seemed indifferent about the whole topic. She accounted for his lack of interest to the fact he was in pain and still tired. Seeing the way his eyes hardened and narrowed, she gave him a quick kiss and set about tidying the room, leaving him to drift back to sleep. But she could not dismiss the feeling something bright had gone out of her day.

Chapter Twenty-one

Morning came all too quickly. Anna battled her unsteady confidence during the long walk to the training grounds. She carried Trean, his legs too short to keep up with her determined stride. Tavish met her on the way and introduced himself.

"How many are against my being here?"

"It seems to be divided between men who are eager to test what ye know and those who look forward to seeing ye scurry back to the keep." His hard expression gave away nothing.

"And which group do you find yourself in?"

"I have seen ye fight before, but will withhold judgment until I see how ye do with men I know to be good fighters."

Nodding her understanding, Anna allowed him to lead to where the others gathered, placing Trean on the ground at her feet. Iain and Malcolm approached and offered polite greetings. Trean eyed them cautiously, but ventured a small wag of his tail in recognition before wandering off to the shade of a nearby tree. Tavish gestured for the men's attention.

"The laird has assigned a new instructor for the morning sessions until further notice. Ye will give yer full attention and respect."

A severe glare from Tavish halted the snickers and hard looks. Ignoring the belittling response, Anna asked to see a demonstration of their hand-to-hand combat techniques. Two volunteers came forward, and at Tavish's command, pummeled each other in a haphazard manner, eventually falling to the ground, rolling around like pigs in mud. Trean left the limb he'd been worrying to stand next to Anna, an eye on the commotion. Seemingly unimpressed, Trean let out a huff, nosed Anna and walked back to his piece of deadwood to resume chewing.

After watching the combatants and the reactions of the others standing, Anna realized their weaponless training was severely lacking. Of the twenty-five men who made up the laird's special guard, she asked Duff—the biggest man she had ever seen—to join her.

"What do you think of when you attack someone?" She gazed up at the giant.

"I hit 'im as I run 'im over". He smashed a fist into his open hand, his eyes narrowed, lips curling into a snarl. As expected, his approach was as subtle as an enraged bull.

"Duff, would you please punch me?"

His features pinched as if he tasted something foul. Anna bit back her laughter.

"You are not going to hurt me." He gave her a half-effort punch. She cocked her head, hands on her hips. "I picked you because I thought you were the biggest, meanest Highlander here. Was I wrong?"

Her gentle taunt elicited chuckles from the men and Duff's face reddened. With new resolution, he threw a hard punch with his right hand. Though powerful enough to end her if he connected, his fist approached so slowly it seemed she had to wait for it. Everything about his motion gave away his intention. From the way he drew back to gather power, to the over-extension of his strike, leaving him off-balance, his was an all-or-nothing approach.

Stepping to the opposite side of his punch, she deflected his strike and grasped his wrist with one hand. Without pause, she curled her other hand around the back of his head. She pivoted in a small circle, pulling both his wrist and head down and toward her, launching Duff into a flip, landing him on his back with a thud. He hopped up, eyes as big as horses' hooves. Murmurs from the men rose noticeably.

"Again, Duff, if you please." She smiled in invitation.

He threw the same slow but hard right-hand punch. This time, she stepped toward it, deflecting his punch outward as she did. Her movement placed them side-by-side, though facing opposite directions. Anna's right hip touched his left hip, as if they were dancing. Holding his right arm, she gripped the front of his tunic, pulling him toward her, disrupting his balance.

With a strong, fluid motion, she kicked her right leg backward into the back of his left leg, calf-to-calf, sweeping it from underneath him. Again, he landed with a thud. This time, Anna held onto his right hand. Grasping it at the wrist, she twisted it outward, painfully locking both his wrist and elbow in the process, leaving him unable to move without causing himself pain. Glancing around, Anna saw big grins from both Iain and Malcolm. They had seen her use this same wristlock on the Graham barbarian, Angus.

Assisting Duff to his feet, she offered an explanation of off-balancing an opponent, the use of angles, and how to harness the strength of their attacker to use against him. She asked for four volunteers, and they positioned themselves all around her. She directed them to attack, taking turns grabbing her however they wished, from all directions. Anna met each attack with a sweep or throw, sometimes throwing them into her next attacker.

After a couple of rounds, Anna asked them to attack faster and harder, and they hit the ground in direct proportion to the speed and strength they employed. She executed throw after throw with no conscious thought, merely taking what they gave, the exercise creating euphoria within her. How she missed this training! Testing her skills against others more powerful than she remained an essential part of her.

Her simple demonstration captured everyone's attention. She noted each man looked at her differently, with the exception of Iain and Malcolm, whose smug smiles spoke of being proven correct amongst a crowd of skeptics. Two men grudgingly handed over several coins to Malcolm. Anna shook her head.

Men.

Starting the men on simple drills gave them an introduction to the concepts she taught. Calling for a brief water break, Anna noticed the laird had arrived and stood speaking to Tavish. When he motioned for her to approach, her nervousness returned.

"My laird." Anna offered a brief bow.

"'Twas a good strategy to choose Duff," he said, a smile on his face.

Ah, he saw it all, then. "I find the biggest are usually the easiest to handle owing to over-confidence. Particularly when facing someone much smaller."

She returned to the group and they switched to swords. Using the same principles of angles and off-balancing, she applied them to armed combat. Anna ran the men through a series of drills, each choosing an angle of attack, rather than merely moving straight forward. Quicker than she thought possible, midday arrived.

"Thank you for tolerating a woman instructor, gentlemen."

Her words inspired laughter from the group of pride-battered men. They broke for the morning and headed to the main hall to eat, Anna in their midst, Trean on her heels. She felt their acceptance, a subtle shift, which reminded her of being around her old clansmen. She wasn't sure how much of the demonstrated respect to attribute to her relationship to Duncan, the laird, or the session they'd completed, but it warmed her nonetheless.

The men invited her to sit with them, which led to discussions of tactics on the battlefield. Trean settled at her feet, gazing expectantly at her for scraps. She smiled and scratched behind his ears while he ate a chunk of venison from the stew.

Once the meal concluded, the men returned to training while she tucked Trean into his box for a nap. She then met with Nessa to address the healing cases Nessa tended the sennight she was away. Anna longed to accompany the men back to the field, but people needed her care. Rory had recovered enough so Liam escorted him carefully home, leaving the room free once again. Anna was pleasantly surprised to see the injuries Nessa treated in her absence. As she suspected, the lass possessed a true gift for healing.

"These stitches are clean and even. His wound looks very good. Excellent work." Anna offered her encouragement after examining a boy who had fallen against a scythe a few days past.

Nessa's confidence seemed to soar at Anna's praise, and her enthusiasm increased when Anna told her of the new medical book Duncan bought. They agreed to spend time each evening reading through it together.

Within a fortnight, Duncan was healed enough to walk around, though he moved gingerly. Anna wanted him to stay away from his duties at the training fields a bit longer, though she knew he was anxious to resume his routine. After their first week back, his wounds had healed enough that no more pretense existed to justify her staying in his room at night.

Duncan stood in the shade of a large oak overlooking the training grounds, legs spread wide, hands on the pommel of the sheathed claymore in front of him. He chose a stance meant to display strength, but in truth it was the only position he could hold for any length of time without falling over. His leg had healed much, but the pain remained, his muscles stiff and weak. He could not sit idle any longer. Not when the clan needed him. Not when he thought he might go mad if he stayed inside another day. And not when men surrounded Anna each morning.

It mattered little he had handpicked these men for their skill and loyalty. Duncan could not bear the thought of *his* woman out here without him present. The powerful emotion of the word *mine* echoed through his entire body, as it did each time he thought of her. He knew better than to voice his possessiveness for fear of angering her. But he would be damned if he allowed her to work with others without him overseeing her safety, and to ensure no one behaved unseemly around her.

His suspicions proved correct. The men followed her about like lovesick puppies, hanging on her every word. She, of course, remained completely unaware of her effect on them. *Damned English beat down her sense of worth because she chose not to wear skirts?* They were as daft as they were blind. In the Highlands, a man or woman showed their merit by their deeds, not their appearance. His men recognized her value and held her in high regard, but part of him didn't like it one damned bit. He wanted to be the only one who perceived her as a treasure.

He stewed, gritting his teeth, clenching the sword in his hands so tightly he lost feeling in them. The urge to pummel every man in the yard grew stronger and stronger as he watched her placing their hands and bodies in proper position, moving from pair to pair, correcting their form. She stole glances at him from time to time, gifting him with a smile warm enough to melt the winter snows. Duncan tried to smile in return, but found his face frozen in vexation.

His temper barely remained under control when he heard her announce a new game she'd devised. Every man would take the opportunity to attack each other at will.

"The rules are thus. You must be outside with no women or children close at hand. You can only use the techniques I have taught. Since I do not wish to spend my afternoons repairing damage caused by inflated pride, you must yield before injury."

Duff raised his hand. Anna gave him her attention. "Yes, Duff?"

"Are ye includin' yerself in the game, milady?" More than a few men chuckled at his question.

Anna smiled broadly. "Indeed I am." The chuckles grew louder.

Shaking with anger, it was all Duncan could do not to storm the group and snatch her away. He had to leave before he did something he'd regret. The jealousy raging through his body would do nothing but push her away. He needed to douse it before he approached her.

He walked back to the keep and grabbed a basket he'd requested for a picnic lunch, since they'd spent little time together the past several days. Simply having her near filled his soul in a way that made him realize how barren he'd been inside. The joy, passion and love she stirred continued to overwhelm him. Duncan knew he watched the other half of his soul. Now he'd found her, he could take no chance of losing her, for fear of losing the rest of himself as well.

He gathered their saddled horses, and Duncan's mind eased as he thought ahead to the afternoon. He missed their time together, the one time they went further than kissing still burned upon his mind. He'd told her it was his turn next, and today he intended to repay the debt. His frown slowly tilted upward as he thought about the seduction he planned.

The morning's session went well, and Anna was happy to see Duncan joined them by watching rather than participating. The stiffness of his body and the hard expression on his face told her he struggled with pain. Hoping he would wait, she was disappointed to see him walk away not long before they halted their practice. However, her disappointment turned to joy when he returned, bringing their saddled horses.

Duncan handed her Orion's reins. "Since we havenae seen each other much lately, I thought ye might enjoy an outing."

"That sounds wonderful. Where do you have in mind?"

"'Tis a place at the loch I like to go to be alone. I will show ye."

They mounted and rode at a leisurely pace, allowing Trean to lope alongside. The days of his being content to ride in her saddle were ending.

"What did you think of this morning's practice?" Anna asked. "The men have come a long way in a short time."

He hesitated, glancing away. "Twas difficult to watch ye put your hands on the men and have them put their hands on ye."

She gazed at him in disbelief. "Duncan, you are *jealous*?" An odd but warm feeling slid through her. Nobody had ever been jealous over her before.

"Aye, I admit I am. I should be the only one who touches ye."

She heard the possessiveness in his voice, which tempted her to anger, but she knew his jealousy revealed the depth of his feelings for her. Though an uncomfortable way of being told how much he cared for her, she chose to see it as a declaration of love, nonetheless.

She kept her voice even. "I am not sure what to say. You know my interest lies only in you. Your men treat me with respect. If one were to act out of line, Malcolm or Iain would step in immediately. Besides, you know me well enough. I can handle myself."

The hard look from this morning returned, and she realized his scowl had little to do with physical pain.

"Aye, but ye dinnae see how the men look at ye, the effect ye have on them."

Anna sat speechless. Never had anyone suggested she'd be attractive to one man, much less a large group.

"The worst was when ye included yourself in this game ye

created. Now I have to stand back and watch as any one of them has yer permission to attack."

"But Duncan, they will be attacking, not stealing kisses. I need this exercise as much as they do to keep my skills sharp. You know they will not harm me."

He closed his eyes and took a deep breath. "I want to spend a pleasant afternoon with ye, not quarrel. I cannae change how I feel, but I agree to not let it get the best of me, if ye promise to be careful."

She didn't want to argue either, but felt his concerns unwarranted and his expectations unfair. After considering his request, there was no harm in agreeing. "I promise to be careful around the men," she replied with conviction. Such a general agreement didn't seem limiting. However, her promise appeared to pacify him.

Arriving at the loch, Anna followed him through a stand of trees until they came upon a deep, narrow finger of water. Shielded by a large outcropping of rock on one side and dense woods on the other, the inlet made a perfect place to bathe uninterrupted.

Duncan took her hand and led her to a flat grassy area below the large rocks. He placed a plaide down, and together they unpacked the food. They laughed as Trean shoved his nose into the basket, eyes wide and pleading as they shared a meal of thick sliced ham, dark, grainy bread and wine. After finishing, Duncan repacked the basket and tossed him a hambone. The pup settled against a large rock, gnawing the bone contentedly.

Duncan strolled to the water's edge and peeled off his clothes. Anna sat and watched, entranced, as he stood bare, climbed onto a rock and dove into the loch.

Seeing his naked body kindled heat deep within her. Her betrothed was a powerfully built man, as well-formed as any of the images of Greek gods in the books in her father's library. As he surfaced, she admired the rugged handsomeness of his face, the sunlight glistening on his wet hair.

"Come join me."

She experienced a moment of modest hesitation, but he gave her a heart-melting smile and chased her uncertainty away.

I want this man as much as he wants me.

Anna swiftly stripped down to her short shift and braies. Grinning at his look of surprise, she took them off and waded knee deep into the lake. He stared at her, his mouth open wide, draining her fragile confidence. Doubt crept in, and she crossed one arm protectively over her chest and the other over her mons.

"What is it?" she asked, her voice small.

Duncan swam to her and she took a step back. He reached a hand out in invitation.

"Sweet Mother Mary, ye are breathtaking. Come swim with me, my *boidheach laoch*, and wash away the sweat of this morning's training."

His beautiful warrior. The familiar endearment renewed her confidence. Anna took his hand and joined him in the depths. He settled her in his arms before she could catch her breath from the cold, rubbing her back as he pulled her tight. The slide of their water-slicked bodies stole her breath more than the chill of the water. The warmth of the sun, combined with the heat of his skin on hers, banished any thoughts of being cold.

He took her mouth in a gentle kiss. As his lips caressed hers, he loosened the leather strip holding her braid in place, winnowing his fingers through her hair until the tresses fell about her shoulders. She opened her mouth, her longing for him pushing away any sense of shyness. His tongue sought hers and softly suckled.

The feel of her nipples brushing against the hair on his chest, coupled with the magic of his tongue, blanked her mind. She sank into the water, but he held her tighter, his arousal bumping against her belly. Inexplicably weak, Anna offered no assistance as Duncan slowly swam them back to shore. He brought an arm under her knees and lifted her out of the water.

"Duncan, your wounds," Anna protested.

"Hush, love. I will gladly take the pain to have you in my arms."

She frowned, but he eased her concern by kissing the furrows in her brow. Gently settling her on the plaide, Duncan lay beside her. Propped on one elbow, he looked her up and down, his scorching gaze telling Anna how beautiful and desirable he found her. His gaze turned her brazen, dispelling all thoughts of modesty. She wanted nothing more than to see yearning in his eyes when he gazed upon her. Nothing more, except to feel his hands and body on hers.

Anna draped a leg over his, offering herself to him as she reached around his neck to pull him into a kiss. He did not hesitate, claiming her mouth possessively, demanding, challenging her to match him passion for passion. Moaning, Anna pushed her leg over, crawling on top, the most intimate part of her pressed against his arousal. She rubbed along his length, yearning to have him inside her.

Duncan growled and stopped her movement. "Nae, my love. We shall save the best for our wedding night. I have other plans for our pleasure this afternoon." He rolled her onto her back.

Anna pushed her bottom lip out in a pout, feigning the sting of rejection. He chuckled, then sucked on her inadvertent offering.

Anna's hands skimmed his back, landing on his buttocks, squeezing the taut muscle.

Duncan smiled against her lips. "Remember, I told ye 'twas my turn next." He palmed her breasts, lightly tracing his fingertips over her skin. Her nipples grew erect as he lightly pulled at them. A soft moan escaped her lips.

As his hot, wet mouth claimed her breast, she arched upward, deepening this new kiss, this new sensation. She moaned louder as his tongue rasped against the sensitive nub and shivers of delight coursed through her body.

His mouth suckled and licked one breast while his hand gently tugged and twisted the nipple of her other.

"Duncan please, I cannot breathe," she gasped. He nipped and pulled at her soft flesh, switching to the other with his mouth, his hand teasing its twin.

The pounding of her blood echoed in her head. A delicious, torturous sensation grew in her belly, centering in the hidden part of her. It pulsed through every nerve, building in intensity.

The sucking, licking and tugging all melded into one sensation. He caught one nipple in his teeth while his tongue rapidly flicked across it.

"Harder, harder," she pleaded, her voice scarcely above a whisper.

She trembled, the sensations too much to take. Suddenly, her body tightened and waves of pleasure shook her entire being. Her hands buried in his hair as she keened his name. A feeling of floating overtook her, her breathing ragged. Duncan kissed her neck, nibbled her ear as his hand smoothed the flesh of her belly in small circular patterns.

New sensations drew her attention. Duncan's fingers brushed along her stomach, lightly stopping at her hipbones and on to her upper thighs. Her legs involuntarily parted at his touch. He kissed and licked the sensitive pulse points along her neck, his fingers never resting as he continued his slow exploration of her thighs.

Anna raised her hips. She wanted him to touch her there, she *needed* him to touch her *there*. He finally brushed her soft curls. Anna sucked in a sharp breath, opening her eyes to see Duncan watching her expression.

"I love ye, my sweet Anna," he whispered on her lips as he kissed her again. "I love the way yer body responds to my touch."

She whimpered and gasped as his fingers lightly grazed her folds. She thrust her hips upward, seeking greater contact with his hand.

As he parted her tender flesh with a finger, she shuddered, twisting the blanket with both hands. He slowly drew his finger up and down her wetness, lightly teasing the center of her pleasure. With each stroke, Anna's body shook in response. She matched the rhythm of his hand with her hips, lost in the pleasure of his clever fingers on her most feminine parts.

Duncan increased his speed and pressure. Again, a warm tension in her core built, escalating faster.

"Duncan, oh Duncan... I don't..."

Waves of pleasure crested and she clenched around his fingers, holding onto them, her body shuddering, blinding her to all else.

Duncan rained light kisses on her mouth, and her tongue swirled lazily with his. He shifted his body and suckled her breasts, taking first one and then the other nipple into his mouth, pulling lightly with his lips, tonguing each sensitive nub of flesh. Then he lightly traced the blue woad lines on her shoulders.

Anna sighed. "I never knew such a thing was possible. I understand now why women chase men if this is what they can expect."

"Aye, 'tis why men chase women, also."

Propping up on an elbow, she asked, "Is it like this for everyone?"

He gazed into her eyes. "Nae. 'Tis so powerful for us because of the love we share. 'Tis why love is considered so precious, and rare. I promise 'twill always be like this for us. What we shared today is only part of the pleasure ye and I have yet to explore."

His answer made the now-familiar warmth bloom again low in her stomach.

"If this is only part, I fear I may never let you leave our bed," she said only half teasingly.

"Aye, 'twill be a problem," he replied with a laugh, clutching her to him once again.

"Ach!" Duncan bounded to all fours, rolling her off with his abrupt movement. "Yer charmed beast stuck his cold nose in a place it should nae go."

Anna chuckled as Trean wagged his tail and cocked his head from side to side.

"He is a wee menace," Duncan muttered, his voice half-teasing. He sprawled against her, one leg across hers.

"You do not feel so menaced to me," Anna replied, swaying her hips gently against his arousal. Duncan buried his face in her neck with a mock growl that ended in a yelp as Trean bounded on top, thrusting his muzzle between them. Duncan rolled away, hands flying to protect himself as the puppy leapt about excitedly.

"Ye wee devil!" Duncan shouted as he rolled to a sitting position, hands in his lap. "She dinnae need your protection from me." He gave Anna an aggrieved look. She quickly bit back her laughter. "Square on my manhood. Has he no compassion?"

Anna cocked her head at him, considering. "Well, 'tis the most prominent part of you at the moment, my love—and most impressive."

Duncan bent over, peering directly in the pup's face. "Arrgh! Be a wee bit more careful, lad, or I shall banish ye to the kennel."

Trean drew to a startled halt. With a hesitant glance at Duncan, he backed two steps onto his rumpled plaide. Anna dissolved into laughter as the pup loosed a healthy stream in the middle of the fabric and the scent of warm, wet wool drifted in the air.

Chapter Twenty-two

By the time they returned to the keep, Anna had rebraided her hair and recovered most of her wits. Her gaze kept locking with Duncan's, re-sharing the passion he'd created with her. She had no comparison for the way he made her feel, and embarrassment edged her thoughts as she anxiously awaited their next encounter.

Heading to the stables, Anna resumed her work with Trean. She'd begun playing games of tug with him, teaching him to bite on command. At his gawky young age, he was more inclined to be silly than serious, and his attention was easily distracted. *Sit, stay*, and *come* were all quickly learned, though he seemed disinterested in repeating the command once perfected.

They also played tracking games. She rubbed raw meat on small pieces of leather and hid them. Each time, he smelled and tracked them, making a game of each one as he found it. As his abilities increased, so would the distances between the bait. Eventually, she would bury the lures, sharpening his skills and creating a more challenging game.

Proud of the wolf pup and the progress they'd made, she smiled and watched him work. A terrible thought crossed her mind as she remembered her promise to Duncan. After spending only a few weeks with Trean, she wasn't sure she could kill him if unsuccessful in his training.

The orphaned pup had wormed his way into her heart. Pushing the dreadful thought from her mind, Anna's determination to triumph multiplied.

After finishing their games, he followed her, always shadowing her, eager to please. She knew he considered her his pack, and slept at the foot of her bed at night, unwilling to be parted from her for long.

Anna turned her attention to the stable. Most of the horses had taken to Trean like the other dogs around the keep and did not fear him as a wolf. She visited Orion, enjoying his company. He now serviced the MacGregor mares as they came into season. Next spring would be fruitful. She would have plenty of new foals to deliver and eventually train. Enjoying her time at the stables, she only returned to the keep to wash for supper once the light of the day waned.

Anna blushed every time her eyes caught Duncan's. With his knowing smile, he told her he, too, thought of their afternoon tryst. She thought about how many such encounters they would have in the future. His words of more to share and explore haunted and excited her.

Anna had a better idea of what to expect, though she almost wished for ignorance. What had passed between them made her crave him more than she could fathom. Every thought seemed to lead back to lying naked in his arms. She now understood why young maidens were not allowed to be alone with their suitors. It also explained why all knowledge of what went on between married couples remained closely guarded until the day of the wedding.

The next morning, the men gathered around the training yard. Anna asked about the first day of their game. While stories were told, a foul odor surrounded the group. In ones and twos, they moved away from Duff, eventually leaving him standing alone.

Anna sniffed the air near the giant. "Duff, why do you smell like rancid fat?"

Looking sheepish, he shuffled his feet before answering. "'Tis a home remedy, milady."

"A home remedy for what? Only the Black Death would be horrid enough to make one wear such a putrid substance."

"Me ma makes it for sore muscles and sprains."

This prompted chuckles from the group. Trying to keep a straight face, Anna glanced around, noticing what she hadn't seen before. All stood rigidly, and many unconsciously rubbed wrists and elbows.

Understanding dawned as she realized she stood before a bunch of stiff-necked Highlanders. Of course, they did not yield as instructed. They would fight any lock or throw, causing themselves more harm than necessary. By resisting, they undermined the exercise. Shaking her head, Anna swallowed the rebuke she wished to deliver. The situation required a different strategy.

"How many would benefit from a balm for sore muscles and joints? I make an effective one which is a bit easier on the nose."

No one was willing to admit to such a need. "Fine, then. I am calling a halt to the game. If you cannot take instruction and yield as ordered, I have no choice. The laird will not be pleased to learn his elite guard is incapacitated because of my doing. Besides, no one learns when resistance is given."

Amid the grumbles, Iain spoke up. "If we give ye our word to yield when we feel the lock engaged, may we continue?"

She glared at him. "Your word then?"

"Aye, milady."

Staring down the rest of the group with narrowed eyes, she did not relent until they gave a collective, "Aye."

She nodded once in return. "We will go another day and see. I expect all those who experience pain in their joints will see me afterward for a proper balm as part of the agreement. No exceptions. And Duff, you are to throw that noxious unguent out. No disrespect to your mother," she added with a smile.

"None taken, milady." He offered a gap-toothed smile in return.

While they worked, Anna noticed the laird at a distance, standing under the large oak with another man she couldn't see well enough to recognize. Though not as tall as the laird, he was broader. Before the group finished for the morning, Duncan joined his father and the stranger. Calling a halt for the noon break, she reminded the men they'd given their word.

Walking toward Duncan, Anna stopped, stunned.

"Grandfather?"

A large grin spread across his craggy face as he opened his arms to her. She immediately ran into his embrace.

"*Tigh Beaghan*. My favorite *Tigh Beaghan*," he said, his voice thick with emotion.

Anna wiped away tears of happiness. "But Grandfather, I am your only granddaughter."

"Aye. And that is what makes ye my favorite." His eyes danced as he laughed out loud and hugged her again.

The MacGregor men left, giving them privacy.

"You are here. Why are you here?" Anna couldn't believe it.

"To see with my own eyes ye are indeed well. We feared ye dead. And now I hear I am to negotiate yer marriage. I knew why ye kept turning down all those English popinjays. There is too much Scot in yer blood to settle for anything less. I also came to tell ye that ye have a choice. If ye love this man, and want to be his wife, then ye shall have my blessing. But dinnae marry because ye think ye must. Say the word, and we will take ye back. Back to yer family."

Anna opened her mouth to speak, only to snap it shut when her grandfather held up his hand.

"The earl may wield power on his side of the border, but he will find more than he bargained for if he tries to cross into Scotland to find ye. The group of men he sent after ye when ye fled never lived to see English soil again. Most of the border clans know of yer fate, and have sworn to protect ye if ye return."

Anna's tears returned, knowing so many were willing to shield her.

"Yer da was an Englishman respected by all. 'Twas a rare thing amongst our people. Because the earl killed Braxton and my grandson, then forced my only granddaughter to flee blindly into the unknown, he earned naught but more enemies."

To be in her grandfather's arms again reminded her of the love she had known all her life. Tears of joy seeped as she held him tight.

"Ye should have come to me, Sprite, I would have protected ye," he whispered in her ear.

Hearing his childhood name for her warmed Anna's heart. "I

knew not who attacked us. After losing father and Edrick, I could not bring those enemies to you."

He held her in front of him and clucked his tongue at her response. "I cannae call ye Sprite any longer. Ye are a woman grown."

A smile spread across Anna's face. "I will always be your Sprite, Grandfather. I do love Duncan and wish to marry. The first week here was difficult, but they have treated me with nothing but kindness since."

Nodding, he held out an arm for her. Anna kissed him on a weathered cheek, then took his offered arm and walked back to the keep. As they passed through the main hall, the group of Elliot men at the table rose as one and surrounded her in greeting. Anna was elated to see her clansmen. Of the twenty men her grandfather brought, an uncle and four cousins were part of the group. With a nod of his head, Moray Elliot signaled his son, her mother's brother, to accompany him to the laird's hall, bringing Anna with him.

Anna, escorted by her uncle Gavin, walked into the smaller room. She noticed the hearth chairs placed in a circle with Duncan, Kenneth and her grandfather already seated. Kenneth gingerly rubbed his jaw, drawing her concern. She took the empty seat between Duncan and her grandfather.

"Laird, do you have a tooth troubling you? I can take a look. Perhaps an herbal posset will draw out any infection."

Kenneth smiled, which apparently hurt, as he clutched his jaw. "Nae, my teeth are fine—mayhap a bit loose. Howbeit, my jaw is sore."

Anna shot him a puzzled look.

"Yer grandda hits harder than one would think. When I told him I held ye prisoner for a sennight, he took offense."

Suddenly embarrassed, Anna muttered, "I am sorry."

Kenneth gave her a reassuring look. "Tis nothing to be sorry for. Duncan would have done the same if he thought he could have gotten away with it." The curve of his lips and the wink he gave her said there were no hard feelings.

She breathed a sigh of relief.

Starting from the time she and Edrick witnessed their home under attack, Anna recounted what transpired until she encountered the MacGregors. Apparently, the two lairds had already covered this touchy ground. She had no wish to open the topic again for fear of further hostilities. Picking up with Alain's attack, she related the rest. Duncan took up part of the tale. Both her grandfather and uncle asked questions from time to time, especially about the ambush. Each time her deeds were told, her grandfather and uncle grinned with pride.

An uncontrollable anger swept over Anna at the news the earl's men had rebuilt her home and now occupied it. She sprang from her chair and paced to the window and back. With no way to vent her rage, it slowly settled into her gut. Trying to control her breathing, Anna told herself this was not unexpected, but to hear it confirmed by family across the border somehow made it more real.

By the time she'd calmed enough to sit again, discussion of her marriage had begun and a bargain was soon struck. Much to Anna's surprise, her grandfather offered a *tocher* on her behalf. Even MacGregor seemed to be surprised by the coin.

The promise of assistance, should it be needed, was agreed upon. Five days of hard riding separated the clans, so immediate help would not be forthcoming for either. They granted permission to have the banns called immediately. Anna and Duncan would marry within three weeks. As they completed the agreement, a shiver ran through her. Whether from anticipation or fear, she couldn't say. Holding her hand, Duncan obviously felt it, sending her a reassuring look.

Uncle Gavin took his leave, along with Duncan, to see the Elliot men settled, and Anna went upstairs to wash and change for the evening meal. Though she immensely enjoyed the company of her family, she remained quiet during the meal. As they settled around the hearth after supper, Duncan asked Elliot for accounts of her childhood.

Escapades she'd long forgotten—some she wished had *stayed* forgotten—were told. Embarrassed by the wildness of her youth, she fidgeted, wanting to find a place to hide. After an hour of such stories, the evening grew late, and her tolerance for embarrassing tales had been exceeded. Excusing herself, Anna kissed her grandfather and uncle then made for her room, feeling Duncan's gaze on her.

Chapter Twenty-three

Duncan offered his arm. "Allow me to escort ye."

With a tired smile, Anna accepted his assistance and climbed the stairs of the tower.

"Do ye wish to speak of what disturbed ye during the marriage negotiations?"

She heard in his voice the soft, reasonable tone he used when he knew her to be upset. "I am surprised you noticed."

He pulled her into an alcove at the second floor landing. "As yer husband, 'tis my job to know when ye are upset and to soothe when I can."

Anna offered a small smile at the fact her braw Highlander possessed a gentle side. "Part of it is the old fear. You will own me as you do your horse. Though I trust you, I struggle with the notion of being someone's possession, at the mercy of their whims or mood."

Smoothing the lines in her brow, he stroked her forehead and hair for a time in silence. "Aye. If I were to be yer chattel, I would feel the same. Ye know I value ye more than my own life, aye? And a wee bit more than my horse." Humor seeped into his voice.

She smiled and nodded.

"Yes, more than your horse." *But more than your own life?* She wished to believe him as strongly as she needed her next breath. The fact remained, she was uncertain. Part of her still believed he would put her aside at some point, or fail to understand and encourage her warrior spirit. She could not bear the thought of losing him or being forced into a role she hated.

"I know ye view our marriage as me taking ownership of ye. In part, 'tis true. However, I see ye as a gift from above, one I dinnae deserve. I am to love and cherish ye, giving up my life, if it comes to it, to protect ye. Some things ye do run counter to those desires. Like charging those men who attacked us by yerself. Ye almost caused my death when ye did. I never want to experience again the feeling of utter helplessness as I stood wounded, unable to protect ye."

Since he mentioned this before, she knew it was important to him. His eyes hardened.

"My mother said she told ye of my brother."

Anna nodded.

"'Twas the same feeling when I watched him disappear under the flow of the river. I couldnae bear to lose ye as I lost him." Unmistakable despair colored his voice. "If I lose my patience or temper with ye, 'twill be because ye make it hard for me to honor my vows to ye and yer family. The *tocher* yer grandda offers is a symbol of payment for my protection and care. Yer grandda and I had a long talk this morning whilst ye instructed the men. He wished to know the man his only granddaughter chose. He also wanted me to know how precious ye are to him. I made it clear I understood how rare ye are."

Anna absorbed his words, weighing them against her fears. Hearing him speak of Callum and his sense of loss helped her better understand his need to protect her.

"I do understand and believe what you say. I also recognize the folly of charging a group of men by myself. But you must understand I feel the same about you. I did so to protect you from further harm."

"What is the rest, then?"

She settled her hands around his waist, nestling her forehead into his neck. She could not tell him the whole nagging fear, so she told part.

"You admire my abilities, but part of you wants me to stay home, tending your keep and raising our children. I fear losing too much of myself in marriage, of coming to resent you over time because of it. Or, I hold onto my independence and have you resent me from worrying about my well-being. Neither of those futures is desirable. I know not how to find the middle ground. There are no couples like us to compare or consult." She glanced up, desperately needing to see his reaction.

Again, long moments passed before he answered. "When ye bought Orion, what was he like?"

She scrunched her brow, immediately recognizing the direction of his question. "He was a wild and powerful colt, not willing to submit to any commands."

"And did ye take his braw spirit and break it during yer training?"

"You know I did not. We worked together. With guidance and patience he came to trust me."

Anna shook her head at Duncan's grin, knowing he'd maneuvered her into the place he wanted. "So 'tis about trust," he said. "Ye say ye trust me. Do ye trust me enough to believe I willnae make such demands on ye or break yer spirit?"

The perceptiveness of his question pierced through her. "Truly, I do not know. I want to say I trust you that much, but I cannot in all honesty say I do without hesitation."

"Ah, then do ye wish to wait? I dinnae want ye to feel pressured into marriage, in spite of our families and signed agreements."

She immediately rejected this idea. "No. I *want* to be your wife. I do not wish to wait. 'Tis not just the pleasure we share, but the joy and contentment I feel when I am at your side. I want to go to bed with you, to wake up with you, to share everything with you."

"Then I need to continue to inspire yer trust whilst ye develop more faith in me, aye?"

She nodded. "I would like us to speak of specifics though. Your reaction to my teaching the men has left me skittish. I did not like the look in your eyes. I would like to know what you think I should and should not do."

He took a deep breath. "Anna, I realized early on, like Orion, demanding yer submission or obedience would do more harm than good. I am trying to walk a different path with ye. Howbeit, I am just a man. Seeing another touching ye, seeing how they look at ye…there are limits to my tolerance. I know ye need to keep yer skills honed, but I need yer assurance I have naught to worry about. I will swear to do my best to keep from killing anyone who touches ye." His voice lightened, but she knew he only partly jested.

"I do understand, and have agreed to keep a respectful distance. I will never do anything to dishonor you. It is easy to imagine we will have our fair share of arguments. I would like to be more strategic than merely stumbling from one conflict to another."

He chuckled. "A battle plan, then?"

Smacking his chest, she glared at him. "Do you mock me?"

He offered up his hands in a peaceful gesture. "*Pax boidheach laoch.* I but admire yer application of combat strategies to our union. Very well, what do ye propose?"

Satisfied with his response, Anna settled against him once more. She inhaled deeply, smelling him, savoring his warmth. This, this was the reason she didn't want to wait.

"What if we listed activities we can both live with?"

"Sounds wise. And what of those items on yer list that dinnae appear on mine?"

She lowered her hand to the front of his kilt, finding the hardness there. She gave him a gentle squeeze and answered in a teasing voice, "I shall convince you once we reach our bedchamber." Hearing him groan with pleasure as she traced the tip of his manhood with her finger made her wish they didn't have to wait three weeks.

"I applaud yer superior tactics. If ye intend on taking such battles to our bed, I fear I will be forced into surrender every time."

She leaned against his chest and sighed deeply. She listened to his breathing, his arms firm around her shoulders.

"Thank you for understanding and speaking with me about this. I know part of my fear has nothing to do with you. I am convinced you will be the best of husbands, and I will soon wonder why I dwelt on this foolishness. There was something about hearing the bargaining, having the banns called, and setting a date which made it more real."

Duncan kneaded the muscles of her neck and shoulders and Anna melted beneath his touch.

"Ye have experienced a number of difficulties in a short period of time. 'Tis expected. I only want to make sure ye have no doubts before I make ye mine forever." Wrapping an arm around her, he escorted her to Nessa's room, where they shared a sweet kiss and said goodnight.

After a few days, word of their training game spread. Men who were not part of the laird's guard expressed a desire to learn and participate. Anna's confidence grew, knowing she contributed to the fighting skills of the clan. She'd been attacked twice, and each encounter only half-hearted. It made her wonder if Duncan threatened the men after all.

Anna received word the weavers had finished her woolens, and went to fetch them. Trying them on, she reveled in the luxurious softness of the Merino wool. Other than silk, she'd not felt anything so fine before. They would help keep her warm when the colder months arrived. She chatted with the ladies, who seemed genuinely glad to see her. Not stopping their work, the talk soon turned to the upcoming wedding. After answering their questions, Anna thanked them and walked out the door.

She immediately noticed four of the guard standing across the way—men who weren't present before she arrived. Iain stood amongst them, and she wondered briefly why they were there. Out of the corner of her eye, Anna detected movement. Dropping her parcel, she turned to face whoever approached.

An arm grabbed her around the neck from behind, and she reacted instinctively by clutching his arm to prevent a choke. She then dropped her right knee to the ground, spiraling her body to the left. The man flew over her right shoulder, landing him flat on his back with a satisfying thud.

His arm still in her grip, she pulled it straight from his body, draping her right leg over his chest. With her left leg at his head, she trapped him on his back. Still on the ground, she stretched his arm out at the wrist, raising her hips. Her move locked his arm at the elbow, causing it to slightly dislocate.

"Yield!" he shouted, as he slapped the ground with his free hand.

Immediately she released her hold, hopped up and assisted him to his feet. She glanced around, noting Iain and the others who had gathered to watch. They all grinned widely, apparently aware of the ambush. She addressed her attacker. "We have not worked chokes from behind yet, Bran. What made you think to attack thus?"

He ducked his head. "I knew ye would defeat me anyway, so I thought to be sneaky."

His answer earned a laugh from the small crowd. As Anna dusted herself off, she spotted Duncan standing several feet away, his arms crossed, the look on his face a cross between rage and disgust. She'd not seen this particular expression before, and her smile faded. Following her gaze, one by one the men took a step back.

Not knowing what else to do, Anna complimented Bran on a good attack, then retrieved her parcel from the ground. Facing Duncan, she waited for a response. When he said nothing, she swallowed her pride and walked toward him.

"You are angry with me. May I ask why?" She kept her voice calm, not reacting to his obvious ire.

"Ye roll around on the ground with one of my men in front of the entire village like a common *siursach,* and ye wonder why I'm angry?" His voice echoed off the surrounding buildings.

At his words, Anna heard the sharp intake of breath from people nearby. Keeping the barest control on her anger, Anna swallowed a curse, spun on her heel and strode toward the stables.

Once at the barn, Anna threw her package against the wall and immediately saddled Orion. *How dare he call me a whore! If he'd seen the whole thing, then he'd know I did nothing wrong. I responded to the attack swiftly and put an end to it. If he thinks he can treat me thus, humiliating me in front of all, he is a fool, and I am a bigger one for agreeing to marry him.*

She jerked the saddle's girth and dropped the stirrup. *I should call the wedding off and accept Grandfather's invitation to return home. I will not tolerate such treatment.* Trean emerged from Orion's stall and pushed his muzzle into her hand. She stroked his head and led Orion through the stable door. Mounting, she sped to the loch, Trean on their heels.

Storming from the village, Duncan loosed a roar of frustration. He knew as soon as he released the words, he had erred grievously. What devil had come over him? Always the one in control, he found himself frequently out of control where Anna was concerned. He knew she did nothing wrong. When Bran surprised her, she took control of the situation. She made no more contact than necessary, nor did she linger on the ground, rising immediately after he yielded.

The jealous rage which possessed him cared naught, hitting him swiftly and completely unexpected. What madness bewitched him to treat the woman he loved in such a way? He'd called her a common whore in front of the men and the village when the previous night he'd asked her to trust him. The anger in her eyes was something he hadn't seen since her capture. He knew better than to approach her now—it would only make matters worse. She needed time to cool off and so did he.

If he did not wrestle his jealousy under control, he knew he risked losing her—if he hadn't already. Her grandda had made clear his offer to take her south to Elliot lands on the border. Fear of her leaving clawed at his gut, and he dropped to his haunches, head in hands. The pull of clan and family presented a very real threat.

If she chose to leave, he'd have no one to blame but himself. He knew he could never allow that to happen and would have no choice but to follow until he convinced her to come back to him. But what would she come back to? A husband so jealous she would never earn his trust? What woman would willingly choose such a fate?

Chapter Twenty-four

*F*or Anna, the loch had become a place of solace, somewhere to think. Staring into the blue-green waters usually brought a feeling of peace, but today was different. She couldn't get Duncan's reaction and words out of her mind. What had she done to earn his mistrust, his anger? He knew she would not dishonor him. He'd witnessed two warriors honing their skills, the way iron sharpens iron—nothing more.

How can I give myself to a man who thinks so little of me? A man who would say such a foul thing to me in public, in front of the men I train? She tried to view from his perspective, imagine a situation where she would discover him on the ground with another woman, but couldn't conjure a fair comparison. Her mind could not imagine him thus.

Surely they could come to some sort of compromise. *Shite! I do not want a compromise!* Hurt and anger bubbled at his reaction, at his lack of trust. Perhaps he would walk away from her sooner than she suspected, disgusted with her lack of delicate feminine skills.

Trean's low growl broke into her musings. She followed his intent gaze to see a dozen men emerge from the trees. A glance at Orion told her she stood no chance of reaching him before she was surrounded. One man leveled a crossbow at her head. A snarled curse rolled beneath her breath as she recognized two men from Alain's group. The others she'd never seen before.

Shite!

"Look what we 'ave 'ere, lads. An' all alone. MacGregor ne'er has known 'ow to protect what's 'is. Come easy, lass, and we can do this without bloodshed."

Reaching for swords not there, Anna slowly dropped her arms in feigned resignation. As she did, the man with the crossbow cautiously approached, a length of rope in his hands. She swiftly drew the dagger from her boot in one hand, and her *sgian dubh* from her sleeve in the other. She slashed him across the throat before he could react, pushing his dying body back to prepare for the next attack.

The men scrambled back in an uproar. "The cat has claws!"

Trean drew his lips back, bared his teeth, and launched himself at the closest foe. The man swung his sword and the wolf pup fell hard with a yelp. Anna took a step toward him, but another man picked up the crossbow, threatening her. Dropping to the ground in a forward roll, Anna popped up in front of him. She knocked the crossbow away, then drove both daggers into his neck. Two down, ten left—hopeless odds, she knew. But more would die before she went quietly. Two in front of her drew swords, their faces murderous as they glanced at their fallen comrades. A blur of movement to her side drew her attention. Before she could react, a blow to her head ended her resistance.

Duncan spotted Orion's empty stall and knew Anna's destination. He waited at the stables for her to return, ready to apologize, beg her forgiveness, and agree to anything she asked. All he knew was the world was not right, that he wasn't whole once she left his side. After two hours of waiting, what little patience he possessed fled. As he saddled his horse, Orion walked into the stables alone. Every nerve in Duncan's body lit as if scraped by a hot iron. He raced to the training fields, calling for the guard to ride with him.

They quickly arrived at the loch and found signs of a struggle and two men dead. Duncan froze, unable to breathe or think. The angry words he spoke rang in his ears, damning him with every breath. Now she'd been taken, no doubt injured, as she would never go willingly. He couldn't bear the pain threatening to consume him. Callum's screams for help rang in his ears as he again saw his brother's head disappear below the turbulent waters for the last time.

Tavish's voice broke through. "Captain, what do ye want done?"

Duncan scrubbed his face with the heels of his hand and considered the possibilities for a moment before answering. "Send a man back and report to the laird, the rest on me now!"

With as much as a two-hour head start, he spurred *Lasair* as if a pack of *cu sith* nipped at his tail. The men who took Anna rode hard, making their trail easy to follow. Duncan needed no tracks to know their destination.

Once Duncan's men realized what had happened, who held her, they required no further incentive. They rode as one, stopping only long enough to rest and water their horses. Duncan was humbled by the loyalty Anna had earned, and shamed knowing his men understood the reason she'd been alone when captured. The hard, angry looks he received said they knew of his actions, and also knew she would bear the brutal cost.

By the time MacNairn keep came into view, gates had been lowered behind the group of riders they'd been chasing, sealing off the approach to the castle. Duncan felt the black shudders of rage threatening to overtake him as he surveyed the shuttered keep. To his surprise, Trean limped along the trail just ahead. Duncan reined his horse beside the injured beast. Blood was visible on one shoulder and he favored his front leg.

"Here, laddie, let me see to yer wound." He reached for the pup, but Trean growled in response, backing away from him. The cut on his shoulder appeared to be superficial, and Duncan let him go. Anna's wolf had pronounced judgment upon him, also. Trean paced just inside the tree line, his limp and mournful whine heaping another measure of guilt on Duncan's heart.

He turned back to his men. "Tavish, send two men back to the laird and report what has happened. The rest remain here and watch. Iain and I will travel to the Stewart laird. If it takes my last breath, we will raze this heap of stones to the ground."

Digging his heels into his horse's side, Duncan drove *Lasair* to his limit, arriving at his grandda's keep hours later, both he and his steed sweat-soaked and spent.

His grandfather granted him an immediate audience, fire lighting his eyes as Duncan related Anna's capture by the MacNairns. Aeneas Stewart rose from his chair in the great hall.

"Assemble the men. Load the siege weapons into their wagons. 'Tis time to put an end to MacNairn!"

His roar sent everyone flying into motion, giving Duncan hope he'd hardly dared look for. He'd been but a lad the last time he'd seen his grandda this angry.

It took a full day to gather the necessary equipment and supplies for the siege. Before they finished, his da and the MacGregor men arrived at the Stewart keep. Riding as hard as the wagons allowed, it took another day and a half for the gathered force to reach the MacNairn fortress.

Anna floated in nothingness. She heard faint voices at the edge of her mind and felt an odd sensation. Something about the voices sounded urgent, insistent, demanding her attention. She wanted nothing more than to resist them, fading back into the blissful state she enjoyed. After some time passed, the odd sensation returned again and with it, the command of voices that would not leave her alone.

Perhaps if she answered them, they would allow her to retreat back into the velvety blackness. Deciding to awake long enough to respond, Anna struggled to reach the surface of consciousness where her body awaited. She found herself deeper than she realized, frightened at how far she had gone. Somehow she knew she wasn't far from the place of no returning.

The strange sensation repeated, this time followed by a sputtering sound.

"Ah, she finally awakens."

The voice was closer, and the strange sensation she now realized was someone splashing water on her. Immediately, a burning sensation shot from her head to her toes. Anna struggled to open her eyes, gain her bearings, to understand what had happened, but her body refused to obey her.

"Hello, my pet. Welcome to yer new home."

Squinting, Anna attempted to see the speaker in the semi-darkness, tried to make sense of his words as pain threatened to pull her back to unconsciousness. She hissed at the intensity of it, a throbbing stab of hundreds of needles. Was she on fire? She looked for evidence of flames but saw none. Surely she'd been captured and brought to the Earl of Northumberland's castle, but the man in front of her was neither the earl nor his son. His long red hair held streaks of gray. His face suggested he would be a few years older than her father. More importantly, she recognized he spoke Gaelic, not English.

"New home?" Her weak, slurred words sounded foreign to her ears.

"Aye, my pet. Ye are finally home. Soon we shall be wed." His voice held eagerness—his eyes, madness.

Something about his statement proved more than her mind could process, and Anna slipped back into the silky darkness.

"Ye great idiot! I wanted her brought back unharmed, not brained! Tis already been two days. At this rate, 'twill be a sennight before she is well enough to stand on her own to make her vows!"

Shrinking at his laird's anger, the man held up his hands in an effort to pacify his chief. "She had already killed two men, m'laird. I dinnae want anyone to run her through in revenge. Ne'er had to knock a lass cold before. I dinnae know 'ow hard to hit her."

'Twas true enough. This hellcat killed two of the men he'd sent to fetch her, and had killed others before. Stories about the lass hadn't been exaggerated. His plans, however, required her to be awake with enough of her wits about her to respond to the priest, with no time to wait for her to convalesce. Even now men searched for her—of this, he was certain.

Once the vows were spoken and the marriage consummated, he

didn't care who knew. He only needed to keep her away from MacGregor until then.

The pain in Anna's head demanded attention. Darkness gave way to muted light that pierced her eyes. Remembering the struggle at the loch, details of her abduction came trickling back. With Herculean effort, she pushed herself upright. She gently probed the side of her head, seeking the source of pain, and encountered a three-inch gash on her temple, the rough, puckered skin poorly sewn shut.

No salve had been applied. By the smell and looks of this hole they'd locked her in, infection seemed imminent. Slowly, she glanced around, blinking to get her eyes working correctly, fatigue and pain sapping her strength. The cell she sat in was one of many. With thick iron bars separating each, they were little more than cages. Her movement must have alerted a guard, as activity sounded outside the door.

A foul-smelling, unkempt man wearing a short sword and set of keys slid a loaf of bread under a slot in the bars. He placed a tall ewer of water through the bars and grunted at her. She didn't move or react, but watched him saunter out the door. Drawing on inner strength, she reached for the bread.

The hard bread had spots of gray and green mold. Not knowing the day, Anna could not recall the last time she put anything in her mouth. Even the look of moldy bread awakened a hungry beast threatening to claw its way out of her belly. She picked away the mold, broke the loaf and inspected it for worms or weevils. Finding none, she forced herself to eat. Sniffing the water before she tasted it, she took a long drink and washed down the stale bread.

After an hour or so passed, the outer door opened again. The older man she'd seen before strode in. This time, two armed guards accompanied him.

"Are ye awake for certain now, my dear?" His grin revealed a mouthful of brown, crooked teeth that matched his sallow, pocked skin.

Anna stared at him for a moment, trying to form words. "Who are you, and why have you imprisoned me?" Her voice was no more than a dry croak.

An evil twist spread across his face. "We are to be wed, my pet."

She stared at him in disbelief, her breath hitching. "Wed? I am betrothed to Duncan MacGregor. The banns have been called. Who are you?"

His smile widened into something more sinister. "Aye, well ye are here, now. Our marriage will give ye the opportunity to replace what ye took from me."

"I have no idea what you speak of. I will never marry you."

His smile hardened into a sneer. "Ye will marry me and bear my heir." The effort he had made to remain calm dropped, his tone a snarl. "Take her."

The two guards placed manacles on her ankles and wrists, and half-walked, half-dragged her out of the dungeon. Her head throbbed and dizziness overwhelmed her, making her unsteady on her cold, bare feet.

They ascended a long stair, through a heavy door, arriving outside into the full sun. The brightness blinded her, increasing the stabbing pain in her head. As her eyes slowly adjusted to the light, Anna saw they walked toward a chapel. She realized his intent, but knew he couldn't legally force her to marry. They would have to kill her. In her present condition, it would be a short journey to death.

The man faced her. "Consider yer words carefully, my pet. Yer choices will decide how ye are treated from here on. Either way, ye *will* bear my heir—that much is certain. A legitimate heir is preferable, but a bastard will do." His lips returned to their sneer, and his over-bright eyes proclaimed his madness.

Anna blanked her expression, saying nothing. As they entered the stone structure, a priest stood at the altar. His expression went from one of nervousness to horror when he took in her appearance and shackles.

Anna's captor inclined his head to the priest. "Father, 'tis time."

The priest glanced quickly at the man, swallowing whatever words came to him, and began the ceremony.

Anna was caught in her worst nightmare, forced into marriage to an evil man who only wanted her to bear his son. Closing her ears to the priest's words, she clung to her love for Duncan. She chose to ignore their bitter parting, replaying only pleasant events in her mind, controlling her instinct to panic.

"Do ye, Baen MacNairn, solemnly vow…"

MacNairn! She was captured by the MacNairn laird? What he'd said earlier now made sense. He'd somehow discovered she'd killed his son, Adair, when he'd stolen Nessa. Her gaze locked onto his face. He gave her toothy smile.

The priest turned from MacNairn and now spoke to her. "Do ye?"

Steeling her gaze, Anna answered, "No, I do not. I would rather die than marry a beast such as this."

The priest's eyes bugged outward in terror and he shrank back.

MacNairn turned to the holy man. "Thank ye, father. Yer services are no longer required." Grabbing her arm, he roughly dragged Anna back to her cell. Throwing her down, he slammed the door. "Rot in here a few more days. Ye will soon beg me to marry ye." He spat on her, turned and left.

Chapter Twenty-five

*B*y the end of the third day, Duncan ensured all were in place and ready for attack. Sweeping through the village took less than a day, as MacNairn had left few soldiers to protect his people. Most of his warriors gathered behind his stone walls, guarding his worthless hide. The villagers gave little resistance once they saw the size of the combined force mounted against them, and several voiced relief to discover an army had come to remove their laird from his fortress, welcoming the end of his rule of neglect and cruelty.

It took all the discipline Duncan possessed to stay in position outside the walls, knowing Anna was imprisoned there. He feared he would lose his mind from worry, anxiety gnawing a fiery hole in his belly. MacNairn had held his Anna, his heart, for four days. Anything could have happened to her, if indeed she still lived.

The lairds and captains assembled for a meeting. After much discussion, Kenneth MacGregor took control and they formulated a plan.

"We will wait until midnight to begin the assault. With four trebuchets positioned around the walls, the attack will come from three sides. Two will focus on the front gate and wall where the main MacNairn force gathers. They will think we try to weaken their defenses and force entry there. The other two will focus on the tower and buildings from the east and the west.

"Duncan will lead twenty men over the south wall with ropes and grappling hooks. The smoke and fire should create enough confusion to mask yer approach. Find Anna then leave the way ye came. We will avoid the back of the keep."

Duncan felt the gaze of all three lairds.

"Five of his group will be my men," Elliot added, his voice leaving no room for refusal.

Duncan nodded.

The plan was simple enough. Burn MacNairn to the ground and free Anna while doing so. Duncan picked a score of men to accompany him, including fifteen of the MacGregor men Anna had trained. The five Elliot men included her uncle and cousins. Now, only the torturous wait until midnight remained.

When Anna next woke, she found leather straps attached to the posts of the bed bound her wrists. Dressed only in her short shift and braies, she knew her helpless position spoke of MacNairn's intent. Shivers of revulsion rippled down her spine to think of the man's hands on her as he undressed her while she lay unconscious. With no soreness between her legs, or sign of blood on the bed she could see, she knew nothing carnal had happened—yet. A hasty scan of the small room showed no sign of her belongings or any other clothing.

A loud commotion echoed beyond the curtain wall, bringing shouts and clamoring from within the keep. *Elliots? MacGregors?* Stark fear shot through her. *MacNairn will not let me leave alive—or unmolested.* Her gaze cut to the door, half-expecting him to charge the room, intent on taking his anger out on her before he killed her. It was doubtful she would live long enough to be rescued. Whatever their plan of attack, she knew if she didn't find some way to escape her current situation, the clans would be too late.

Though the night was cool, perspiration trailed down her face and her body shivered. She feared infection had set in the poorly treated wound, further limiting the amount of time she had to escape before she became disabled by weakness.

The new moon offered scant light, but provided a shadowed

covering to hide her if she could escape this chamber. She shifted again on the bed and discovered she could bend enough to reach the bonds with her teeth. In a frenzy of hope, she struggled to untie the first, then used her free hand to quickly untie the other, rubbing blood and warmth back into her cut and bruised wrists. Retying the leather, she reluctantly slipped her hands into the loosened bonds and lay back on the bed, waiting for the devil or one of his lackeys to appear.

It wasn't long before voices sounded in the corridor. The MacNairn stationed a guard at the door, then placed the key in the lock. As he entered the room, Anna closed her eyes to slits, feigning sleep. He loomed over her and she felt his presence, smelled it, suffocated in it. Every muscle in her body screamed for her to attack and it took all the discipline she possessed to remain relaxed.

Climbing onto the bed with her, MacNairn straddled her hips, crouching above her on all fours. Anna felt his hot, vile breath on her face as he leaned forward and licked her cheek. Without warning, she thrust her hips upward in a violent motion, throwing him forward into the stone wall, face first. Blood splattered warm across her skin.

He moaned, stunned from the impact. Quickly, she slipped her wrists from the loops. Bringing her legs up around his head, she trapped his neck and one of his arms in a vise-like grip. She pressed her legs tighter, the pressure on his neck cutting off the blood flowing to his brain.

Unable to utter more than a guttural protest, he flailed about, throwing them off the bed, almost dislodging her hold with the fall. Anna hit the edge of the bed frame hard, and a sharp, stabbing pain lanced through her side. She ignored the pain and flexed, squeezing tighter as his face turned a dark purple-red. His body flopped forward as he passed out, and she released him to scramble quickly onto his back. Grabbing his chin in one hand and his hair the other, she twisted his head with all the force she could muster. The resulting crack sent MacNairn to meet his son in the afterlife.

She listened for the guard to react to the sounds of their thrashing about, but realized he likely believed his laird to be simply enjoying himself—vigorously. Dismissing the thought with a snarl of disgust, she rechecked the room for clothing, finding none. Left with no option, she took the laird's. Dressed in a leine that stank of him, Anna forced the revulsion out of her mind as she put on his kilt, buckling his broad leather belt about her much smaller waist, and more importantly, snatched his *sgian dubh*.

Looking closely, she recognized the small blade Duncan had given her with the MacGregor crest. No doubt MacNairn had considered her dirk a sort of trophy. She shoved her feet into his boots, but they were much too large, more of a hindrance than help, and she kicked them aside.

Calming herself for the next part, she made sure MacNairn's body lay hidden by the bed. Lifting the bar from the door, she opened it only a crack. Dagger drawn, she crouched behind the portal.

The guard stole a look into the room. "Laird?" he called tentatively. Placing a hand on his dirk, he stepped into the room and took a sudden step toward the bed before he halted. Springing from behind the door, Anna kicked the back of his leg, driving one knee to the floor. A quick draw of her dagger across his throat sent him sprawling, bleeding his life out into the rotted reeds. She shut the door and barred it, kneeling to unbuckle the guard's belt and collect his weapons. In addition to his *sgian dubh,* he carried a bollock dirk almost as long as her short swords, and a broadsword of questionable quality.

Out of breath from exertion and weak from fever and lack of food and water, she fought a wave of dizziness as she wiped sweat from her brow. With the immediate danger eliminated, she attempted a deep, calming breath, but the pain in her ribs cut like a blade. She hissed through the agony and waited for it to pass, then strapped on every weapon, feeling more confident now that she was armed.

She glanced out the window as the noise outside rose. From the distance to the ground, she appeared to be on the second level of a three-level tower with a wood-and-beam structure above her. Searching the guard's sporran, she withdrew a large flask of whisky.

After opening the shutters on the window to allow more air, Anna piled the small wooden table and two chairs atop the bed. She used the whisky to soak an old tapestry hanging on one wall. The top of the moth-eaten fabric reached high enough for flames to ignite the floor above. She emptied the rest of the contents of the flask on the heather-stuffed mattress, first lighting the tapestry, then the mattress, with the candle before exiting the room.

Checking the hallway, she inched her way to the stair, sword and dagger in hand, each step feeling as though a knife pressed deep into her side. Closing her mind to the pain, Anna stopped in an alcove to listen for footfalls and voices. Nothing within the keep made a sound. All noise came from outside. The stairs ended in a large hall filled with tables, benches and a large hearth. She found it empty.

The double doors stood ajar, allowing the sounds of battle at the walls inside. A glance around the bailey showed no activity, though the top of the walls were thick with MacNairn warriors armed with bows, most concentrating on the main gate. She scanned the wall and spotted a small postern gate unguarded from below. Only two men stood above it.

Needing an additional diversion and way out, Anna silently made her way to the stables, sticking to the shadows along the way. She had to move quickly, as the fire in the tower would soon alert the men. Her muscles protested, echoing the pain in her side and head. Dizziness threatened to take over, but she willed it back. Slipping through a side door, she entered the stables.

The horses stamped their nervousness, sensing the tension in the air from the battle raging outside. Stalking the length of the stables, she spotted a young man of no more than ten and two summers on duty, his attention on the window. Not wanting to seriously injure him, she quietly approached from behind.

She struck a blow to the side of his neck with the flat edge of her hand, rendering him unconscious. Grasping his shoulders, she dragged the lad out the door and into the bailey. She grabbed a bridle from a hook and fitted a large, dark horse. Leading him to the rear of the stables, she opened each stall along the way, allowing the horses to walk out the large double doors.

The score or so horses seemed confused to be free and entered the yard slowly. Anna tossed a lantern into a large stack of hay at the back of the stables, then led her horse outside. She clasped his bridle tightly and led him toward the unwatched smaller gate, the rest of the horses milling behind her.

She picked the rusted lock, then jammed the guard's smaller dagger into the upper hinge, bending the blade slightly, leaving the gate wedged open. The fires at the stables and tower grew larger, the men's shouts warning her they'd been spotted. Forcing herself onto her horse's back, she struggled upright, gasping at the pain in her side. The fires further agitated the horses, and they stampeded, neighing loudly in alarm. Discovering the open gate, they funneled out of the yard as fast as the small opening allowed.

Pressing against the neck of her horse, Anna kept to the middle of the herd, hidden by the mass of frightened horseflesh. Once outside the gates, she rode directly to the edge of the forest a few hundred yards away. Reaching the shelter of the trees, she halted and glanced toward the keep for signs of pursuit. Only an empty field lay between her and the curtain wall. Flames lit the sky from the burning keep. She had escaped.

Though the thin moon allowed little light, she could discern formations of men on the edge of the forest, and she made her way to the closest group. More than a dozen men armed with claymores, broadswords, crossbows and axes immediately surrounded her. Several carts rested near them. She'd apparently interrupted them loading a small trebuchet. Large ceramic jars rested in the carts beside the wooden apparatus. From the smell, they contained Greek fire.

Anna slid to the ground and raised her hands, leaning against her horse's shoulder. "I am Anna of clan MacGregor, betrothed of Duncan MacGregor."

A squat, bald man, who seemed as broad as he was tall, eyed her narrowly. "If ye are who ye say ye are, why are ye dressed as a MacNairn?" His voice rumbled as gruff as his appearance.

"I had no choice of clothing and took what was available. If I can be brought to any MacGregor or Elliot, you can confirm my identity. I assume my capture is the reason forces are gathered here. Once it is known I am safely away from the MacNairn, many lives can be spared."

The bald man spat on the ground. "Aye, the Stewarts fight alongside the MacGregors and Elliots this day, but naught will save Baen MacNairn from his fate. His death is long overdue. If ye speak the truth, the MacGregor captain will be relieved his bride-to-be is free."

A warrior took her horse. Anna nodded her thanks. "The MacNairn Laird is no more. I broke the foul beast's neck with my own hands," she said, her voice harsh with pain and anger.

Her claim brought a buzz of speculation from the group of men surrounding them. The leader gave her an appraising look, suggesting he didn't believe her.

"Just the same, I will be taking yer weapons, lass."

She handed over the weapons she'd taken from the MacNairn, but hesitated in giving up her *sgian dubh*. Feeling the effects of her wounds—along with lack of food or water during captivity—bearing down on her, Anna hit her limit and staggered. She raised her chin and fixed her gaze on the man.

"This was a gift to me from Duncan MacGregor. I shall not give it up willingly."

Seeing the MacGregor crest on the hilt, the man gave a hint of a smile and nodded. He turned his back and walked toward the main body of retainers. Anna followed, along with five other men behind, one of whom led the horse she'd stolen.

They passed behind several more groups of Stewart warriors before finally arriving at a group of MacGregors.

"Lady Anna!"

She turned at the sound of her name and saw Liam break into a run toward her. Overwhelmed at finally seeing a friendly face, she stumbled the last few steps and embraced him.

"Easy now, lass. The lairds and captain will be glad to see ye safe. I told ye, attack one MacGregor, ye attack us all."

Exhausted, she staggered behind Liam as they headed toward the lairds. In the darkness, Anna couldn't see the rocks, and her bare feet suffered for it. She was past caring, and a little more pain made no difference. She heard her name spoken as others recognized her, some offering thanks for her escape. Anna was about to tell Liam she had to stop to rest when she spotted her betrothed seated on his bay horse.

"Duncan." Though it was barely a whisper, he swiveled in her direction. Before her next step, he held her in his arms.

"Thank the saints, Anna. I thought I had lost ye."

The warmth of his breath brought comfort as he buried his face in her hair. But the weight of the past sennight caught up with her and she shook uncontrollably, clutching him as if her life depended on the contact. He brushed her hair back, his fingers grazing her wound. She winced.

"Ye are hurt." His expression of relief twisted into angered concern. He pulled her closer to examine the poorly stitched gash in her head, uttering a curse when she flinched as he touched her ribs.

Tears streamed down Anna's cheeks, drowning her attempt at a brave smile. She remembered what he'd called her the day she'd left. If he thought it then, what must he think now after spending days—and nights—in MacNairn's dishonorable care?

Taking her by the hand, he led her away from the front line. She managed only a few wobbled steps before he swept her into his arms. Carrying her to a large tent many yards behind the rear of the formation, he lowered her onto a pallet, calling for food and drink. Someone brought a water skin, bread and cheese.

MacGregor entered, followed by her grandfather and a strong-looking older man she had not seen before.

"Anna, thank the heavens ye are safe." Morey Elliot addressed her first, squatting on the floor by her side. Seeing her wound in the lantern light, he asked, "How fare ye?"

"I am feverish, fear—fear my wound is infected." Still shaking, she fought back tears.

"Anna, this is Aeneas Stewart, Mairi's father, my father-by-marriage," Kenneth told her, introducing her to the older man.

The Stewart smiled warmly and nodded. "I see ye are as strong and brave a lass as my grandson tells me."

They waited patiently for Anna to gather herself before pressing for information. After taking a few drinks of water and a few bites of bread, she took as deep a breath as her injured ribs allowed and recounted what she could remember. Much of it was muddled, particularly her memories of when things happened. She had no idea how many days she'd been in MacNairn's grasp. As she described what the beast intended, Duncan stood abruptly, hands curling into fists as he paced the small space of the tent.

Anna knew better than to try to calm him, so she continued her tale. As she came to the point where MacNairn tried to take her, Duncan stiffened, his eyes closed. Mutters and gestures of disbelief filled the tent when she described how she killed the vile man. She quickly finished her story.

"'Tis my Sprite, for certain. More strength and courage than a tower full o' those bastards!" Elliot exclaimed as he hugged her gently.

Anna's body shook. She gazed at Duncan, hoping to draw from his strength. Moving to her side, he carefully cradled her in his arms, muttering tender words in her ear. She didn't know why he comforted her, only that he did.

She knew it wouldn't last. Couldn't. She wanted to relish every moment before he acknowledged her ruined. For all he knew, she'd been taken while unconscious, even though she knew she had not. Breathing in his scent, the feel of his arms around her, Anna let them imprint on her mind for when he would let her go. It would have to be enough. She knew with a certainty as strong as the mountains before her that she would never love another man like she did this one. Though he offered her kindness now, Anna knew he could no longer want her.

Her grandfather kissed her forehead and followed MacGregor out of the tent, the Stewart laird on their heels. Closing her eyes, she focused on the man whose arms surrounded her. She used his warmth to push back the fear and shock. After a while, she realized he'd not moved at all. Had the reality of events finally sunk in for him? Would he continue this comfort as he emotionally withdrew, or would he turn her over to family for tending?

It didn't take long to gain her answer. Laying her on the pallet, he took a blanket and covered her. As he sat next to her, Anna watched the twitch of tension in his body. More telling was the cold creeping in, now that he no longer held her.

Fiona pushed through the tent flaps.

"What dammed fool patched up our lady? A blind man could 'ave sewn straighter. There, there, lass. Fiona will see ye right." The healer cleaned the wound on Anna's head, then applied an herbal dressing.

"Check her ribs on the right side. I fear they are broken." Duncan's voice was low, detached, sparking a deeper chill within her.

Fiona probed her injured ribs and wrapped them tight, allowing Anna to breathe more freely. Producing a brewed tisane from a small kettle, she poured the hot liquid down Anna's throat as Duncan helped her sit.

Too exhausted and feverish to struggle, Anna allowed them to handle her as they would. Her eyes heavy and burning, never left Duncan, searching for signs of his love she craved so desperately. His stiff actions and rigid body language said everything she needed to know. Too fatigued to mourn her loss, Anna closed her eyes and allowed sleep to bear her away.

Chapter Twenty-six

Duncan had seen Anna approach, barely able to stand, supported by Liam, and had never moved so fast in his life. Though she embraced him, he knew something remained amiss. She shivered, her skin scalding hot. He pulled away to look at her and brushed her hair from her face, grazing a wound on the side of her head. Though not large, the wound appeared poorly tended and very angry.

Realizing she was hurt, he'd quickly checked the rest of her. She recoiled as he touched her ribs. Another injury. A cursory check in the dark would not do. Taking her hand, he'd walked her back toward the main tent. She took two unsteady steps before he saw her feet were bare. Enough. He scooped her up and carried her the rest of the way.

Entering the tent, Duncan laid her on a pallet of blankets and furs. He called for food, drink and Fiona, using the lantern light to examine Anna further. Beyond her head, ribs, and a vast assortment of hateful bruises, no other serious injuries appeared. Her eyes told a different story. She ate a small amount, drinking as if the bastard hadn't given her as much as a drop the entire time he'd imprisoned her.

The lairds arrived and waited until she sated her thirst and regained her composure. The weakness in her voice unsettled Duncan, but the deadness in her eyes was his undoing. Her expressive green eyes always told exactly what she felt. They snapped when angry, blazed with enthusiasm when they sparred, and darkened with passion when they loved. Now her eyes stared lifelessly from her pale, drawn face. He stood frozen, feeling as though someone had carved out his heart with a rusted blade.

As she told her tale, rage rose and licked at his body as though he were staked to a raging bonfire. Anger roiled in equal parts at MacNairn for committing such brutalities and himself for setting the circumstances in motion.

The killing of MacNairn and her daring escape would be talked about for years. When she finished her account, she could no longer speak properly, her voice failing. The lairds took their leave but Duncan had no desire to follow. Anna gazed at him, need heavy in her eyes, and he offered his arms. As she made a movement toward him, he gathered her in, gently rocking back and forth, murmuring reassurances that sounded empty to his own ears. She lay beyond comfort, but he gave what she allowed. He was uncertain how much of this night she would remember—for mercy's sake, he hoped not much.

Fiona entered the tent and gave Anna a thorough examination, clucking her tongue and muttering against the treatment she'd endured. Duncan lay Anna on the pallet and the healer first tended to her head, mixing an herbal paste to draw out the infection, then bound her ribs. Producing a steeped a tisane, they coaxed Anna to drink.

"How bad is she?" A tremor of fear wavered in his voice.

Fiona cocked her head to the side. "She appears to have cracked two ribs, but I am fashed aboot her head. The fool who tended it did her no favor. 'Twas poorly done and 'tis infected, giving her the fever. We must keep pouring this brew of feverfew and yarrow down her and keep her cool. She should be in a proper bed where we can see to her, not on a cursed battlefield."

The command and concern in Fiona's voice told him all he needed to hear. Once Anna fell asleep, Duncan left her in Fiona's care and sought his father. He found the lairds gathered with the other captains. They'd altered the battle plans now Anna was safe and MacNairn dead.

"What does the healer say?" Elliot asked.

"She needs to be in a bed so we can fully tend to her."

"Choose some men and take her home. Ye are in no shape to fight with yer mind on her condition," Kenneth said.

Duncan nodded. He summoned five men, and they moved her pallet to a cart. Trean rose from the shadows outside her tent, and Duncan gingerly placed him into the back of the cart, where he curled up at his mistress' back. The men mounted and started the trek back to Ciardun.

The day-and-a-half trip proved uneventful, though the fever never loosened its grip. Fiona stayed by Anna's side, cooling her with wet cloths when she burned, wrapping her in blankets when she was chilled. Trean repeatedly licked her face, but Anna did not regain consciousness. As soon as they arrived at the castle, Duncan carried her to his chamber. Trean trailed him up the stairs and lay in the corner by the hearth. Mairi and Nessa stripped her out of the foul clothes she wore and Duncan took and burned them, cursing MacNairn as he did. When he returned, the ladies had cleaned Anna as much as they could, ridding her of the foul MacNairn stench, and dressed her in a night shift.

"Ye must be tired and hungry from yer journey. Go, eat and bathe. We will watch," Mairi encouraged him.

Duncan's eyes did not leave Anna. "I cannae. 'Tis my fault she lies so close to death. I willnae leave her side until she is well."

Duncan felt his mother's hand on his arm. "How is this yer fault?"

He took a deep breath and confessed his actions the day Anna was abducted. Mairi didn't hide her shock. Neither spoke for several moments. Finally, Mairi squeezed his shoulder.

"Ye of all people know how strong Anna is. She will make it through this."

He met his mother's gaze. "Ye dinnae see the condition she was in when she escaped. MacNairn starved and imprisoned her the entire time in his dungeon, in spite of her wound. She was in shock, barely able to stand when she found us. I know she is strong, but a body can only take so much. I fear for her life. I willnae leave her side until the fever releases its grip."

A soft kiss touched his cheek. "Ye will find a way to make it up to her, and ye will put these petty jealousies aside. I will have a meal sent."

When the tray came, so did Fiona with a fresh kettle for the fire. "I am off to sleep, but will return on the morrow. Keep her cool.

Make her drink a small amount of this brew every two or three hours. Ye need to eat and rest yerself. 'Twill be a long battle afore she comes round."

The door closed softly, leaving Duncan alone with his thoughts as he sat vigil over the woman he loved. They both slept fitfully. Duncan stirred at every groan and movement she made. Anna muttered in her sleep, speaking to unknown people in different languages, including a language unlike any Duncan had heard before. He guessed it was the tongue of her mentor.

As she rambled, bits and pieces fell together. Duncan listened closely to her whispered words, and what he heard broke his heart. She pled for acceptance and spoke of longing to find a place in a world which considered her neither English nor Scot. Her words faded in and out of coherence, but her heartache remained.

Duncan touched her hot, dry cheek, tracing his fingers along the face he loved. She turned into his caress, tears leaking onto his hand.

"Duncan, I am sorry...please don't leave me." Her voice cracked and she quietly sobbed.

He wanted to reply, realizing she spoke from the depths of her torment. Her fevered state lowered her protective walls and her anguish poured forth. He sat powerless, listening to her beg for his love, hearing her admit her feelings of unworthiness—all because of his words of jealousy.

'Twas too much. The shame of what he had done to her tore through him without mercy. He had grievously injured her, mind, body and soul. He'd been right all along—he didn't deserve her. Selfishly, Duncan also knew he could not live without her. He pledged he would never allow anything to happen to her again if the Fates would only allow her to live. He would spend the rest of his days winning her trust, her love.

At the end of the third day, the fever released its grip, her skin cooling. However, she remained deep asleep.

"Her breathing is shallower than it should be," Duncan observed.

"Tis likely due to the pain. Broken ribs dinnae allow deep breathing," Fiona answered.

Broken ribs didn't explain her pallor or weakened heartbeat.

He turned to the pot on the fire. "What is that?" Finally, something out of Fiona's kettle smelled pleasant.

"'Tis an infusion of peppermint and thistle. 'Twill help spur her body to wakefulness when she's ready. She was verra weak when she came to us. 'Tis no surprise she needs more rest to heal."

Her words provided a small comfort. Nothing could be done but watch and wait. Trean's wound had scabbed over and appeared to be healing nicely. Duncan barely detected signs of his previous limp. The two of them maintained a silent vigil over Anna. Slow agony as the sun rose, traversed the sky then set again. Meals were brought, but Duncan could have been eating sand for all he knew. The morn of the fifth day brought a change.

"Water."

'Twas a mere croak of a whisper, but it brought him out of his torpor. Trean whined and placed his paws on the bed. Starting from his chair, Duncan looked into Anna's eyes, relieved at last to see life behind them. He filled a cup of water and gently raised it to her lips. She took a few sips, then returned to sleep. 'Twas enough. Hope soared in his chest.

News of her progress spread throughout the castle. Mairi and Nessa took turns sitting with her. Her grandda sat at her bedside each day for an hour or so, creating an uncomfortable silence between him and Duncan. Word of why she was alone at the loch had spread. Though he never said anything, Duncan knew Elliot seethed. Part of him hoped Elliot would thrash him, if for no other reason than to assuage his guilt. On the day her fever broke, Moray Elliot made his daily afternoon visit.

Pouring wine into two cups, he handed one to Duncan.

"When I first married Anna's grandmam, God rest her soul, I was a stubborn and foolish young man, and laird, so I thought I always knew best. Morna had a way of seeing into people that was canny and unexplainable. She told me a cousin, who was like a brother to me, plotted my death, hoping to take my place. At first, I was shocked to hear such a thing. When I asked for her proof, she told me she had naught, just her intuition. I became furious, accusing her of creating dissention. I said terrible things to her in anger."

Duncan shifted in his seat, unable to hide his surprise.

"She ignored the hateful words and tried to reason with me, but I wouldnae have it. I told her she was wrong and to never speak of it again." The pain of remembering was etched on his face.

"What happened?"

"My brother overheard our cousin making plans to ambush me with men he paid to do the deed. This way, my blood would be on their hands. He wouldnae be suspected. We went to the elder council, which included my uncle, with the story. They suggested we allow the plan to play out, insisting at the last minute my cousin accompany me. Our men surrounded them at the ambush site, stopping the attack. My uncle confronted his son. He denied it, but it dinnae take much persuasion to loosen the tongues of his hired thugs. He was hanged for his betrayal. 'Twas a dark stain on our clan for many years."

Elliot took a long drink, as if to wash away the bitterness of the memory. "Morna and I lived as strangers for three months, from the time she told me, to the time I discovered the truth. I knew I had badly damaged the one person who loved me above all others—the one I could truly trust with my life."

"How did ye get her to forgive ye?"

Elliot pinned Duncan with a hard expression. "I did exactly what ye will do when Anna wakes. Beg her forgiveness. Convince her 'twill never happen again. Tell her she is the most important thing in yer life, and ye cannae live without her. If ye dinnae, I will thrash ye within an inch of yer life, then take her home when she is well enough to travel. Ye willnae be welcome on Elliot land, and 'twill be a cold day in hell before ye get close enough to hurt her again. I can protect her from the evil of such men as the earl. She will be safe amongst her kin."

The force of emotion behind his words startled Duncan, but no more than he deserved. "What if she willnae come around? I dinnae deserve her forgiveness."

"Nae, neither did I, but she will forgive ye if she is convinced ye love her and vow not to indulge in such foolishness again. Women have a greater capacity for forgiveness than we men. 'Tis especially true with the ones they hold most dear. We mock the softer feelings of women until 'tis is the verra thing we need. Swallow yer pride, son. Win her back."

"Pride?" Duncan spread his hands. "I have no pride in this. I watch her every day and live with knowing I am the one who hurt her." Duncan buried his head in his hands, ashamed of the tears threatening to fall.

Elliot placed his hand on his shoulder. "Aye, ye have the right of it. Ye will do just fine then. 'Twill be a wedding soon enough."

Early that same evening, Anna opened her eyes. She glanced around the room, trying to understand why she felt like she'd picked a fight with Duff—and lost. No part of her body felt unbruised. Her head, especially, throbbed with pain. *MacNairn!* She was a prisoner of that foul beast. No, that couldn't be right. She was in a familiar room—Duncan's room. She blinked a few times, trying to reconnect all she knew. Threads of memory reformed. The abduction, MacNairn's intentions for her, her escape. After that, details grew a bit fuzzy. Turning her head, she saw Lady MacGregor in a chair next to the bed, working on a square of embroidery.

Mairi noticed her wakefulness. "Thank the saints ye are awake! What can I get ye?"

Swallowing hard in an effort to speak, Anna whispered, "I need to use the privy." Weak as a newborn lamb, Anna leaned heavily on the older woman while they stepped into the garderobe. Merely making her way back to bed exhausted her.

"I will fetch Duncan and Fiona," Mairi said and moved toward the door.

"Wait," Anna feebly replied, but Mairi had gone.

Duncan entered a few moments later, a haggard, yet hopeful look on his face.

She puzzled at his appearance—he looked as bad as she felt. "Duncan, what has happened to you?"

He smiled faintly in return. "I am fine, love. Ye are the one everyone has been fashed over."

He called her 'love'. Hope surged in her breast, but she warned herself not to put too much meaning behind it. "How long have I been here?"

"What do ye last remember?"

"I recall escaping that evil man, but everything after is murky."

Duncan described events after she stumbled into camp, including her three days of fever, along with the past two. She absorbed his story, remembering more of her time with MacNairn. 'Twas then she felt a familiar cold nose on her hand.

"Trean!"

"Aye, he has rarely left yer side since we returned."

"I thought him dead. I saw him felled by one of MacNairn's men at the loch."

"He has a wee scratch on his shoulder—all but healed. We found him following the trail of the men who took ye. He is a braw laddie. Other than being a mite skittish of people, he seems as tamed as a wolf can be."

Anna stroked his muzzle while he licked her other hand.

"You still haven't explained what has happened to you." She took in Duncan's gaunt appearance and the bruised circles under his eyes.

"He has nae left yer side these past five days," Fiona answered as she bustled into the room. "We had to threaten him to eat what little he did, and he has nae had a full night's rest for worry and watching over ye."

Anna didn't know how to respond to this news, but the hope she felt earlier increased tenfold.

"I will tell Cook to prepare a broth and to soak some bread in it. Isla will see a bath is sent up afterward. Do ye need anything else?" Fiona asked.

Anna shook her head. The one thing she needed, only Duncan could supply.

Fiona hurried from the room. Duncan sat in the chair next to the bed. He picked up her hand and, holding it to his lips, he kissed each finger.

"Anna, I beg ye forgive me. I cannae lose ye. Ye are my life. My words that day—I knew they were wrong the moment they left my mouth."

Anna saw tears pool in his eyes. Though she regretted his pain, her heart leapt with the knowledge he still loved her.

"Duncan, 'tis not your fault. I was the one who rode away."

His jaw clenched and his expression hardened. "Dinnae think to absolve me of this. I shamed ye in front of the men and others. I drove ye away with my senseless jealousy and anger. Because of my actions, ye almost died. I am the one who is supposed to honor ye, protect ye." Bitterness filled his voice.

"Duncan, I am not Callum. It was not your fault then, and it is not your fault now. I will be well soon enough, and an evil man is dead. I should have been able to ride to the loch in peace to clear my head whilst you cleared yours. 'Tis not your fault an enemy took advantage of my solitude."

He leaned over the bed and kissed her on the forehead. "Does this mean ye forgive me?"

The tortured look in his eyes was more than she could bear. She would have said or done anything to remove it. "Yes, I forgive you. I love you. You are to be my husband, aye?"

He hugged her, burying his face in her hair. "Aye, I will be yer husband if ye will still have me."

Anna nodded. "Duncan, my love for you does not change simply because of a few harsh words spoken in anger."

"Anna, the past nine days have cured my jealousies. If the words are important, ye have my vow I will never behave that way toward ye again, nor will I ever speak to ye out of anger in public. I am not foolish enough to believe we will never quarrel. Howbeit, I will save those words for when we are alone. The fear, guilt and humiliation I have lived through have conspired to scour my very soul."

His confession and promise reassured her, but somewhat confused her. "I do not understand. Humiliation?"

Duncan gave a grim chuckle. "The men—*yer* men—knew exactly what happened. Though not a word was spoken, the anger aimed at me for days was unmistakable. I would fear for my life if ye were to leave us. Those same men volunteered without hesitation to rescue ye."

She considered his words. While deeply moved by their loyalty, Anna didn't wish it to be at Duncan's expense. Not knowing how to respond, she reached for his lips instead. The kiss was born out of desperation and a hunger for what they'd almost lost. As it ended, he pressed light kisses all over her face and neck, until Anna couldn't help but smile. When she opened her eyes, his gaze told her they were whole again.

Epilogue

*B*efore dawn on her wedding day, serving lads brought a bath upstairs, fragrant oils scenting the water. Isla scrubbed her mercilessly and used a special mixture on her hair, creating a mass of glossy black waves. Wrapped in a warm robe, Anna sat while Nessa and Mairi dressed her hair.

They wove flowers and thin strips of gold fabric into the gathering of curls atop her head, allowing tendrils to drape loose around her face and shoulders. At last finished with her hair, the women carefully placed a gossamer-fine silk chemise over her head. Anna fingered the fabric in wonder.

"Mairi, where did you get this? It is quite beautiful, but is much like wearing nothing at all."

Anna's soon-to-be mother-by-law gave her a knowing smile and leaned in to whisper. "I never properly thanked ye for yer special gift to me. Kenneth was too embarrassed to thank ye, though he has enjoyed it as much as I. 'Twas only fitting to return the favor."

Anna's cheeks heated and her nervousness spiraled upward until she found it hard to breathe. Mairi poured her a cup of wine.

"I remember my wedding day. I was tender of nerves, also. The only advice I can offer is to think on the love ye share with Duncan. Remember the plans ye have made together. They will banish yer fears." Mairi gave Anna a wink. "Taking a deep breath and a long drink helps also."

Anna considered Mairi's words as she drank. Perhaps a bit more wine to settle herself would be advisable. Not too much though. She didn't want her wits addled when it came time to say her vows. She had time to drink another cup before the ladies finished buffing, fluffing and adjusting every part of her. With a bright smile, Nessa took her hand and led her to stand before the reflection disc mounted on the wall. Staring back at her was a woman Anna had never seen before.

Small white blossoms, interlaced with gold ribbon contrasted with her dark tresses. Her creamy complexion held a hint of pink, likely due to the wine. Her deep green eyes glowed, wide with anticipation, and the full pink lips of her mouth formed a graceful bow. The green velvet gown with gold trim highlighted her features, drawing the eye to a modest décolleté. Taller than the younger woman standing next to her, the dark-haired beauty in the mirror bore an air of nobility and grace. Anna continued to stare at this stranger, mesmerized by her reflection.

"I am—beautiful," she said in disbelief.

"Ye have ever been, my dear. We only added a bit of polish," Mairi replied.

"Do you think Duncan will be pleased? He has never seen me like this." Uncertainty crept into Anna's voice.

"I predict my son willnae be able to tear his eyes from ye."

"What's more, I dare say every man who sees ye will experience the same." Nessa added, a pert grin on her face.

Anna did not care about the rest. She only wished to please Duncan.

A knock on the door signaled it was time to leave for the kirk. Anna floated down the stairs, her feet scarcely touching the stone. As she reached the bottom step, her grandfather waited, a tremulous smile on his face.

"Forgive an old fool. Watching ye walk down the stairs reminds me of the day I gave away my Rossalyn in marriage to yer da."

Anna accepted his arm with a smile on her face, gripping him firmly. "I think Mother and Father would be happy today, don't you?"

"Aye, they would indeed. Verra happy. 'Tis a good man ye marry. I can go to my maker knowing ye will be loved and well cared for. Before I depart, howbeit, I would like to hold some great-grandbairns."

Anna laughed at his request. "I will speak to my husband. We shall see what can be done."

As they exited the hall, Anna gasped, astonished by the crowd of people gathered in the bailey. They stood on either side of a flower-decorated path leading to the kirk, its doors open wide. From where she stood, the small chapel appeared packed with people. Glancing through the doors, her eyes sought only one. She found him standing at the door with the priest. When she met his gaze, every care dropped away, and she hardly noticed her grandfather place her hand in Duncan's.

As they bowed before the priest, Anna tried to concentrate on the words said, repeating her vows in a clear and confident voice. Entering the kirk, they bowed at the altar according to the priest's direction. When they rose, she faced the man who held her heart. He placed a simple gold band, with a knot etched into the metal, on her finger.

Pulling her into an embrace, Duncan lowered his head. Without hesitation, Anna met him, offering her lips for his possession. The kiss was tender, but too short for her liking. She reminded herself this would be but one of thousands of kisses they would share from henceforth.

Duncan tucked her hand against his chest and turned her to face the cheering crowd before them.

"Are ye ready for the festivities, love?"

Heat flared in her cheeks. "Tonight?" she hissed, her gaze darting to the side to see if anyone else heard him.

He threw back his head with a hearty laugh. "Och, that, too. But I referred to the feasting and games and exhibitions." He tilted his head at her. "Will ye compete?"

Pleased he considered her wishes, Anna turned sultry eyes on him. "Aye, milord. Let the games begin."

DDs Note to the Reader

The inspiration of Anna was born of two things, my 35 years of love of martial arts and fascination with the Crusades. She is actually a composite of two women I used to train with. With the exception of her archery, the other skills are held by a combination of both of these ladies. I attempted to keep the weaponry and abilities authentic to the period. In Chinese martial arts, it was common to learn the art of healing along with, or before one learned to fight, hence Anna's knowledge of acupuncture and other herbal healing. History tells us acupuncture goes back thousands of years.

The trick was to figure out a way to get Chinese martial arts and weaponry, along with healing arts, into medieval England, and the 9th Crusades provided the vehicle. During this period, the Silk Road, which was a means for many cultures and peoples to mingle, was dominated by the Mongols as they and the Muslim Mamluks fought for superiority in the region. When Edward (Longshanks), son of Henry III, came crusading after arriving too late to aid Louis IX of France in the capture of Tunis, he headed toward the Holy Land. Edward negotiated an alliance with the Mongols to fight the Mamluks in the region.

While seeing some success in places like Tripoli (modern day Lebanon and Syria) and Acre (Northern Israel), Edward withdrew due to pressing needs back home. The 9th Crusade wasn't a loss per se, but rather the campaign ran out of steam as its principals were needed elsewhere.

The backstory for Highland Escape gives us Sir Everard Braxton, a English knight, who proved instrumental in the campaign in Tripoli and was in turn rewarded with a small barony in the borderlands. It was common for second sons who wouldn't inherit and other knights to go on crusade for the opportunity to earn land and wealth in the Holy Land, or purchase land for themselves with the spoils back home. Some would say such a title and holding wasn't much of a reward, as the borders were a dangerous and tumultuous place, particularly at this time. Longshanks would want men he knew to be loyal and strong at the border.

Having won victory at Tripoli, it wasn't a stretch for Braxton to have freed Mamluk prisoners. Zhang was a bodyguard to a rich merchant who plied the Silk Road who met with a foul end. Attaching himself to Braxton in exchange for his freedom, Zhang provided the means of cultural transfer to the borders of Northern medieval England. His time in captivity would have changed his perspective on training, much like US POWs in Viet Nam changed how military training is done today. Anna and her brother Edrick became beneficiaries of his experience.

Braxton used diplomacy rather than war to keep the peace on his piece of the border by marrying the daughter of the local Scottish laird. While this made him a peacekeeper in his territory, it set up an impossible situation for his daughter, who was despised for her Scot's blood south of the border, and for her English heritage north of it. This provided enough conflict for Anna to become someone other than a pampered English noblewoman.

We hope you enjoyed Anna's story and the rich history behind it.

Other Books by Cathy MacRae

The Highlander's Bride series:

The Highlander's Accidental Bride (book 1)

The Highlander's Reluctant Bride (book 2)

The Highlander's Tempestuous Bride (book 3)

The Highlander's Outlaw Bride (book 4)

Kinnon's Story (working title)(book 5)
coming 2015

Enjoy an excerpt from

KINNON'S STORY
(working title)

CATHY MACRAE

Chapter One

1380, Châteauneuf-de-Randon, France

Kinnon Macrory stared into the face of death.

'Tis nae fair. After all the battles I have survived, to arrive at this.
He would have sighed at the injustice of it, but he was, quite frankly,
afraid to make an unnecessary move.

The black mask surrounded dark topaz eyes, burnished fur, and a
fine set of strong, white teeth revealed from beneath snarling black
jowls. The Alaunt's ears pressed flat against his skull in warning, and
his hair stood up along his neck and shoulders. As did Kinnon's.

Shite.

He lifted his gaze carefully from the reddened hand laid across the
dog's neck. The slender fingers could have belonged to a nobleman's
daughter, but the nails were short and the skin rough. Amazing what
the mind registers when death is imminent. The owner of the hand
wore a serviceable gown, patched areas meticulously sewn, sleeve cuff
turned back on itself, almost hiding the raveled edges. A smudged
apron covered the gown, the bucket of milk at her feet attesting her job
before he walked up. And came face-to-face with death.

"Do ye mind calling off yer beast?" He offered a winsome smile,
splaying his hands at his side, a small bag of coins in his left palm.
The young woman stared at him, hardly giving the bag a look.

He tried again. "*Chien?*"

The young woman's gaze did not waver—clear, cold blue eyes bore into his. Wisps of black hair curled damply against her temple, attesting to her work ethic. Her thin nose sat atop full, red lips that neither smiled nor frowned at him.

The dog growled, a deep menacing sound originating from his enormous chest that warned Kinnon from making a further move—if he wanted to keep his throat intact.

Kinnon did.

His heartbeat kicked up. The impressive muscles in the dog's forelegs rippled, his claws gripped the ground, his hindquarters bunched. Endless moments passed as Kinnon roundly cursed the man who sent him to this farm on an errand better suited to one of the camp lackeys.

"*Se calmer*, Jean-Baptiste," she murmured as the dog leaned forward.

"Jean-Baptiste?" Kinnon couldn't help himself. "Ye call this beast John the Baptizer?"

The woman gave him in inscrutable look, but the edge of her lips quivered, threatened to smile. "He has changed the religion of more than one man, *monsieur*."

Kinnon's eyebrows shot upward. "Aye. I can see that happening." He eyed the enormous beast, his shoulder almost even with the woman's waist, his possessiveness clear. With his mistress's soft command, the dog settled, but his eyes did not waver, his threat remained unmistakable.

"I was sent here to ask ye for what supplies I could buy." Kinnon gently flipped the small bag in his hand. The movement and clink of coin drew the woman's attention.

"You brought coin?" She snorted and hefted the milk bucket in one slender hand. Kinnon moved instinctively to take the burden from her but froze at the snarling response from Jean-Baptiste. Cool blue eyes met his, and this time, the young woman smiled.

"*Merci,* but I can manage. If you would like to keep yourself intact, please take a step back. Jean-Baptiste and I do not like to be crowded."

Kinnon let out his breath and took the required step backward. "Aye. And I thank ye."

She raised her eyebrows. "For what?"

"For not letting yon beast change my religion."

About The Authors

Cathy and DD MacRae have been critique partners for several years and worked together to create the book you just read. Cathy has authored 4 books in her Highlander's Bride series (with a 5th one on the way). DD writes both contemporary and historical romance books, one of each scheduled to be released in the next year.